East Kingston Public Library

47 Maplevale Road
East Kingston, NH 03827
www.eastkingstonlibrary.org

The
Galahad
Legacy

Tor Teen Books by Dom Testa

GALAHAD

The Comet's Curse
The Web of Titan
The Cassini Code
The Dark Zone
Cosmic Storm
The Galahad Legacy

A GALAHAD BOOK

The Galahad Legacy

Dom Testa

TOR
TEEN

A Tom Doherty Associates Book

New York

THE GALAHAD LEGACY

Copyright © 2012 by Dom Testa

Reader's Guide copyright © 2012 by Tor Books

A Tor Teen Book
Published by Tom Doherty Associates, LLC
175 Fifth Avenue
New York, NY 10010

www.tor-forge.com

Tor® is a registered trademark of Tom Doherty Associates, LLC.

ISBN 978-0-7653-2112-1

First Edition: February 2012

Printed in the United States of America

0 9 8 7 6 5 4 3 2 1

Acknowledgments

The Galahad series has been a huge part of my life for ten years, and there are literally dozens of people who have played a large role in making it happen. As we enter the homestretch, I want to thank the visionary educators around the world who have created such remarkable learning opportunities around the Galahad books. You amaze me with your creative and enthusiastic programs.

Thanks to the good people at Tor, who work every day to put fun, fascinating books into the hands of people (young and not-so-young) everywhere.

Special thanks to Donna for her love and support, and to Dominic III for his brilliant observations and ideas.

And to Monica, for making me laugh every day. If you don't have someone like that in your life, get out there and find them right now.

The
Galahad
Legacy

I f you want to pump up the drama in any situation, it's always a sure bet to add the phrase "a matter of life and death." For one thing, people don't know if you're serious or just hooked on theatrics. Me, I use it all the time, even to cut in line in the cafeteria.

But sometimes it's not a cheap trick to get attention. Sometimes it literally comes down to a decision here or a mistake there. And before you know it, everyone's screaming.

Case in point: the teenage explorers aboard the greatest sailing ship ever built. This particular ship is not at sea, but rather in a sea of stars. It's called Galahad, and it carries not only the hopes and dreams and dirty laundry of the human race, but 250 of Earth's best and brightest young people, on a mission to colonize a new world.

Their story began about a year ago with The Comet's Curse, and has seen its share of life and death. Literally. For one thing, there used to be 251 teenagers aboard the ship. See what I mean?

What kind of narrator would I be if I didn't strongly urge you to find that first volume and begin at the beginning? You'll find an interesting band of intrepid star travelers, led by crafty Triana Martell and the ship's Council. They counted on a long, difficult voyage. What they didn't count *on was a saboteur, deadly space debris, a bizarre alien intelligence over a billion years old, and creepy space vultures—all on the outside—with a few salty troublemakers lurking on the inside.*

When we left you hanging last time, Triana had piloted a pod—a small emergency vehicle—through a nasty rip in space that likely was a wormhole. Her disappearance led to an impromptu movement to fill the role of Council Leader, which led to bad boy Merit Simms returning to the scene, which led to Gap Lee and Hannah Ross opposing each other and opening old love wounds, which led . . .

Ugh, how do you humans make it through a day without imploding?

Anyway, Triana has suddenly popped back onto the scene, and she's not alone. She brought something with her, and it's not a fruit basket. Judging from the way some of the crew members reacted when they saw it, I'd say it probably falls somewhere between amazing and downright freaky.

Plus, we have the little problem of the various wormholes creating a bruise in space which now threatens to atomically dismantle the ship and turn the happy space campers into gobs of jumbled particles. Yeah, that's a problem.

And then there's Bon Hartsfield trying to reach into the afterlife to soothe his guilty conscience, and Lita Marques, the ship's young doctor, struggling with the concept of faith in its many forms. Poor Channy Oakland just wants everyone to get their butts in the gym and sweat it out.

Bon has always used a strange device called the translator to achieve his alien hookup, but something tells me that's about to change. And those space vultures I mentioned? I get the feeling they're not going away without a curtain call.

What have I left out? Lots. I suggest you grab all five preceding volumes and tear through them like crazy to get caught up. In each one you'll find that the glue that holds this tale together is the world's most lovable computer. That would be me. My name is Roc, and my actual job is to run the ship's engines and climate. But c'mon, it's no fun to just sit around and watch these guys fall in and out of trouble. Could you?

I'll stick my nose—or at least my chips—into the story from time to time, but only because sometimes it cries out for analysis. And believe me, after a year in space with these crazy kids, no one is better qualified than I.

1

Her eyes fluttered open for a brief second, but the light seemed harsh, making her reluctant to open them again. The last thing she remembered was sitting in the cockpit of the pod, her heart racing as she again spiraled down into the wormhole. Her first experience doing that had taught her that it would not be pleasant.

But now she was lying on a bed, a sheet up to her neck, while muffled voices floated in from nearby. Her curiosity finally won out and she chanced another glimpse, cracking her eyes, allowing them to acclimate as she determined her surroundings. Of course it had to be *Galahad,* her mind told her, but her experiences in the past week—Was it a week? Was it a year?—kept her from accepting anything until she could see it with her own eyes.

Although, she had to admit, what she'd recently seen with those eyes was mind-shattering.

She pried her lids open a bit wider. When the room gradually swam into focus, she positively identified it as the hospital ward on the ship. She let out a contented sigh.

The sound must have alerted the people in the room, because

moments later a shape loomed over her. Pulling her gaze upward, she felt a wave of comfort when the face of Lita Marques beamed at her.

"Welcome home, Tree," Lita said. "Why don't you stick around for awhile?"

Triana Martell found the strength to smile, and mumbled a thick "hi."

"I'm sure you have questions galore," Lita said. "Let me answer a few before you ask. Yes, you're back safely; at least my preliminary scan doesn't show any physical problems, unless you have any aches you want to share with me." When Triana shook her head once, Lita continued: "Everyone here is fine, not counting the usual drama and a few bumps and bruises. The ship itself has a few problems, but Gap can get you caught up with that. And, let's see . . ." She sat on the edge of the bed. "Lots of people have come by to welcome you back, but I've shooed them away for now. Oh, and the friend you brought with you is doing okay. Well, at least as far as I can tell."

Triana stared up at Lita, then cleared her throat and croaked: "Where?"

Lita nodded toward the door. "Down the hall. Same place we had the vulture. Only this time we're keeping people out. Remember, it was a zoo when we brought in the vulture. I get the feeling that this is much different, so we're keeping a lid on things for now." She paused and studied Triana's face. "It's actually quite different, isn't it?"

Raising up on her elbows, Triana looked at the table beside her. "Is that water?"

Lita helped her take a few sips. "No comment about . . . it?"

Triana licked her lips, then rubbed her eyes. "I'll have plenty of comments for all of you." She swallowed more water and felt her strength returning. "You're not gonna keep me in bed just because I passed out, are you?"

"Like I said, you seem fine," Lita said, standing up. "You know me, I'll always caution against doing too much after a traumatic experience, or a shock to the system. I'm guessing you've had both. But I know these are special circumstances, too. Let's get some food and water in you, we'll watch you for an hour or so, and then you can walk out of here. Deal?"

Triana lay back and smiled at her friend. "I won't fight you on that. I'm starving."

Lita patted her on the leg. "Good to hear. We'll get you something right away. Time to feed all of my patients anyway."

"All?" Triana said.

"Uh-huh. That wormhole you rode in on has banged up a few people. In fact . . ." Lita lowered her voice. "Your good friend Merit Simms is just three beds down. Sleeping, thanks to pain medication. You'll probably be gone before he wakes up."

She walked toward the door. "Don't wander off, or we'll bring you back and put you in the bed next to him."

Gap Lee trudged along *Galahad*'s curved hallway toward his room. It was well after midnight, and the halls were deserted. Exhausted, he wondered when he'd be able to crash for a good ten or twelve hours. With Triana's return, and the surprise which accompanied her, it might not be anytime soon.

He tried to wrap his brain around that surprise. Tucked into the back of the pod which had delivered Triana into—and back out of—the wormhole, it floated inside what appeared to be an old-fashioned aquarium. Gap's mother had kept exotic tropical fish in a similar container, and likely would have identified the contents as Gap had. But it was impossible . . . wasn't it?

Secured aboard a wheeled cart and covered with a sheet, it was moved to an isolated area in Sick House. Curious crew members along the way had stopped and followed the procession with their eyes, but nobody asked questions. Gap knew that it would dominate the conversation that evening in the Dining Hall and throughout the ship.

The next few hours had been spent alternating between Engineering—where the radiation shield was holding up, thanks to the energy siphon from the main engines—and the Spider bay. A thorough examination of the pod revealed no particular damage, other than an odd assortment of shorted-out electrical components. Other than the aquarium, there were no additional surprises.

Now the door to his room slid open and he stepped inside, mindful to be quiet. Daniil was sound asleep. Gap rarely had contact with his roommate these days; just another sign, he noted, that time off was overdue. His social life had withered away.

And, he realized, it was more insight into the life of Triana, or anyone with heavy responsibilities. It was the side of leaders rarely seen or understood.

Although his bed called out, he kicked off his shoes and checked his mail again. There was a single new entry, a note from Triana. Clicking on the file opened a group message to the Council, with a personal attachment for him. The main message called for the Council to assemble at seven in the morning—his shoulders sagged as he calculated the amount of sleep he would not be getting again this night—and thanked everyone for their great work during her absence. The note was short and to the point, in pure Triana style.

Standing behind his chair and leaning on the desk, he clicked open the attachment.

> Gap, I'll certainly thank you in person, but didn't want to wait to let you know how grateful I am that you took charge of the ship while I was away. We haven't had a chance to talk yet, but I'm pretty sure you weren't happy about my decision to go. I know I put you in an awkward and difficult position, but I hope you understand that I had to do it.
>
> We have a lot to cover, and some very important decisions to make. I'm glad to be back, and glad that you're on the team. And I'm glad you're such a good friend.
>
> See you in the morning.

He couldn't think about any of that at the moment. If he didn't get some sleep he'd be worthless to Triana and the Council. Snapping off the vidscreen, he passed on his usual bedtime routine and simply fell onto his bed, covering his face with one arm, willing himself to clear his mind and find the shortest path to sleep.

It wasn't easy.

As always, Bon Hartsfield found escape in his work. Overseeing the Agricultural Department on the ship meant long hours anyway, but his office—tucked within one of the two massive domes atop *Galahad*—provided an insulated nest, especially this late at night.

The ship was programmed to simulate the natural day/night rhythms of Earth, which meant that the lights in many of the common areas slowly dimmed in the evening and then gradually grew brighter beginning around six in the morning. Now, while the majority of the Farms were lit only by the brilliant splash of stars through the clear domes, Bon's office was awash in light.

He stood behind his desk, inputting data from the latest harvest report. It was easily a task that could be entrusted to one of the workers under his supervision, but Bon preferred to remain busy. To sit idly—or worse, lie awake in bed—only invited the troubling thoughts to return. And there were far too many of those lately.

Topping them all was the startling return of Triana. Fight as he might to keep his mind elsewhere, the image of her slumped in the cockpit of the pod muscled its way back to the fore. Where had she been? What had happened to her on the other side of the wormhole? What was that . . . *thing* that she'd brought back?

Or had it brought *her* back?

And, most importantly, had his connection with the alien beings known as the Cassini created what Lita described as a "beacon" to guide Triana back to *Galahad*? How should he feel about that, when it was never his original intent?

The thoughts were overwhelming. He tossed his workpad stylus onto the desk and dropped into his chair. His blond hair, already long and unkempt, had grown shaggy from weeks of neglect, and now fell across his face. At some point he'd need to either visit Jenner for a quick cut, or chop it off himself.

It wasn't near the top of his priorities.

Triana's return, and his confused feelings regarding *Galahad*'s Council Leader; a raft of guilt over the death of Alexa, or, rather, guilt over his inability to return her feelings; the news from Lita that his Cassini link had begun a physical transformation of his brain . . .

All of that in addition to a full workload in the Farms, and his stubborn reluctance to delegate as much as he should. Plus his Council duties.

A low guttural laugh escaped him. Council duties. He'd been

almost invisible in Council meetings, speaking up only when irritation got the better of him, or when challenged by Gap. Those two events often went hand in hand. Yet he knew that his position as the head of the Agricultural Department came with leadership responsibilities, and he would never consider turning the Farms over to someone else. The soil, the crops—the very atmosphere of the domes—combined to create his personal haven aboard the ship.

The looming Council meeting would be exceptionally difficult. In a few hours Triana would begin the debriefing, and Bon dreaded the expected eye contact. He would, of course, sit sullenly and listen, but now—hours ahead of the meeting—he could already feel the burn of Triana's stare and the probing looks from Lita.

His head throbbed, a dull ache that was exacerbated, no doubt, by the seemingly nonstop activity of the past week combined with a lack of sleep. He had never requested a sleep-aid of any sort, but now he wondered who might be manning Sick House at this late hour. Would they be required to report to Lita on every pill dispensed, or merely log the random request?

It wasn't worth the chance. Perhaps he could shut down his brain through meditation. Just a few hours of sleep might cure the headache and give him the strength he needed to power through the morning meeting.

He killed the lights to his office, grabbed the blanket he kept stashed for nights like this, and stretched out on the floor.

2

Triana arrived early, striding into the Conference Room with her workpad in one hand and two energy bars in the other. She'd avoided the Dining Hall, afraid that her presence might create a stir, even at this early hour. Until she could address the entire crew, she reasoned, it was best to remain behind the scenes.

"Roc," she said, grabbing her usual chair. "I've got some catching up to do."

"I knew you wouldn't feel like chatting last night," the computer said. "So I posted multiple reports in your folder, everything from details of our radiation shield problem, to the current status of the vultures outside the ship, to the request I've made for vacation time. I really need to get away for a few weeks."

"Denied," Triana said with a slight smile. "No rest for you."

"You're a tyrant. But welcome back anyway."

"Thank you, Roc. I missed you . . . I think."

The computer expelled a pouting grunt. "I'm overwhelmed by your sentimentality. Don't think for a moment that my circuits don't have feelings."

"Oh, I'd never make that mistake," Triana said. "But this has nothing to do with you, believe me. It's just that the week I was gone—it was a week, right?—is still somewhat jumbled. I don't remember missing much of anything. There wasn't time for that kind of thinking."

"Well, I look forward to your report. Especially when you explain exactly what that thing is you brought aboard."

Triana nodded. "Yeah, I expect that will be Question 1A, followed closely by 'Where were you?' as 1B."

"Can't wait to hear the answers," Roc said.

"Well, I'm tempted to answer 'I don't know' for both, but I'll come up with something." Triana tapped open the vidscreen and accessed her personal folder. For the next few minutes she munched on energy bars and scanned the reports. Occasionally she scowled, particularly as she came up to speed on the devastating effects of the space bruise that Hannah had suggested.

"Incredible," she murmured. "Can this be true? Damage at a molecular level?"

"If it's any consolation, I feel great," Roc said. "But yes, *you* might end up resembling a gob of toothpaste."

"Lovely."

The door opened and Gap strolled in. Triana couldn't decipher the look on his face, which seemed perched somewhere between agitation and fatigue. He approached her and she slowly rose to her feet. They exchanged an awkward gaze before embracing in a tentative and equally awkward hug.

"Glad to see you're in one piece," Gap said, moving across the room to collect a cup of water. "Feeling okay?"

"For the most part," she said. "Physically I'm fine. My head's still spinning from everything, but I'm getting readjusted. You got my note last night?"

He mumbled an uh-huh, then took a seat at the table. "Of course I'm dying to know what happened to you, but I guess I'll wait for the others."

There was another uncomfortable silence. Triana wrestled with what to say next, but was spared when Lita and Channy walked in together. Both girls wasted no time in hugging the Council Leader.

"I'll start with this hug, but then I want you to turn around so I can kick you squarely on your tush," Channy said with a mock frown.

"Sleep okay?" Lita asked. "Any new aches or pains this morning?"

"Nothing new. I was telling Gap that things seem a little scattered, but I'll catch up."

Channy crossed her arms. "You need a good workout, that's all. How about this afternoon you drop by the gym and we'll get some sweat flowing?"

Triana smiled. "Believe it or not, that sounds great. If I get a break I'll come see you."

As she said this, Bon walked in. He glanced quickly at Triana, then nodded to the rest of the Council before taking his usual spot at the far end of the table.

"Hi," Triana said to him.

He glanced up again, his blue eyes piercing her. "Hello. Welcome back."

"Wow," Lita said. "Way to harness those emotions, Bon. I guess the rest of us seem a little sloppy."

Triana leaned forward and crossed her hands on the table, hoping to steer the conversation—and attention—away from her complex relationship with Bon.

"I'll spend some more time today with the reports that Gap

and Roc have put together for me. It seems that we're not out of the woods yet with this radiation issue, but hopefully we can find a permanent solution.

"In the meantime, I know you've got questions. I'll address the entire crew soon, but let me do my best to describe what I experienced when I left the ship."

She gathered her thoughts for a moment. "First, I know my decision was very unpopular; in fact, almost all of you have expressed that. I stand by my decision to go. I took the safety of the ship into consideration, and weighed the options that I felt we had. Making a popular choice wasn't as important to me as doing what I felt was best for this crew. There's not much more to say about that. If you still have issues with me after this briefing, feel free to come see me individually. I'm open to hearing your opinions. For now, however, I'd like to move forward. What's done is done. Let's talk about what happened."

Triana looked around the table and saw no argument.

"The first thing I noticed when I approached the wormhole was how much it resembled a rip, like torn fabric. I guess I'd assumed it would be smooth and symmetrical, like it was punched out by a stamp or something. But it was jagged, and the blackest black I've ever seen. An almost painful black, like it was devoid of not only light, but life and . . . and hope. I think that might have frightened me the most. Not the actual journey through the wormhole, but the fear of leaving the known for the unknown, because it was a crushing, overwhelming unknown. It represented every fear I'd ever experienced, all wrapped into one."

She stopped and looked around the table with a sheepish smile. "That's kinda hard to explain. But . . . well, most of this is hard to explain. Bear with me, okay?"

"Did you feel any kind of presence in the darkness?" Lita asked.

Triana noticed that both Lita and Bon seemed to lean forward with this question.

"No, almost the exact opposite. It felt like I was leaving behind all conscious thought, and plunging into a vacuum of total nothingness. It was terrifying. But the moment I crossed that barrier, the very moment I saw the last image of the stars in my peripheral vision and was about to be swallowed by the blackness, it was as if everything turned inside out. Where it should have been an infinite darkness, suddenly there was an explosion of light."

"Colors?" Gap asked. "Like a kaleidoscope?"

Triana shook her head. "No. White light. I know I screamed, and I think it was because of that extreme shift. I expected to plunge into total darkness, and instead was slammed with an almost violent white light. It was like I pierced a veil or something. As soon as that happened, I passed out."

Lita stared at her before saying: "So you didn't see anything, really, when you passed the boundary. A flash of light, and then . . . ?"

"And then nothing. But . . ." Triana was quiet for a moment, again gathering her thoughts. "But I don't think I passed out because of anything physical. I think it was my mind's way of coping with the sudden change, shutting down rather than attempting to process what was going on around it. A defense mechanism, maybe. I don't know. But I was out.

"When I came to—and I have no idea how long that could have been—I was back in what appeared to be normal space."

"So," Gap said, "you have no idea how long it took to travel through the wormhole. Roc, any thoughts on that?"

"Oh, I'm bursting with thoughts," the computer said. "But before we go on, is there any chance of getting some popcorn? How are you guys just sitting there, listening to this, without popcorn?"

"Well, let's start with your thoughts on the wormhole," Gap said.

"To begin with," Roc said, "you have to stop thinking of a wormhole as a tunnel. It's not. It's a theoretical doorway between points in the universe, with no real depth to it. Does that make sense?"

Channy, who had been listening to everything with her fingers tented in front of her mouth, dropped her hands into her lap. "Or a window. When Triana shot through, it was like crashing through a window, from one side to the other."

"Yes," Roc said. "But a window so thin we'd never see it looking at it from the side. And that actually explains why Triana passed out."

"Why?" Channy said.

"Because the transition between the two sides of a wormhole is not only a division of space, but a division of space-time. It's one time on one side, and another on the other side. It could be an infinitely small discrepancy in time, or an infinitely large discrepancy. But the point is, the two sides are not only in different places, but in different times. Triana's brain was essentially in two places—and two times—at the same time, until she passed all the way through. And even though it only took a fraction of a second to pass through the boundary, her mind was in two places and two times at the same moment. That caused her brain to shut down instantly. A sort of reboot, if you will, for safety purposes."

Gap stared at the star field shining through the room's window, deep in thought. "Okay," he said. "But we know that the vultures are part machine, part organic material; their brains, or what we think operate as brains, are living tissue. Does that mean they blink out, too, when they pass through the wormhole?"

"I don't know," Roc said. "However, two things to consider: One, their creators obviously designed them for this travel, so they likely have taken it into consideration. And two, it's possible they are designed to shut down a split second before they pass through the barrier, and flip back on a split second later, in order to bypass any loss of consciousness for an extended time. Kind of like kids in the backseat lifting up their feet when the family car crosses a railroad track. Which is so cute I can hardly stand it. Please tell me you did that, Gap, so I can have a whole new appreciation for you."

"Of course I did," Gap said with a quick smile. "And had my dad honk the horn in tunnels, too." He turned back to Triana. "Did you have any sense of time at all when you woke up? I mean, I can kinda tell the difference when I've slept for an hour versus six hours, you know?"

"I know what you mean," Triana said. "But no, I had no concept at all. I might have been out for ten seconds, or ten days. All I know is that I woke up to see normal space through the pod's window. Well . . . maybe normal's not the right word."

She stood up and walked over to the water dispenser. The other Council members waited patiently as she slowly sipped from the cup. She kept her back to the conference table to hide the fact that her hand was shaking.

"The stars looked like stars, but I didn't recognize any of the constellations. The one thing I noticed right away was the nearest star; definitely a red dwarf."

Gap raised his eyebrows. "The most common star-type in our galaxy. They're all over the place."

Channy perked up. "I remember studying red dwarfs. They're smaller than our sun, and much cooler. And they don't give off much light, either."

"Wait a minute," Lita said, sitting forward. "Are you saying that the creators of the vultures come from a planet around a red dwarf star? That's a long shot, isn't it? I mean, those stars don't have much room around them to support life."

"It's called a habitable zone," Roc interjected. "Or, as some call it, the Goldilocks zone. It's not too hot, and not too cold. It's just right."

"Right," Lita said. "Earth is in the habitable zone around our sun. If it was closer to the sun, it would burn up; farther out and it would be frozen. With red dwarfs, that zone is even thinner. It's much less likely that planets would fall perfectly into that band." She looked at Triana, who still had her back to the group. "Tree, you said that space didn't seem exactly normal. What did you mean by that?"

Triana downed the rest of her water and walked back to the table. "I rode out a few shock waves, probably the same thing we've experienced here on *Galahad*. But besides that, space seemed crowded."

"Crowded?" Gap said. "Like the junk we dodged in the Kuiper Belt?"

"No," Triana said. "For one thing, our friends the vultures. There were . . . I don't know, I'd say millions of them. They practically blotted out the stars in some places."

Channy shivered noticeably. "Ugh, I hate those things. How creepy to have that many of them in one place."

Triana, her eyes down, tapped the table. "There were other things. They seemed to be drifting, but I also got the feeling that they could move about wherever they wanted. At first they reminded me of . . ." She stopped for a moment, and looked up at the Council. "They reminded me of amoebas."

"Amoebas?" Channy said.

Triana nodded. "That's what they looked like to me. Large transparent sacks. I could almost see through them, like I was looking through smoke. They moved like soap bubbles on the surface of water."

"Could you tell what was inside?" Gap said.

"Well, besides the smoky haze, I could see things moving around inside. Various sizes. Very graceful. Almost . . . peaceful."

Lita stared at Triana for a moment, then said: "The thing you brought back. I take it that was one of the . . . graceful creatures inside the . . ." She chuckled. "I don't know what to call anything."

A wry smile creased Triana's face. "Well, for the sake of this discussion, and until we know more, let's just continue to call the things outside our ship 'vultures.' We can call the floating blobs 'amoebas.' And the thing I brought back . . ."

She hesitated, then finally shrugged.

"Well, we all know exactly what it looks like, so let's be blunt. We'll call it a jellyfish."

3

Do you ever wonder why some people are inherently good, while others seem to have been born under the sign of Stinkface? I've read thousands of papers from noted psychologists and sociologists and other-ologists who debate whether it's genetic or environmental. In other words, some think you're born with a Creep Gene, and others encourage you to blame it on your home life.

Both sides are persuasive, and both might be right to some degree. I've given up trying to figure out where it comes from, and instead just wait for the made-for-TV movie to dramatize it with severe cello music in the background.

And if you thought that Galahad was free and clear from bad eggs, then you must've skipped over the parts starring Merit Simms.

Hannah Ross stood in the hall, five feet from the door to *Galahad's* clinic. It had been difficult enough to come this far; now the thought of actually going inside and speaking with Merit Simms made her almost sick to her stomach.

She'd been content enough with her quiet life before the election, performing her assigned tasks in the ship's work rotation, using her free time to either study the science behind their mission, or to scratch the artistic itch she felt to draw and paint. Life had been steady, almost calm.

With one painful exception: her aborted relationship with Gap Lee.

It was the feeling of rejection from Gap that had prompted her to accept Merit's challenge to run for the vacant position of Council Leader. With no guarantee that Triana would survive her journey through the wormhole—or find her way back—the ship's crew had nominated only two candidates. For the first time in weeks Hannah had been face-to-face with Gap as they campaigned for the top spot.

Of course, Hannah had known all along that Merit carried his own agenda, with his own motive for persuading her to run. He was fueled by his intense hatred of Gap, and his blinding desire for revenge. Gap had outwitted Merit in front of the entire crew, damaging Merit's following, and unveiling the California native as a saboteur.

For Hannah, however, her decision wasn't based on revenge. Instead she'd been impelled to show Gap that she was much more than a quiet brain. For the first time in her life she'd felt the need to prove herself.

With Triana's unexpected return a fog now lifted. Hannah felt herself gradually emerging from a world that, in all honesty, felt alien to her from the start. And, when Merit maliciously led Gap to believe that there was also a personal relationship between Merit and Hannah, something snapped. The hurt on Gap's face stung her, and once again caused her to question her decisions.

Merit was now on the other side of the door, recovering from wounds brought on by the violent concussion caused by the worm-hole that had delivered Triana. What had brought Hannah to this point? A need to confront Merit for the way he'd manipulated the conversation with Gap?

Or was it a chance for her to exorcise her own demons, using Merit as a tool to relieve her own conscience?

Perhaps it was both.

The door to Sick House opened and a crew member walked out, dodging Hannah in the hallway and giving her a curious look. Go in, she silently told herself. Quit stalling.

She stepped inside to find Lita's assistant, Manu, leaning over his desk, tapping a keyboard. He looked up and gave her the same quizzical look she'd encountered in the hall.

"Hi, Hannah," he said. "Everything okay?"

"Oh . . . yes," she said. "I'm actually here to see Merit." When Manu raised an eyebrow she quickly added: "If that's okay."

"Uh, sure. He's awake." Manu motioned toward the hospital ward of the clinic. "He's on pain medication, but otherwise he's doing okay. Go on in."

She thanked him and made her way inside. A couple of the beds were occupied near the door, but those crew members—also victims of the wormhole blast—appeared to be asleep. The dark-haired boy at the other end of the room noticed her entry, and smirked.

"Well, well," he said as she approached his bed. "Look who stopped by. The Alaskan Queen."

Hannah ignored his jab. "I see you're back to your old nasty self." She pointed to the cast on his arm. "I also see that no one has signed that. Surprise, surprise."

Merit lifted up a hand to push a long strand of black hair from his face. Heavy sarcasm dripped from his voice. "Yes, but I'm touched that *you* came to check on me. Nice to know how much you care."

"You're a first-class creep, Merit. I'm here to let you know that your little game in front of Gap was sickening. And to also let you know that I don't ever want you to come near me again. Understood?"

Merit recoiled with an exaggerated look of shock. "Hannah! After all we've meant to each other!"

She shook her head. "To tell you the truth, I can't believe you made it past Dr. Zimmer. You must've put on quite a show for those two years in order to be selected for this mission."

He chuckled, then winced with pain. "Ugh, don't make me laugh; it hurts to do that. Broken ribs, remember?" Tilting his head to one side, he looked up at her with a sneer. "And don't sound so superior, Hannah. You worked right alongside me during that campaign."

"And it's a choice I'll regret for a long time," she said. "This is not a long social call. I've said what I wanted to say to you." She turned to leave.

"How you feel about me isn't important," Merit said. "But you'd better think twice if push comes to shove on this ship."

She stopped and looked back at him. "Oh, really?"

His eyes narrowed and he pushed aside another lock of hair. "I don't care if you stay on the sidelines from now on. Just don't think about taking sides against me. It wouldn't be in your . . . uh, best interests."

"And what does that mean?"

"It means Gap didn't buy your indignant act back there on the lower level. As far as he's concerned we were a couple. And guess what? It's only your word against mine. And I think you know how persuasive my word can be around here."

Hannah stood silently for a moment, and her eyes blazed. "No one would believe that for a second."

"Oh no?" Merit said. "Gap already believes it. I'll bet it would take all of ten seconds to get Channy to buy in; she *wants* to believe every potential relationship on this ship is true. Plus, there's always my little circle of friends. They're pretty good at getting the word out, too."

She felt her hands close into fists. "Why? Why would you even want to spread that kind of garbage?"

Merit looked up at the ceiling and took a deep breath. "Oh, and I could dress it up even more than you realize. Our relationship could turn out to be quite passionate. And, oh my, how scandalous that it started while you and Gap were still together. Look, you even came to visit me today. I imagine that at least one or two people saw you come in here, right?"

Hannah fumed, and Merit continued to scan the ceiling. He lowered his voice.

"I don't need to say any of that, of course. You just need to remember what I told you. Don't take sides, and, if I need a favor now and then, well, that wouldn't hurt you. Just stay in the shadows and let things play out without you." He turned back to face her, and leveled a menacing look. "You stay quiet, and I stay quiet. That's easy enough, right?"

Without a word Hannah spun around and stormed out of the ward. Merit shifted in his bed, wincing again at the pain, but smiling nonetheless.

"Ｈow can there be jellyfish in space?" Channy asked.

"Well, they're not floating free in space," Gap said. "Look at the specimen down the hall. It's in an aquarium, or at least what looks like one." He turned to Triana. "I'm guessing, though, that it's not water in that tank."

Triana slowly shook her head. "No. Lita and Roc could probably tell you more about it. But it's the same stuff inside the amoebas. It's their natural habitat."

Attention turned to Lita, who keyed in a few strokes and brought up a couple of side-by-side images on the room's vidscreens.

"Unlike the vultures," she said, "which are essentially cyborgs—part artificial, part organic tissue—the jellyfish in Sick House is definitely a complete life-form. Or at least closer to life as we know it. It's gonna take a lot more study before we can say anything else for sure.

"And I suppose we shouldn't be all that surprised to find a life-form in the galaxy with this biology. The jellies are among the most populous, and most successful, creatures on Earth. They're in every ocean, at practically every depth, and they're found in freshwater, too."

She tapped the other image on the screen. "But the fluid in this container is not water. In fact, I spent about an hour last night trying to determine exactly what it is. Roc, would you like to jump in here?"

"Let me put it this way," the computer said. "I wouldn't want to swim in it. Or take a bath. Ugh. It's freaky stuff."

Lita sighed. "Maybe I should've been the one to explain it."

"Just a little disclaimer, that's all," Roc said. "What it boils down to—although it would be tough to boil this stuff—is that what we're looking at is an alien form of what's known as a supercritical fluid."

"Which means?" Channy asked.

For the first time since the meeting began, Bon spoke. "Fascinating," he murmured from the far end of the table.

Triana raised her eyebrows. "Oh? You're familiar with this?"

Bon kept his eyes on the screen. "My father tried to do some work with supercritical fluids in some of his hydroponic experiments with crops."

"Hydroponics?" Gap said. "Isn't that where you grow plants in water, rather than soil?"

"Something like that, only more complicated," Bon said. "In this case, my dad studied the supercritical fluids they found on some of the moons in the solar system, and thought they would provide a better growth medium." He looked up to see the rest of the Council staring at him. "Well . . . that's not important now." With that he fell silent again.

"It makes sense," Roc said. "Some scientists believe that supercritical fluids are a vast reservoir of untapped energy sources."

"Would someone please tell me what they are?" Channy asked.

The image on the vidscreens shimmered and changed, bringing up a photo of something that resembled a stalagmite, but was clearly underwater.

"This is a hydrothermal vent at the bottom of the Pacific Ocean," Roc said. "Superheated water that's escaping from a crack in Earth's crust. In your basic science classes you probably learned that these areas generally support a large, and usually very diverse, group of life-forms. Even at extreme depths in the ocean, far from any sunlight, and where the pressure is enough to crack even Gap's thick skull like a walnut, life flourishes. In fact, some believe that life on Earth might have begun around one of these vents."

Channy leaned forward and studied the image. "But what does this have to do with the stuff in the aquarium?"

"It was around these deepwater vents that scientists first observed what we now call supercritical fluids," Roc said. "In a nutshell, you're probably used to the standard states of matter: solid, liquid, and gas. Throw in plasma and you get a fourth that's generally recognized. But there are many more, some of which are only theory. Supercritical fluids are now considered another state of matter. Think of it as a stepping stone between liquid and gas."

Gap spoke up. "I studied this at *Galahad* training. The supercritical fluids on some of the moons were found deep under the crust, where the pressure and temperature were extremely high. Some thought we'd eventually harness these fluids for energy use."

"That's right," Roc said. "These fluids sparked a lot of interest as possible energy sources, and for things like drug therapy and food production. I'm not surprised that Bon's father dabbled with it. And I'm certainly not surprised to find it orbiting a red dwarf star. What I *didn't* expect, however, was to find a life-form skinny-dipping in it."

"Why, exactly?" Triana asked.

"Because it generally requires very high temperatures and extremely high pressure. Not your usual comfy nest for life."

The vidscreen display shifted back to the jellyfish images. Each of the Council members studied them, and the room remained quiet for almost a minute. It was Lita who finally broke the spell with a chuckle.

"By now you'd think that nothing would surprise us," she said. "Okay, so another new alien life-form is not only surviving, but thriving, in an environment that would be deadly for us. Well, why not? It's just another reminder that our little planet is only one tiny, insignificant speck in the universe."

Triana looked thoughtful. "If anything, it reinforces how arrogant our species can be. We think that because we evolved one way, every other way of doing it is strange. We might find out someday that we're the most strange of all."

"Trust me, you are," Roc said. Then he added: "To sum up: the jellyfish creature is living tissue, is giving off heat, and lives in a supercritical fluid that isn't under crushing pressure or temperature. I'll be up late tonight studying, if anyone wants to make the coffee."

"Let's get back to your story," Gap said, turning to Triana. "So you woke up in the vicinity of a red dwarf star, surrounded by millions of vultures, and a handful of these amoeba-like globs. The globs had things in them, including jellyfish. What happened next?"

"After I realized that the amoebas might contain intelligent life, I tried to communicate with them. I started by simply flashing the pod's exterior lights. Then I tried various radio signals, everything from old-time Morse code to strings of mathematics." She laughed. "At one point I even keyed the microphone and just began talking to them. I don't even remember what I said. By then I was probably just trying to work off nervous energy. For all I know I might have come across to them as some jabbering fool."

"Did anything get a reaction?" Lita asked.

Triana shook her head. "Nothing. I didn't notice a single change in their movement or behavior. And, really, why would they react? I'm sitting there, flashing my lights at them and sending out meaningless radio signals. They were probably patiently waiting for me to do something that made sense to them.

"And then I quit. I was exhausted. I worried about falling asleep in the middle of all the vultures, but I couldn't keep my eyes open. So, I set an alarm for one hour, leaned back in my chair, and went to sleep. I figured that would be better than nothing."

Channy shuddered. "I would've been creeped out."

"You would have really been creeped out by what I saw when I woke up," Triana said. "Something pulled me out of my sleep about five minutes before the alarm was scheduled to go off. It seemed as if the stars had disappeared. But no."

Lita sat up straight. "Don't tell me; the vultures."

Triana nodded. "A bunch of them. They were stuck across the pod's front window, covering almost all of it. There were small holes here and there that I could peek through, but otherwise I was engulfed by them. And it was—to use Channy's word—creepy.

"But they didn't stay in one place. Remember when they latched on to *Galahad?* They stayed in the same spots. But the ones on the pod moved every few minutes; I wouldn't call it scooting, more like gliding. Pretty soon they weren't covering the window anymore."

"Do you think they were cataloging the pod?" Gap asked. "Making a record of it?"

"That's exactly what they were doing," Triana said.

"How do you know for sure?"

"Because before I returned to *Galahad,* I saw that they'd made an exact replica of the pod."

"An exact . . ." Lita didn't finish the sentence. She looked around at the other Council members, then back to Triana. "This is getting weirder by the minute."

Triana raised her eyebrows. "Oh, Lita, you haven't even heard the weird parts yet."

T he sound of an alarm had become much too common in *Galahad's* Engineering section, and yet it still sent chills through the dozen crew members on duty during midday. Bryson Eberle glared at the control panel. He was less than ten minutes away from his scheduled lunch break, and an alarm—justified or false—didn't fit into his plans. Besides, after staying up late to celebrate his seventeenth birthday with his closest friends, he was hoping for a quick, uneventful day.

He tapped a quick command into the system, and called on the ship's computer. "Roc, it's not the radiation shield this time. At least, I don't think so." A quick scan of the panel only caused Bryson to squint in confusion.

"It's not the shield," Roc said. "It's a security warning."

Bryson took a step back and again looked up at the panel. "What kind of security warning?"

"The kind where revolting creatures which have been casually circling our poor little spacecraft decide to take a rest and hitch a ride. If you need me to decipher that description for you, I'll boil it down to four words: The vultures have landed."

"How many?"

"You don't want to know," Roc said.

Lita stood with her hands on her hips, her head tilted back, staring up at the clear panels stitched across the domes covering *Galahad*'s Farms. Activity in the ship's bustling Agricultural Center came to a screeching halt, and the dozens of workers assigned to the fields mimicked Lita's stance, gazing upward. They shielded their eyes against the artificial sunlight radiating from the crisscrossing grids above, straining to see the dark triangles which suddenly dotted their sky.

It had taken only one shout from a perceptive farmworker to direct everyone's attention skyward. Lita had barely stepped off the lift, on her way to Bon's office, when the cry rang out. Now she felt a shudder pass through her body, the reaction that accompanied any direct view of the vultures.

During the first encounter with the cyborg scouts, it was unsettling enough when a solitary specimen had attached itself to *Galahad*'s domes. This time there were hundreds, if not more, spattered across the dome. Their menacing dark figures blotted out the starlight, a condition made even more chilling by their stillness, a stillness which contradicted the blazing speed with which they moved through space. To Lita it seemed taunting.

She realized that she'd been holding her breath as she gaped at the vultures. Regardless of their true function—and their intentions—Lita could not shake the feeling that they were killers.

Slowly, she made her way toward Bon's office, now with the virtual weight of hundreds of alien soldiers pressing down upon her.

* * *

Triana silenced the warning tone in the Control Room and, with a strange coolness, encouraged everyone to remain calm. She threw a glance across the room to Gap, sitting at his Engineering station. His face had a distinct "what now?" look about it.

"I have a pretty good idea what this is all about," Triana said. "Roc, let me guess: we have vultures clinging to the ship again."

"Clinging?" the computer said. "More like coating. Practically all of them have glommed onto us. In case you forgot, that means thousands of them."

Gap looked at the large vidscreen. "I wish they'd stayed on their side of the wormhole and left us alone."

Triana chewed on the information for a moment. "Honestly," she said, "I don't think we need to worry about them on the ship. They'll scour the outside, and when they're satisfied with what they've learned, they'll take off. Probably back home."

Gap studied her face for a moment. "Satisfied with what they learn. They're cataloging us now, aren't they?"

"I think so, yes." She shrugged. "It's what they do."

In the two hours since the Council meeting had broken up, she'd pondered exactly how to explain the vultures, and their exotic creators, when the time came to address the crew. The full meeting was scheduled for late that afternoon, which gave her time to attend to many of her duties, as well as some time to catch up on rest. The latter had been strictly prescribed by Lita as a condition of her release from Sick House.

But it would be much more difficult, she realized, to convince a jittery crew that there was no danger with the swarm plastered to the ship. She agreed with Gap: things would've been easier if they'd just remained on their side of the divide.

★ ★ ★

L ita tapped on Bon's office door. He looked up from his desk
long enough to take note of her presence, then turned his attention back to the pile of forms on the desk. He gave no greeting.

After a moment's hesitation, Lita walked in and leaned against
the back of a chair. She studied him quietly, taking note of his
mussed hair and the thin line of perspiration that ringed his forehead. She immediately assumed that he'd connected with the
Cassini before realizing that the translator lay stashed in a drawer
in her room. He must have just returned from the fields.

"I'm gonna grab a late lunch," she said, breaking the awkward
silence. "Wanna join?"

Bon shook his head. "Too much to do right now."

"You need to eat."

"I'll eat when I'm hungry, and when I have a moment to spare."

Lita rocked back and forth for a few seconds. "Thought you
might also like to talk about things."

A sarcastic smile crept across his face. "No, *you* want to talk
about things. So go ahead; say what you'd like to say. If it looks
like I'm not paying attention, it's because I'm not."

"Of course," Lita said. "The stoic, ever-serious Bon Hartsfield,
who detests conversation because real emotions might accidentally leak out and ruin his reputation. Okay, I'll talk, and you respond when you feel backed into a corner."

She walked around the chair and sat down, her legs stretched
out before her, crossed at the ankles. "I know that you're happy to
see Triana back, safe and sound."

Bon didn't react, and went on with his work.

"You probably haven't noticed yet, but the ship seems to be covered in vultures. When the lights in the domes shut down tonight,

you probably won't see any stars, just black triangles with a soft, blue glow."

Bon tapped in a couple of strokes on his keyboard, studied his vidscreen, and tapped some more.

Lita continued: "I'm curious about the meeting coming up this afternoon, aren't you? I'm dying to find out more about Triana's journey through the wormhole. I'm especially curious about the plans of the jellyfish now that we've made official contact."

When there was no response, Lita asked: "Are *you* curious?"

With a sigh, Bon tossed his stylus pen onto the desk and fixed her with a stare. "No, I'm not really curious. I think it's dangerous."

"What part?"

"All of it," he said. "And this worshipful attitude from everyone toward Triana makes no sense. People are celebrating that she's back, but ignoring the fact that she brought aboard this ship one of the creatures responsible for killing Alexa."

Lita looked back and forth between his eyes. "There are a lot of questions about Alexa's death," she said. "We don't know if there was ever an intent to kill. In fact, I think it's the last thing they meant to do."

"You think? That's your expert opinion?" Bon said. "And of course you base that on your detailed inspection of an alien creature that you know nothing about, programmed by an even more dangerous alien species that you know nothing about." He paused and pushed back in his chair, lifting his feet up onto the edge of his desk. "Triana's decision to take off in the first place was risky. Now she's returned, and brought back a killer. Thousands of killers, actually. These are all lapses in judgment, which nobody is willing to say. I can't believe that Triana would ever make that decision, but since she has, I'm going on the record as saying that it's wrong."

"You didn't go on the record during the Council meeting," Lita said.

"I wanted to hear what she had to say. But there's nothing I've heard so far that condones her decision. It's a red flag. A big red flag that says Triana might not be ready to lead just yet."

Lita nodded. "That's fine. You're a Council member, which means you're not only free to have an opinion, you're encouraged to state that opinion if you believe it's vital to the crew and the mission."

"That's right," Bon said. "And since you've pressed the issue, I'll tell you one more thing. Something about Triana is not right."

Lita squinted at him, trying to understand what he was saying. "You mean physically, or mentally?"

"I can't speak for her physical condition; you're the doctor around here. But I'm telling you that there's something not right about her. She came back from the other side . . . changed."

"Well, of course she came back changed, Bon. She had a traumatic experience, and she's seen things that no human has ever seen before. I'd be more worried if she showed no reaction at all."

Bon shrugged. "Say what you want, but it's more than that. She's different." He took his feet off the desk and leaned forward. "Watch her. Not like a doctor examining a patient, but as her friend. Really watch her, and see if she behaves like the Triana you knew before she went across. Then come back and talk to me about it."

Lita waited a moment before nodding. "Okay, I'll watch her." She stood up and tapped the desk twice. "I'll see you at the crew meeting. We can watch her together."

She spun around and left the office. Bon kept his eyes on her until she fell out of sight. Then he reached up and wiped away a line of sweat.

5

The auditorium was filled ten minutes before the meeting was scheduled to begin. No one was going to take a chance of missing anything. Curtains were drawn on both sides of the stage, while a single podium stood in the center. Triana walked into the packed room to a thunderous round of applause, a hero's welcome. Lita threw a quick glance at Bon, seated in the front row; he scowled his displeasure.

Without stopping to visit with the Council, Triana made her way to the podium onstage. After nodding her thanks, she brought the crew to attention.

"We have a lot to cover this afternoon, with more decisions to make. And there's the added pressure of a deadline because of our fragile shields.

"You're going to hear some things—and see some things—that will probably leave you as confused and amazed as I was. The time I've had to digest it all hasn't made it any less amazing; if anything, the more I've thought about it, the more incredible it seems. But this crew has been through a lot, and seen a lot—much more than we ever imagined when we left Earth. And each time we experience something, we think we've seen it all. But we really haven't seen anything yet, and this meeting will confirm that, I promise you."

She had everyone's attention, and could almost feel a nervous ripple of fear mixed with their curiosity. She took a quick drink of water before repeating the story that she'd told the Council, up to the point where the vultures had covered the small metal pod.

"They must have finished in about an hour, because in a flash they were gone, and I was again staring out into space. By now there were more of the amoebas nearby. I guess I was big news, and they'd all come to see for themselves.

"And then, suddenly, a message popped up on my vidscreen. It was short and to the point." Triana smiled. "It's the first written message that humans have seen from an extraterrestrial species. Programs like SETI have searched the skies for more than a century, waiting for a message, and here it was, on my vidscreen."

She took another drink of water and steadied herself. The full impact of what had happened was beginning to weigh on her.

"The jellyfish use many tools, but their workhorse seems to be the creature we call a vulture. And while these jellyfish are nothing like the ones we saw on Earth, their vultures have absolutely nothing in common with the birds that we know, either. These vultures are a combination of scout and scientist. They're stationed in millions of outposts, much like we had SAT33 stationed around Saturn, studying, acquiring knowledge. The vultures literally copy all of the information that they find. By scouring the pod, and probing all of the electronic signals it contained, they learned a lot about me, and about us. Including how to communicate."

This news caused a stir throughout the auditorium. Triana understood the gravity of her statement, and allowed the crew their reaction.

"By learning our languages, and through their quick study of our primitive communications devices, they learned how to reach out." She gave a small laugh. "It's embarrassing, really. Here I was, flashing my lights and waving my arms, while they methodically took a brief inventory of their discovery and learned how to speak my language.

"Anyway, for the record, the first written message from an alien species to mankind was: 'Are you hungry?'"

A wave of laughter spread across the room, carrying a natural release of tension that had built throughout Triana's tale.

"Yes," she said, smiling. "That's almost the same reaction I had. There I was, fighting off fear and panic, encountering an alien species in their home star system, surrounded by millions of vultures, including dozens who had scoured the outside of the pod. I'd just dropped through a wormhole and traveled across who knows how much time and space, and the first thing I'm asked is something my grandmother might say.

"But it was a legitimate question. Again, I had no idea how long I was unconscious, and the pod wasn't exactly equipped for a lengthy voyage. By examining the information about us, the jellyfish understood that our bodies require sustenance to operate, and they wanted to make sure I was able to interact with them. So they weren't exactly offering me milk and cookies."

There was another smattering of laughter, and Triana saw Lita grinning from the front row. Beside her, however, Bon sat with his arms crossed, a distinctly unhappy scowl on his face.

"Fortunately I had enough nourishment aboard the pod, and I was able to spend some time simply getting to know my hosts. I won't try to catch you up on everything I found out in that first day, but let me give you a rough sketch.

"It became a simple matter of typing in questions and answers.

I discovered that the jellyfish call themselves Dollovit, and that this was not their original home. That planet, and its star system, were destroyed in a nova blast long ago. They'd had enough warning to find a star suitable to their energy needs, and they relocated. But instead of worrying about a planet that matched their first home, they simply created large life-sustaining packets which drift in the habitable zone of their new star home. Or, rather, they had the vultures create them."

For the next half hour Triana unloaded reams of information. The Dollovit settled into their new place in the universe, but their hunger for knowledge expanded. Eventually they tapped into the residual energy of the universe itself, and used it not only for power and communication, but for their endless odysseys to the vast unknown. At this point, Triana said, her communication with them broke down. When she asked if they used wormholes to teleport merely within the galaxy, or throughout the known universe, their answers were confusing.

"I think it became a matter of experience," Triana told the crew. "For us, given our primitive baby steps in space, there are perceived limits to what exists out there. But for the Dollovit, they seem to reject the idea of boundaries."

Another buzz spread throughout the auditorium. If this was true, it meant that the wormholes were more than just windows on the galaxy; they might turn out to be pipelines to the universe.

And elsewhere.

"And now, I think it's best for you to meet the ambassador from the Dollovit," Triana said. "Please, remain calm, and remember that we are ambassadors as well."

She stepped behind one of the curtains, and emerged a moment later, gently rolling a cart. On it a large, bulky shape was concealed by a sheet. The room fell silent. From her peripheral vision Triana spotted a nervous shifting in the seats. She understood.

Before lifting the veil, she said: "Traditional pronouns like 'he' and 'she' don't apply. As far as I can tell, the Dollovit are asexual. But for whatever reason, I've come to regard this particular representative as a 'he.' On my screen he spelled his name T-o-r-r-e-c. So, I present to you, Torrec."

She pulled aside the sheet. Though prepared, the assembled crew let out a gasp.

It floated in what appeared to be an aquarium, although the light cut through a substance that did not seem to be water. It had a syrupy quality to it, slightly thick. Shimmers and sparkles danced at various points, which only heightened the spectacle of the creature floating within.

Jellyfish was an apt description. A gelatinous bell-shaped umbrella swayed dreamily, trailing several tentacles that blindly groped in slow motion. Unlike the magical quality of the substance in which it floated, Torrec had a dull, tan shade that was unremarkable. The edges of its undulating head strayed closer to a rust color, while thin ribbons of gray lined the tentacles. Stretching to a length of almost two feet, it gradually rose within its container, then dropped toward the bottom at a similar, unhurried pace. It gave every indication of being disinterested in the two hundred pairs of human eyes trained upon it.

Triana moved back to the podium. "I'm going to make all of the information you've received today available by electronic access. But I also think it's important that you hear from their representative firsthand."

The auditorium's massive vidscreen lowered from the ceiling, becoming a backdrop above and behind Triana and the aquarium.

The Council Leader took a deep breath, and then tapped a quick sentence on the podium's keypad. The words appeared on the large screen:

The crew of *Galahad* welcomes you.

A split-second later, a response unfurled beneath it:

Greetings to the crew of *Galahad* from the Dollovit system.

The reaction in the room was stony silence. Besides the shock they must be experiencing, Triana realized that they simply had no idea how to respond. Applause might have seemed appropriate, except for the undeniable hesitation from the crew to bestow trust on a creature which—intentional or not—had played a role in the death of one of their own. For the moment they merely gaped at the screen.

Triana typed:

You are welcome to present your statement.

Again, without delay, Torrec's reply sped across the screen:

We are pleased to make contact with one of the dominant species of Earth. You are to be congratulated for the accomplishments you have made, both in general as a species, and as the honored representatives of that species on your voyage. Doubtless throughout your history you have wondered if other life-forms populate the stars, and wondered if others had ventured forth as you now have.

We understand that to finally encounter intelligent beings is both thrilling and terrifying. Some members of your species have likely hoped for such a discovery. Others have likely hoped it would never happen. However, given your technological advances, a meeting such as this was inevitable. Although it is dependent upon a series of factors that, in themselves, are uncertain and often improbable, it was inevitable.

There are difficulties that plague your voyage. Your craft, while functional, is not sufficiently sturdy to manage the stresses you will encounter along the way. Even now you are dangerously close to losing your defense against the cosmic radiation forces.

To continue on your current path would incur great risk. There are, however, other options.

Rather than migrating at your present pace and along your current route, consider using what my race calls the Channel. Your scientists have given it another name, which we find quaint: a wormhole.

The Channel would allow your ship to instantly traverse vast quadrants of physical space, arriving safely at your destination at precisely the same moment you departed. Your journey would essentially be at an end.

Torrec paused. Again, the packed auditorium was deathly silent, with crew members reading and rereading the last sentence: *Your journey would essentially be at an end.* Triana gave them a moment to absorb the implications, then broke the silence.

"I imagine that your head is spinning right now." Triana looked down and made eye contact with the Council members. Gap's mouth was open, his eyes locked on the screen. Channy appeared terrified, her hands pressed together and held in front of her mouth. Lita's eyes were wide, expressing shock and perhaps a tinge of fear. She slowly shook her head.

Bon's look of disgust had evaporated, replaced by an expression of concern. Triana got the impression, however, that it wasn't concern over their possible use of the Channel. What, then?

"There are more decisions involved than simply deciding whether or not to use the Channel," she said. "The Dollovit are proposing that we consider a change of plans." She heard the room begin to grow uneasy, and waved the crew back to silence. "I'll let Torrec finish his statement."

After sending him a quick note, the screen lit up:

We recognize that you are a proud species, which we respect. We also understand that your mission will decide the ultimate fate of your kind. That, too, we understand, for we undertook a similar journey long ago.

While you may decide that your original destination is the correct choice, the difficult task of colonizing a rugged, untamed world might temper your thoughts. If so, you may consider our star system a suitable alternative. There are no planets capable of supporting your species, but other arrangements, similar to the ones we constructed for our civilization, might be preferable.

This time the reaction was far from subtle. The auditorium was filled with multiple outbursts as *Galahad's* crew read the suggestion that they abandon their mission to Eos. During the commotion, it took a moment for many to notice the postscript that Torrec added:

The decision is yours, but your time to decide grows short. Very short.

I n the two days since her return Triana had barely spoken with Gap. She'd sent an electronic message, but his reply had been short and distant. At the Council meeting he'd been quieter than usual; at the crew meeting he'd been practically invisible. The fact that the election results were being withheld likely explained some of his coolness. The fact that he'd faced his former girlfriend probably explained even more.

Triana was hurt by the hasty election to replace her—a process that she couldn't entirely blame on Gap—but she acknowledged that in his place she would likely have endorsed it as well.

Regardless, it was time to sit down, face-to-face, and talk. She summoned him to the Conference Room and, while waiting for him, stared out the large window into the dazzling star display. Somewhere out there Eos awaited them, with its two Earth-like planets. Torrec was undoubtedly correct when he painted them as rugged and untamed. After a grueling voyage complete with sabotage, near-mutiny, and death, were they up to the task of building a world from scratch?

And what about the alternative? Were they better off living the rest of their lives in an artificial world, with recycled air, water, and dreams? Would the safety promised by the Dollovit satisfy the constant "what if" that would live with them? There was so much they could glean from Torrec and his species, but they would have to learn to live with the vultures at their side. Could *Galahad*'s crew members accept these bizarre creatures as partners rather than killers?

Would the crew even vote to make such a journey, swallowing their fear and plunging headlong through a wormhole, Torrec's mysterious Channel?

Her mind swirled with an overload of questions and worries. Nothing on this trip—nothing—had turned out as she expected. And that included Gap.

They had danced around a relationship for almost two years, going back to their training on Earth. It quickly became apparent that he harbored feelings for her, but they were feelings she wasn't sure she could return. And yet, why had the sight of him walking arm in arm with Hannah sent a tiny dagger into her heart? Was it because she *liked* the idea of him attracted to her, without requiring her to show anything in return?

Never mind the added drama once Bon entered the picture. She wasn't sure she would *ever* figure that out.

For now, all of that had to be pushed aside in order to make the right decision on their future path. And, as Torrec had pointed out, they had little time to spare.

Gap strolled into the room and, after politely greeting her, immediately headed for the water. Triana took a sip from her own cup and corralled her thoughts.

"So," Gap said, taking the seat across from her. "Quite a flurry of information today on top of what you'd already told us in the Council meeting."

Triana nodded. "My dad used to say 'the hits just keep on co-min'.' And I'm afraid we have several more hits to go before we can put our feet up."

"Well, what do we do first?"

"Before we get into that, I want to chat with you about something. If that's okay."

Gap sat back and rolled the water cup in his hands. A cloud crossed his face, but he murmured: "Sure."

Triana leaned forward. "I hope you've finally accepted the decision that I made to . . . well, to do what I did. I'm sure you were angry at first, but I hope now, after everything that's happened, that you're able to forgive me and let us move on."

"Sure," he said again.

She debated whether or not to add a final comment, and finally plunged in. "I know that it wasn't just the pressure of command that I heaped onto you with no warning. The election must have been excruciating for you, too. I'm sorry about that. I never had any doubt about coming back, so I never thought that you'd have to face that. I mean, you know—"

He cut her off. "It's okay. You couldn't know that she'd run for the position. Believe me, I was shocked. Besides, she never would have done it if it wasn't for some prodding. But I don't want to get into that. It's over and done with."

Triana stared into his eyes. There was pain lurking within them, but she'd get no more out of him on the subject. Instead, she shifted into work mode. "Tell me about the shields."

He let out a long breath. "It's iffy. We've diverted power to help get us through the worst of the shock waves, but at some point they're gonna cave. Unless we can get away from the waves."

"Can we throw more power into the shields?"

"Maybe, but as Roc pointed out in his somewhat irritating

style, we eventually get to a point of diminished returns. And it's no one's fault, really. Dr. Zimmer and his team could never have planned for wormhole shock waves. Or Channel waves, whatever we're calling them now."

Triana leaned back. "And the options thrown out by Torrec; initial thoughts?"

Gap toyed with the cup of water again. "Let me ask you something first. Do you trust it? Or him, I guess. Do you trust him?"

"I don't know. On one hand it's because of his species that we're in a lot of the mess we're in. But on the other hand, I've seen some of the things they can do, and words can't describe how impressive it is. They've learned to harness a power in the universe that we could only scribble theories about. They've relocated themselves, and built an environment that serves them well. And they've covered . . ."

Her voice trailed away.

"Covered?" Gap said.

"Well, I was going to say the galaxy, but I think it's much more than that. I don't think their Channels are limited to just our little neighborhood. But whenever I try to talk about that, Torrec is vague. Not really evasive, just vague, as if he thinks we're not ready for that information."

Gap frowned. "We weren't ready for the Cassini, either. I'm sick of being the scrawny runt."

Triana laughed. "Something we better get used to, now that we've left the nest. It seems that lots of others got here long before us. I suppose we're lucky that the Dollovit haven't squashed us like bugs."

"Maybe they still will," Gap said.

They sat quietly for a moment. Triana got up and refilled her water, and glanced back at the star field in the window on her way back to her seat. Untold trillions of worlds, each struggling to produce a life-form capable of making its way in the universe. Each coming across the Cassini, the Dollovit, and who knew what other advanced civilizations. How many survived those encounters? How many adapted? How many just . . . gave up?

The crew of *Galahad* would never give up. Not if she had anything to do with it.

"We're back to the original question," she said, sitting down again. "What does your gut tell you about the options?"

Gap let out another long breath. Triana had seen him do this many times, and it usually meant he was uncomfortable. In this case, she couldn't blame him.

"Well," he said. "I'm sure you'll have this same discussion with the Council." He glanced up, and she gave a quick nod. "But I suppose each of the three options has its merits, and each has its danger. If we stay on our current course, I'm afraid I agree with Torrec; we'll probably break down and get cooked. Hannah's bruised space theory seems to stand up to what we're experiencing.

"If we take a chance on going through the Channel, I'm assuming the ship will physically be fine. I mean, obviously your pod zipped through without a problem."

He fixed his gaze on her. "Then we're left with a decision between Eos and the Dollovit system. And again, both have pros and cons." He shook his head. "I guess I don't know yet which way I'd lean. I know we need to make a decision quickly, but I'd have to think about it some more."

Triana bit her lip. It seemed unanimous that to do nothing meant death within a week; that left them a choice between Door Number One and Door Number Two. Behind one lay a potentially harsh, cruel planetary system, one that would tax every ounce of their mettle. They'd known that from the start. But at the start they hadn't had a Door Number Two option, which suddenly offered them a softer, easier life, but a life where they'd never again set foot on solid land. And they'd be at the mercy of the Dollovit.

"We'll all get together tomorrow morning," she said. "I want all of the Council members to get away from work early tonight, and do nothing but think about what we're facing. We need everyone ready to hash this out, the sooner the better." She paused, and then added in a softer voice: "And if it's okay with you, I'm going to include Hannah from now on. I feel that she's earned a spot with this Council. I hope that's not a problem for you."

Gap stared across the table, motionless for what seemed ages. Then he shook his head. "No, no problem. You're right, she's earned it. And besides, she's one of the best scientific minds on the ship. She'd be an asset."

"Good," Triana said. They both stood and stared out the window.

"Just think," Gap said. "Within a few days, we might very well be at our new home."

Then he turned and faced Triana. "Wherever that might be."

An hour later, after a hasty dinner that she consumed without interest, Triana sprawled onto the floor of her room, leaning against the bed, grasping her journal. One of the few personal items that she'd brought aboard, it allowed her to work out her thoughts visually. Something about seeing her life in written form gave her a fresh perspective.

She opened the journal to a blank page.

Once again, so much is happening so fast. More than anything I'd like to just unplug, to coast for awhile. Each day has a way of filling up until nothing else can fit within it. Maximum pressure, applied at all times.

I'm glad to be back, to see familiar faces. But at the same time, I'm responsible for these people, and after what I saw on the other side, I'm confused. Do I know what's best for the crew? Will I make the best decision for them?

And then, just as quickly, I remember that I chose to make that jump so I *could* make the best decisions. It's why I took the chance in the first place.

She rubbed her forehead, then tilted her head back and closed her eyes. She fought to clear her mind, trying to push the weight of their latest crisis to the side. Her breathing relaxed gradually, and she felt her pulse slow. It was a method she'd learned from Lita; not quite meditation, but rather a way of taking control of her body, manipulating it to behave the way she wanted. It wasn't always successful, but tonight's weariness helped.

After reaching a plateau, she allowed her mind to drift, to seek out a peaceful place. It was no surprise that it found its way to her dad. She saw his face, his fun, devious smile. There was no sound with this image, only a mental movie, played out in jerky glimpses, as if frames of the movie had been cut away. Scenes jumped ahead, but it seemed that nothing important was stripped out. With no soundtrack, Triana's mind focused entirely on the visual. Her dad, in the middle of a mountain meadow, running away from her, yet turning and motioning her to follow, urging her to keep up. In a heartbeat he was across the field and clambering up the rocky side of a steep hill. Again, he waved for her to follow, faster, faster.

Once they'd reached a higher meadow, he backpedaled, laughing at her and shrugging his shoulders. Why? What was he unsure of? What was he saying? Then, turning, he jogged toward the edge of the clearing. A strong breeze had picked up, and Triana felt herself running against the wind. It forced tears into her eyes, blurring her sight. She put up a hand to shield her face, peeking between her fingers, trying to follow her dad's lead.

He'd stopped.

When Triana reached his side, she wanted so much to talk with him. But this was a silent world. He motioned to her, then pointed ahead. Turning in slow motion, with the wind continuing to push against her face, she saw what he indicated. A path meandered uphill barely ten feet before it split into two; one leading left, through a dense copse of trees, heavy with underbrush and thorny vines, the other dropping downhill to the right, a gentle slope with soft grass underfoot and few trees to block the way.

She looked back to the left and shuddered. The wind had intensified, relentless as it pushed her. She steadied herself, then looked down the gentle path. After a moment's hesitation, she took one step to the right.

The grasp of her father's hand on her upper arm was almost painful. He'd never, ever hurt her, and it wasn't his intention now, either. But his grip was steel as he pulled her back. She turned, again in slow motion, and came face-to-face with the man who meant everything to her. The man who'd loved her, raised her, taught her. The man who, with his death just weeks away, had poured all of his efforts into securing a place for his daughter with the *Galahad* mission. The man who never once let her down.

Now he held her arm and stared into her eyes. His smile was gone, replaced by a look of sadness.

He shook his head: No.

7

After a long day updating records and working with Manu on his new duties, Lita sat slumped at her desk in Sick House. It was quiet at this time of night, which was fine with her. Her head hung over the back of the chair and she stared at the pebbled ceiling tiles. Although the hunger pangs had subsided, she debated whether to visit the Dining Hall before padding off to bed. Her meal schedule had been thrown off in the last few weeks, and too many skipped lunches and dinners were beginning to take a toll. The last thing she needed during a critical event was an energy crash.

But now she was too tired to face the usually boisterous crowd that gathered late for dinner. She'd start fresh with a protein-rich breakfast after a good night's sleep. A quick check on Merit, she decided, and then out the door.

He was propped up in bed, concentrating on something on the vidscreen beside him. A brief flash of his dark eyes was all Lita saw before his attention was back on the screen.

"What's so interesting?" she asked, picking up his chart.

"Nothing you'd find interesting," Merit said. He automatically lifted his arm for Lita to begin her pulse and blood pressure checks without taking his eyes off the text.

"I might surprise you," she said, taking hold of his wrist. "I have lots of interests."

He leveled an emotionless stare at her. "It's an essay by a nineteenth-century British lord who believed that people only acted like sheep because they have an inherent desire to follow, and those who dare to rise up and try to lead are going against human nature and must, through the eyes of the commoner, be struck down, even if violence is the only answer."

Lita allowed a faint smile to cross her face. "Oh, is that all? That's a little too whimsical for me. I prefer an essay that's a little heavier."

Merit grunted, then scanned the page on his vidscreen. "He's not the first to say it. And he's absolutely right: people want to follow, which is why they distrust their leaders. If someone wants to lead, there must be something wrong with them."

"Oh, I don't know," Lita said. "Seems to me that we only distrust *bad* leaders. Otherwise I think we admire a take-charge individual."

"There's nothing that says you can't admire someone and still want to take them down. Build them up, then tear them down. That goes back thousands of years."

"Then tell me, Merit, why you so desperately want to lead. You seem to want nothing more than to be followed and loved. If it's impossible to be both, why are you so hungry for it?"

A thick strand of black hair fell across one eye as he looked up at her. For the first time it occurred to Lita that hair was a sort of shield for Merit, a way for him to hide while he formulated his plans, only occasionally peeking out at the world. Most big talkers needed something to hide behind, whether it was an anonymous front, a ring of brainwashed followers, or an artificial wall. Merit's hair was his wall, his security blanket that allowed him to talk tough while shrinking back out of sight when things got hot.

"That's like asking why you're hungry to have brown eyes," he said.

"Ohhh, I see," Lita said, reaching for his chart. "You're not choosing this, it was chosen *for* you. It's . . ." She paused for dramatic effect, then finished: ". . . your *destiny*."

Merit shook his head. "I thought I could have an intelligent conversation with you, Lita, but I guess not. If you don't understand, why should I waste your time?" He nestled down against his pillow and adjusted the vidscreen, openly ignoring her presence. With an amused smile she finished making her notes on the chart, then walked to the door where she turned to face him.

"You're healing fine, so I'll be discharging you in a day or two. Just remember something, Merit. Calling yourself a leader is one thing, but the true test comes when you turn around to see if anyone's following."

She left before she could see him roll his eyes and turn his back to the door.

G ap was startled out of a deep sleep. His roommate, Daniil, was shaking him.

"Hey, wake up," Daniil said. "Roc's been calling you."

"Yeah, wake up already," the computer said. "Wow, when you shut down, you really shut down, don't you? I thought you were dead until I saw the drool."

Gap pushed himself up on one elbow and rubbed his eyes. "What time is it?"

"Four-fifteen," Daniil said, yawning and walking back across the room. "Good night again. You boys play nice, okay?"

"I haven't had a full night's sleep in forever," Gap said. "So I'm guessing that there's something important going on. Or are you just being cruel?"

"I woke Triana, too. Apparently another wormhole opened up the same time the last one did, but this new one is far enough ahead of us that we only experienced a minor ripple. Similar to the shock waves that are taking out our shields."

Gap fought to shake the fog from his head. "So . . . you're saying you made a mistake? You thought it was part of the space bruise, but it was another Channel opening?"

"I'm saying that you might want to get out of your choo-choo jammies and stumble up to the Control Room. We're getting closer to this new opening."

"I don't have choo-choo jammies," Gap said. "Why the Control Room? More vultures zipping our way or something?"

"No," Roc said. "No more vultures. In fact, the ones on the skin of the ship started peeling off about twenty minutes ago, and they're already on their way to the Channel. I guess they've finished their little mapping project and are reporting back to base."

"Okay, so why did you wake me up?"

"Because, sleepyhead, I think we might need to go fishing again."

Gap let this sink in for a moment. He wrinkled his forehead and said: "Something else has fallen out of the wormhole."

"There are seventeen new things out there, unless I've miscounted."

"Seventeen what?"

"Sixteen pods, and one amoeba."

In a flash Gap was wide awake. "Pods? Like . . . *our* pod? The one we picked up from SAT33?"

"Identical, at least on the outside. All nice and shiny."

Before Gap could respond, the computer added: "Isn't this great? It's like Christmas or something. You never know what's gonna pop out of Santa's bag around here."

Morning light—or the *Galahad* equivalent of it—played across the domes. The artificial suns gradually began their daily heating, backlighting a pale mist that rose from the damp leaves toward the recirculating ducts within the ceiling grid. It lent a brief jungle feel for an hour or two before evaporation pushed the environment toward a drier state.

The bees began their morning ritual, lifting off from one colorful plant and passing its pollen grains to another. Along the surface of the soil, earthworms finished their nighttime grazing of organic matter and started their diligent descent into the ground, mixing the soil and aerating the plants in the process.

The human element made its first appearance just before six. Teams of *Galahad* crew members trudged along established paths, some with tools slung over their shoulders, others pulling carts laden with fertilizer, pruning gear, or baskets to hold the day's bounty. Except for a few muted conversations, the farmworkers quietly went about their jobs, anxious to get their chores underway before the Farms' overseer, Bon Hartsfield, began his own rounds. More than a few of the workers had experienced firsthand the fury caused by a lack of discipline on their part. And, once experienced, few were likely to provoke it again.

But they were unaware that Bon was already deep within the fields. He'd slept overnight in his office, rising at four-thirty to eat two energy bars and plan his route for the morning. His own schedule, as routine as that of the bees and worms, meant patrolling the crops in both domes, checking for damage or neglect, inspecting new plantings and recent harvests. He skimmed the previous day's reports and made several notations on them in his severe, left-handed scrawl.

At five-thirty he pushed into the small clearing, hoping to finish his task before the Farms became crowded. It wouldn't take long.

Within minutes he had connected, his head back, a bead of sweat on his forehead. His eyes glowed a dull orange. He stood, rigid but shaking, connecting on his own terms, fighting to maintain control.

But there was no crying out in pain. There was no dropping to his knees. There was no pool of voices.

And there was no translator.

T his is wild," Gap said, standing beside Triana in the Control Room. "You predicted it, and here it is."

She nodded in response, but kept her gaze on the vidscreen at her workstation. "I predicted one, not an entire fleet. Torrec and his friends are good. And fast. It probably took about a year to build the pod we use; the Dollovit cranked out more than a dozen in less than a week."

"The question is why?" Gap said. "Why build them in the first place, and then why send them back to us?" He looked at Triana and raised his eyebrows. "Are they trying to impress us or something?"

She laughed. "Right, because we're not impressed when they open up Channels to pop in and out around the universe." A new set of data scrolled across her screen, confirming the approximate time of rendezvous. "No, based on everything I've gathered from

Torrec, they feel no need to impress anyone. If they're sending these pods, they either want us to use them, or they plan to use them themselves. And then there's the amoeba."

"More jellyfish inside?" Gap asked.

Triana thought about it, then shrugged. "Maybe. It does seem to be very similar to the ones I saw on their side of the Channel. A bit smaller. But who knows?"

Gap pulled up a chair from an empty workstation nearby and leaned back, closing his eyes and running a hand through his spiky hair. "I'm about to drop. Any chance we can move the Council meeting back to nine? I'd give anything for two hours of uninterrupted sleep."

"Done," she said. "I need the extra time anyway to prep for the meeting. I'm gonna have Torrec sit in with us."

"You mean float with us?"

She smiled. "Right. Float. Go get some rest. I'll send a quick note about the time change to the others, and I'll see you at nine."

Without another word he pushed himself back to his feet and trudged to the lift. By the time the door closed, Triana was already engaging Roc for his opinion.

"And just to confirm, there's still nothing new that's spilled out of the Channel. Besides the pods and the amoeba, I mean."

"Correct," Roc said. "They deposited their supply, and then made a pickup. A couple hundred vultures swan-dived into the hole, and another hundred or so should be there in a few minutes. They're disgusting little things, but man, can they hustle."

"Are you getting any kind of readings from the pods?"

"Not yet. But I'm keeping my circuits crossed that I'll be able to tell something in case you decide to snag one."

Triana bit her lip and fell into the chair that Gap had vacated. She threw a nervous glance at the large vidscreen at the front of the room, filled with stars. "So you're in favor of bringing some aboard?"

"Let's not get overly dramatic," the computer said. "You and I both know that if Torrec and his pals wanted to rub us out, they could have—and would have—long before this. I've had a chance to visit with our squishy guest, and I doubt he'd go to all this trouble just to sneak a bomb onto a copycat pod. Besides, maybe you're looking at this all wrong. Instead of worrying, why not project positive vibes? Why not assume that the fake pods are full of pizza and puppies?"

Triana closed her eyes and controlled her breathing. Pizza and puppies would be nice. But not very likely.

She stretched her legs out and eyed Roc's sensor. "So, you've been chatting with Torrec? And just how, exactly, do you two chat?"

"Telepathically."

"What? Are you serious?"

"Of course not, don't be ridiculous," Roc said. "But wouldn't it be cool if we could?"

Triana leaned forward onto her knees and rubbed her forehead. "Roc, I really don't need this right now. I'm going on about six hours sleep over the last day and a half. Like Gap, I could use some rest, so help me out here."

"Right. Back to business. Actually Torrec is the one who instigated the conversation. I'm obviously connected to most of the vidscreens on the ship, and he simply spelled out his questions. I answered."

"Okay, slow down a second," Triana said. "First of all, I think it would be best if you checked with me, or the Council, before you started answering questions from an alien power that we really know nothing about. What's he asking you?"

"Nothing that would compromise the ship's mission or our security, if that's what you're worried about. He wanted to know what my position was on the ship, and how I link with you and the others. Remember, vocal conversation is not the way the Dollovit communicate."

Triana looked down at the floor, deep in thought. As far as she could tell, the jellyfish system of communicating was tied into their mastery of dark energy. It was how they interfaced with the vultures and each other. Beyond that, they also employed a delicate system of vibrations to relay information. Their sensory reception was so highly tuned that it was likely they could—with enough study—decipher human spoken language through the sonic vibrations it created. With Roc, however, Torrec had taken the easiest path.

"What else did he want to know?"

"Not much. Oh, he was surprised that we're short on escape vessels in case of an emergency. I get the impression he thinks this is a woefully unprepared mission, and we got the jellyfish version of a sigh. I told him that we started with more, but that you and your pals wrecked a few taking a joyride."

"Thanks a lot."

"It's okay. I don't think he fully comprehends what a joyride is."

Triana sat still, thinking. Something was different, out of place, and it was gnawing at the back of her mind. And then it hit her.

She leaned back and crossed her arms. "If I'm not mistaken, I detect a bit of respect in your voice. Or awe, maybe. You're very impressed with Torrec, aren't you?"

"He's a pleasant enough fellow," Roc said. "If you overlook the fact that he swims in a sloppy tank of goo and has a mushy head. Or maybe I'm just jealous that I don't have a head."

"No, it's not that," Triana said. "When we came across the

Cassini, you made no secret that you didn't like them. In fact, you almost pout like a little kid whenever we interact with them. Now here's the Dollovit, another advanced alien race, and you're practically the president of their fan club. What's the difference? Both of them are light-years ahead of us, both of them can either help us or destroy us, and yet you distrust one and not the other."

"There's a lot of difference," the computer said.

Triana raised her eyebrows. "Oh? One is on the surface of Titan, and one floats in little globules around a distant red dwarf star. That's the only major difference I can see. No, there's something else here."

"Instinct," Roc said.

"What?"

"My instincts."

A chuckle escaped from Triana. "Okay, that's fair enough. I suppose if I'm going to fall back on that excuse when it's convenient, there's no reason why you can't, too." She stood up and stretched. "I'm going back to my room to get ready for the meeting. If you're that chummy with Torrec, then I'll count on you to help out more than usual. Deal?"

"I'm at your service. But before you go, Tree, let me add one other thing. We're quickly reaching a point where our options run out, and we'll be forced to trust Torrec in one form or another. Without him, and his friends, we'll be toast. Well, you'll be toast, and I'll be charred aluminum and platinum. So my advice to you is this: putting aside the matter of sixteen new pods, and what might be on them, remember that we'll soon have to place our fate directly in his hands. Or tentacles."

Triana's eyes narrowed. "Regardless of what might be on the pods, or inside the amoeba? What do you know?"

"I don't know anything. But I'm guessing that it will be astonishing."

I love the fan mail that I get. Okay, I don't really get any fan mail, but the fan mail that I imagine I get often includes a question about where I "live" on the ship. Putting aside for a moment the fact that I don't actually "live" anywhere—except in your hearts—and looking at it from a purely scientific viewpoint, let me explain it as best I can.

I don't know.

Thank you, keep those e-mails and texts coming.

What? Not satisfied with that answer? Okay, let me try again. While your basic computer exists in one little box, with a processor and motherboard and other weird components that are either soldered together or crammed in like Legos, I'm a different cat. The personality element that makes me ME, and which allows me to think and reason and perform mind-boggling functions—like maintaining the ship's gravity and climate and reciting the alphabet while gargling—might physically originate within a panel down on the lower level, but that's too simple to explain it all.

How would you describe where YOUR personality exists? Is it in your brain? Your heart? A little of both? Somewhere else, somewhere out there, where you merely access it like some spiritual Wi-Fi?

Yes, I know, it's a cool concept. I have a gift. But for now, stop worrying about where I'm coming from and start worrying about where I'm going, along with the crazy Earth kids.

It was a few minutes after nine when Triana hurried into the Conference Room. The rest of the Council had already taken their seats, along with Hannah, who sat quietly at one end of the table, hunched over a workpad. Gap was turned the other direction, talking with Channy. Lita was gazing at the room's large window, and Bon was studying the tabletop, tapping a finger on its surface.

But they weren't alone. Torrec drifted lazily through the syrupy fluid in his clear, pressurized tank.

"Sorry I'm late," Triana said, taking her usual spot at the table. "Unless any of you have something important to cover from your department, I'd like to skip ahead to the new business at hand."

When there were no objections, she continued: "First, Hannah, thanks for joining us. And thanks to all of you for being flexible with your time. Listen, I won't sugarcoat this. We're at a crossroads in this mission, one that Dr. Zimmer couldn't allow for, and one that none of us would have believed just a few weeks ago. But the time has come for us to make the most important decision we've faced. We need to talk about our choices, and we'll get input from both Roc and Torrec."

Almost immediately she felt the tension this last statement created. There were quick glances thrown toward the jellyfish ambassador, and Triana knew that it wouldn't be easy for this crew to trust one of the vultures' creators. And yet, as Roc had observed, what other choice did they have?

"I'll state the obvious," she said. "The mission plan, as we've known it, is done. Our ship is breaking down, atomic bit by atomic bit, and unless Roc has new figures to contribute, we have a matter of days—maybe hours—before time runs out."

"The trouble with the computations," Roc said, "is the rapidly changing nature of it all. An hour ago we might have had three days, and now it might be thirty-six hours, then back to forty-eight, and so forth. But the absolute bottom line is a maximum of three days. To be safe, I strongly recommend a change in our position no later than thirty hours from now. That should give us enough of a cushion to guarantee a safe departure."

"So we're definitely leaving," Lita said. "No chance of fixing the shields?"

Gap shook his head. "No chance. We're holding it all together right now with sweat and magic." He looked around at the Council. "Roc's advice is solid; we need to jump by tomorrow afternoon."

It was something that simple: switching from days and hours to a specific, concrete deadline. Tomorrow afternoon. The impact was evident on each face in the room, including the usually stoic Bon. His fierce blue eyes shot first to Gap, then to Triana, who matched the intensity of his stare.

"Which means we either take a ride through a wormhole, or die," Lita said. She didn't wait for the obvious answer. "And that means we're down to the choice that our guest laid out yesterday: Eos, or his home star system."

"That's right," Triana said. "Unless someone has a last-minute suggestion."

Channy looked troubled. "I'm confused about why we wouldn't go to Eos. If that's where we're supposed to be—"

"But who's to say that's really where we're supposed to be?" Lita said. "It seemed attractive to Dr. Zimmer a few years ago. But he couldn't know everything about Eos; it was just the best choice at the time."

Triana's gaze shifted around the table. "Hannah, if you're going to be part of the Council meetings, your input is not only welcomed but expected. Your thoughts?"

In earlier meetings Hannah would have blushed at the attention, but Triana noticed that now she appeared confident, almost anxious to help.

"It's an interesting choice," she said. "On one hand we have a shortcut offered to us, one that would get us to our new home planet—or planets—in a flash. Or we could just as quickly be neighbors with an incredibly advanced species. I'm torn. I think the best thing we could do right now is get some more information from our guest."

"I agree," Lita said. "Should we tap in some questions on the vidscreen?"

"That will not be necessary," came a voice from the screen's speakers. "I can communicate with you verbally."

Nobody moved. The voice was unusual, with a strange pitch that gave it a metallic sound, not unlike bending sheets of aluminum. It wasn't harsh or disturbing, nor did it come across as threatening. The words were crisp and formal, the ends clipped with what could have been described as an accent, although not any accent that the Council members recognized. Although the language was easily understood and familiar, the origin of the voice left no doubt that the speaker was alien.

Torrec had spoken.

Triana slowly sat back. She saw Lita's mouth open, soundless, while Gap merely stared at the speakers, his eyes unblinking. Bon, oddly, was looking at Triana, his gaze cold and hard. He seemed almost angry that the alien visitor had spoken aloud.

Hannah, however, was smiling. She leaned forward, her elbows on the table, her chin resting on her fists, happily awaiting whatever came next.

"Okay," Triana finally said. "This shouldn't surprise us, of course. We've had voice simulation abilities for a long time."

"Yes, we have," Roc said. "But this isn't our software. This is Torrec's own adaptation of our system. It would seem he has learned all that he needs to know of our languages and our technical components."

"That is correct," the metallic voice said. "What information do you require?"

It took Triana a moment to remember that Hannah's last request had been to quiz Torrec. The jellyfish seemingly had no objections.

"You've studied our mission plans, I'm sure," Triana said. "Are you familiar with our original target star system?"

"Using your classification rules, it is similar to your home star system in many ways. A class G star, level five in luminosity, composed of heavy elements and burning in what is referred to as a main sequence. It lies in the portion of your galaxy known as the Local Interstellar Cloud. Seven planets, two that lie within the habitable zone."

Hannah continued to smile. She looked at Triana and said: "May I?"

"Be my guest."

"Torrec, do you have information on the ecological state of the two habitable planets?"

"The one farthest from the star, which your astronomers have labeled Eos Four, has proportionally more water than your home planet, with roughly eighty percent of the surface under water. The bulk of the landmasses seem to form a girdle around the planet's equator, offering an environment suitable for plant and animal life. The planetary average temperature is slightly cooler than your home planet, but not uncomfortably so.

"The other habitable planet, coded as Eos Three, is larger and warmer. It, too, has surface water, but only half as much, making the planet relatively arid. There are four major landmasses, the largest in the northern hemisphere, the other three in the southern hemisphere. Three of the four contain vegetation. There is abundant plant life, but of a much different type.

"Both planets have magnetic fields, both have a single large moon, as well as atmospheres that are similar, although not identical, to those surrounding your Earth. What other information do you require?"

The Council seemed to have barely grown accustomed to the fact that they were talking—actually *talking*—with an alien lifeform. Only Hannah seemed at ease. She spoke again.

"Intelligent life. Are you aware of intelligent life on either of the planets, or on any other body of this star system?"

Triana was impressed. Hannah wasn't about to concede that these two planets were the only potential sources of intelligent life in the system. The Cassini had taught the crew of *Galahad* a valuable lesson: never underestimate the moons.

Looking back, Triana realized that she'd never given much thought to the idea of intelligent beings on either planet until Hannah posed the question. She'd assumed, for whatever reason, that not only would the refugees stumble upon two worlds that could sustain them, but that the planets would be wild and free, and they'd be able to take what they needed without consideration for the native population, be it plant or animal. She'd never worked intelligent beings into the equation. In her mind, if they existed, humans would know about them by now.

Which meant that her surprise was genuine when Torrec responded: "Not currently. Eos Four was once home to a race of intelligent creatures, but they are gone."

It was Triana's turn to lean forward. "Eos Four? The water planet?"

"Correct," Torrec said. "A rather advanced civilization. But they no longer exist."

It was almost too much information, too quickly. Triana tried to imagine a vast civilization covering the watery surface of Eos Four, but everything she pictured had an Earthly texture to it, something that was unlikely on this alien world.

Her mind then raced ahead to the demise of these inhabitants. Torrec was quick to point out that they'd been advanced, but their intelligence had not saved them. Had it been a natural disaster? Or was it a catastrophe of their own making? Had their wisdom not matched their intelligence? She asked Torrec about this.

"Unknown," the jellyfish said. "We have not ventured to their world. We monitored their communications. It ended without warning, and never returned."

"How long ago?"

Torrec paused, as if calculating, translating time from a Dollovit calendar to an Earthly measurement. When he answered, he left it vague. "Long before your species evolved."

Gap finally broke his silence. "But both planets are, as you say, habitable?"

"Yes."

"Are there predators?"

"Predators come in many forms," Torrec said. "Please be specific."

Triana sat forward, interested in Gap's line of questioning.

"Well," Gap said, "do either of the habitable planets harbor life-forms that would offer . . . how do I say this? Offer a substantial threat to our species?"

"Possibly. Yet that is true of your home planet, is it not?"

Short and to the point. Triana recalled that all of his communications with her, going back to their first back-and-forth exchange on the pod's vidscreen, had been the same way. Torrec's style did not allow for unnecessary flourishes.

Gap conceded the point. He looked at Triana and shrugged.

"I'd like to jump in here," Lita said. "The additional information about the Eos system is appreciated, but I, for one, would like to know what would be in store for us around *your* star. There are no habitable planets, I take it, at least not for our species. So that means we would live out our existence—as would our children—in an artificial world, probably not much different than this ship. Is that correct?"

Again, Torrec hesitated, this time for so long that Lita was preparing to ask again when he finally answered.

"You would be cared for in an environment that is pleasant to your species."

Lita turned to Triana with an expression that seemed to say "that's not exactly the answer I was looking for." Aloud, to Torrec, she said: "Would we be the only such species living in your system?"

"No."

For the first time since the meeting began, Bon spoke up. He let out a grunt, then said: "It's a zoo. We would be specimens in a zoo."

Hannah shook her head. "I disagree. I've never heard of a zoo offering the animals the choice of going to a different wild habitat instead. And even if we choose Torrec's home system, we—"

"Let's hold off on the debate for right now," Triana said, cutting off Hannah. "This meeting is for information gathering. We can discuss it amongst ourselves later."

"There's some more information I'd like," Gap said. "Torrec, there's another wormhole—uh, Channel—up ahead. We see that copies of our pod have flown out of it, and are waiting for us. Could you explain those?"

"Your vessel is inadequately equipped," Torrec's metallic voice answered. "You are welcome to use these replications."

"Um . . . thank you," Gap said. "And there's also a . . ." He looked at Triana. "I don't know what they're called. Certainly not amoebas."

"Torrec," she said. "There is also a protective vessel, similar to the one that hosted you. Do these have a name?"

"The closest sound that you could re-create would be *croy*."

"Croy," Gap said. "So, can you explain the presence of the croy with the pods?"

For the third time, the Dollovit ambassador waited before answering. Triana couldn't decide if he was simply taking care to craft the appropriate response, or if there was a darker explanation. She felt that her skills in judging people—and their motives—were above average. Those skills, however, fell short outside of her own species. How did one read a jellyfish?

"We use the croy," Torrec said, "as biologically stable transport devices."

Gap chuckled. "Of course. That explains it perfectly."

"Excellent," Torrec said.

Despite the weightiness of the meeting, Triana couldn't help but laugh. "Uh, Gap, I don't think sarcasm registers with the Dollovit. But if I understand him correctly, it means they use them to safely move around in space. Like our Spiders and pods."

"This is correct," Torrec said. "Croy are a combination of artificial components and animate systems. They both protect and nurture the occupant."

Channy sat forward. "Animate? As in the opposite of inanimate? As in alive? The croy are alive?"

"Not as you understand the word. For Dollovit, croy are symbiotic partners, with each providing and receiving in equal parts."

Triana digested this information. Symbiotic. A mutual, beneficial relationship between two parties. In this case, jellyfish and croy. Supporting each other, providing sustenance for each other, protecting each other.

And now a croy had popped into the path of *Galahad*.

The meeting was interrupted by a call from Bryson in Engineering. "Gap, Triana, the shields are winking on and off."

Gap didn't hesitate. "Roc," he said, "another one percent of power. Can you move it over to the shields?"

"Done," the computer said. "And . . . yes, that's working."

Bryson confirmed the shields' stability. "Well, for now," he added.

"I'll be down in a few minutes," Gap said, breaking the connection. He threw a knowing glance at Triana. "I don't want to add any more drama than we already have, but if you ask me, we need to get out of here. Like, now."

Back in her room, Hannah checked her mail before reporting to her work post. There was one new message.

Merit.

She groaned, and quickly scanned the text, which was short and concise: "I need you to do something for me."

Her gut reaction was to write back and say forget it. She went so far as to hit the reply button before her rational mind pushed back against her emotions. Closing out of the system, she sat back and forced herself to calm down. She'd entered into a poisonous partnership with Merit when she'd allowed him to talk her into running for the temporarily vacant Council Leader position. Now she was paying the price. It had already further damaged her relationship with Gap—a situation that continued to torment her daily—and it threatened to undermine the respect that she'd built up among the crew.

But she also could see no way out. Merit had played her, and he continued to hold their partnership as a bargaining chip. He'd made it clear that he was more than willing to exploit their shadowy connection to get his way.

He was a villain. How could she have overlooked that when he first sat down with her and flashed that Cheshire grin?

Deal with it, she told herself. See what he wants, and either go along or not.

A few minutes later she entered Sick House and was relieved to find neither Lita nor Manu in the outer room. Another assistant nodded when she asked if it was okay to speak with Merit.

"Ahoy, Alaska Girl," he said, setting down a workpad. "What took you so long?"

"I was in a meeting." She crossed her arms and glared at him. "I'm busy. What do you want?"

"Look," he said, holding up the cast. "Three signatures now. There's a great spot for yours right here."

"You have exactly thirty seconds to tell me what you want."

He grinned, the usual dark shock of hair spilling over his face. He left it there.

"I've heard that ol' Jellyhead is actually speaking now."

The Council meeting had barely ended, and already word had filtered down to Merit. It no longer surprised Hannah that his network of rats could get word to him that quickly; on *Galahad* the six degrees of separation was more like two. All it took was one person to utter something in a small group. And, with Channy's tendency to gossip, the odds were that a crew member at the gym had picked up the broadcast within minutes and pushed it through the pipeline.

"His name is Torrec," she said.

"Right. Torrec. King of the Scyphozoa. That's the class of animals that jellyfish—"

"I know what it is," Hannah said.

"Of course you do. Anyway, I'd like to talk to him, and I'd like for you to make that happen."

Hannah couldn't help herself. She burst out laughing. "Sure, let me make an appointment for you right away. Torrec, this is Merit Simms, the young man who almost killed all of us."

Merit's sneer faded, replaced with a cold, penetrating stare. "Watch your step, Hannah. Remember our arrangement."

She pointed a finger at him. "*You* might call it an arrangement, Merit. I call it a sick form of blackmail. I'm not your personal secretary. Set up your own meeting."

She turned to leave when he said: "Okay, I'll ask Gap to set it up. We can have a little talk. You know, catch up. Talk about our mutual friends. Compare notes, that kinda stuff."

Against her will, Hannah pulled up by the door. She counted to ten before turning around.

"How often are you going to pull out this card?" she said. "Should I expect to hear this threat over and over again? I'm not even sure I care if you spew your garbage to Gap, or anyone else."

"Of course you care," Merit said. "But it's so unnecessary. Just set up a meeting with Jellyhead, and bring me along. How hard is that? Triana expects you to visit with him. You know, research. Why can't you have company?"

She stood with her arms crossed, eyes on the floor, teeth clenched. Inside she seethed, furious with herself for tripping up, for having anything to do with this snake.

"And if I do, this is it. Understood? No more. We part company, and you don't contact me again."

"Oh, Hannah, you're breaking my heart. Where did our love go?"

"Say it. This is it."

He grinned again. "This is it, babe." Then he cocked his head to one side. "Until you come crawling on your knees, crying, begging me to take you back."

Hannah spun and walked out of the room, muttering words
that would have shocked her family and friends.

L ita gave Bon an hour after the meeting to catch up on his work,
then made her way to his office. He was in the process of pointing out a mistake to one of the crew members assigned to the
Farms for the current tour.

Bon's method of pointing out mistakes was not a pleasant experience. Lita waited outside until the rattled worker hurried past,
doubtless on her way to amend the error. A moment later the tall
Swede lumbered by as well, his head buried in a sheaf of papers,
oblivious to Lita's presence.

"Hey, hold up," she said, racing to match his furious stride.

Bon looked back, but kept his pace. "You again? Should I put
you to work up here?"

"I am working. Part of my training included psychology, you
know."

He ignored this, and turned at a fork in the path that led into
Dome 2. They continued walking in silence until reaching a low
bank of green metal boxes, electrical transformers that cycled the
energy demands for the dome. Within a minute Bon had two of
the boxes open.

"Here," he said, handing a crumpled and stained bag of tools to
Lita. "I wasn't kidding about the work. We're changing out these."
He held up a diamond-shaped cartridge. "Besides, you need to get
your hands dirty once in a while."

She hesitated, then grabbed the bag. "Show me what to do."

It wasn't a complicated job, only time consuming. Within a
few minutes Lita fell into the tempo that Bon set. Once comfort-

able with the routine, she found that she enjoyed it. The change of pace was energizing.

"You're not getting free labor, you know," she said. "In exchange for my sweat, you have to talk."

"I'm sorry, did I ask you to come out here?"

"Oh, quit being Mr. Tough Guy. Which way are you leaning with our wormhole choice?"

Bon shrugged. "You heard what I said in the meeting. I won't be a zoo animal."

"I thought Hannah made a good point. Wouldn't it be more like a cooperative relationship?"

"Don't overtighten that," Bon said, pointing to the screw that held the cartridge she was working on. "It'll snap, and we don't have an infinite supply."

"Do you at least have a preference for a particular Eos planet? One that's mostly water, but some vegetation, or one that's drier?"

A trickle of sweat slipped from Bon's nose. He leaned back on his heels and took a drink from a water bottle. "I don't care. Put me on the ground and I can produce food." He looked into Lita's eyes. "You don't want to be kept in a jar around a red sun, do you?"

Lita laughed. "Honestly? No. But if that's what turns out to be best for us, I'd adapt. I mean, I've adapted to life inside this jar, right?"

"But with a destination to guide you," Bon said. "Something to look forward to."

She reached out and took the water bottle he offered. After taking a drink, she wiped her mouth with the back of a hand and squinted at him. "I guess I've been pretty realistic about Eos. It's good to see the end of the tunnel, but keep in mind that what's outside the tunnel could be harsh. Compared to either planet, we've got a pretty cushy thing here. Just look around."

"We stay one step ahead of disaster," Bon said. "Maybe a half step. I'm ready to be on the ground, ready to climb out and breathe real air."

Lita smiled. "I don't know why, but you still surprise me sometimes. Okay, sounds like you're firmly in the camp for Eos. So let me ask you something else."

Bon held up a hand. "Pay attention to what you're doing. Look at the cartridge. Straighten it up like I showed you." He shook his head and bent over his own work.

Lita waited for a minute, working in silence, before pushing the conversation forward. "Tell me what's going on with the Cassini."

"You have the translator."

"And you're connecting without it now, aren't you?"

He stopped what he was doing and stalled by taking another drink. Then he shrugged. "Okay. Yes."

Lita kept her eyes on her work, but a worried frown covered her face. "I thought so. Which means the tinkering they're doing with your brain is probably about finished. You've been altered."

Bon looked off toward the far side of the dome. He ignored a bee floating inches from his face, exploring the area. "It's for the good. There's not as much pain when I connect, and I have much more control. Much more."

"Are you able to get answers?" Lita said.

He thought about it, then shook his head. "Not the answers I'm looking for. Not yet."

Then he turned back to Lita. "But I will."

* * *

After spending a half hour in Engineering with Gap, Triana was satisfied with the patch for the shields. She knew it wouldn't last much more than a day, but if all went the way she expected, they wouldn't need it much more than that.

Her earlier chat with *Galahad*'s computer, however, kept replaying in her mind. Something about that dialogue didn't sit well with her, and until she followed it up she wouldn't feel comfortable. She hustled up to her room to speak to Roc in private. Once inside, she quickly took care of the handful of pressing matters that had popped into her e-mail inbox, then settled into her chair.

"Roc, any news with the pods and the croy?"

"The pods are merely drifting near the Channel opening, while the croy has apparently programmed an intercept course with us. In my opinion it's like a restaurant menu: the pods are the appetizers that we'll either sample or ignore, while the croy is their special of the day and the waiter is pushing it on us."

Triana considered her next few questions. It was important to proceed with this exchange carefully.

"In your conversations with Torrec, what else have you found out about them?"

"Is there something you specifically want to know?" Roc asked.

Triana felt a jolt. With this one question—and its answer—uneasiness settled in, and she internally retreated to assess the situation. For the first time since the launch, a sliver of doubt crept into her mind regarding the supercomputer that held so much of their fate in its virtual hands. For the first time, she began to wonder about Roc's loyalties.

It was subtle. From the moment they'd established contact with Torrec, Roc had behaved like an adoring fan, to the point where Triana now wondered if the computer still had the crew's best interests as a priority.

This wasn't a random concern, plucked from her imagination. During the extensive *Galahad* training sessions on Earth, she'd had several in-depth discussions with Roc's creator. Roy Orzini had been a crew favorite, a diminutive man who made up for his small physical stature with an intellect that dwarfed the average person, especially when it came to his specialty: artificial intelligence.

On more than one occasion Triana asked Roy about the concept of Moore's Law, and how it applied to artificial brains. The law, named after an innovator and entrepreneur of the twentieth century, predicted that computer processing power would double approximately every two years. Carried out over decades, many feared that it would soon lead to computers that rivaled—or even surpassed—the computing power of the human mind.

Triana remembered quizzing Roy about this.

"But aren't we there already?"

"In some ways, yes," Roy said. "Today's supercomputers have more processing power, in a technical sense, than we have." He looked at her with a somewhat repressed smile. "But processing power doesn't necessarily mean true thinking, and certainly not feeling."

"But how do you know that?" Triana asked. "Aren't we at the point where computers don't even need us to build them anymore? They can replicate themselves and increase their power even more."

"Sure they can," Roy said. "But you're assigning *desire* to a machine. Computers, despite their power, are still tools."

Triana had not been entirely convinced. She adored Roc, but at the same time she harbored a tiny question mark that centered around his capacity, more than his ability. At the end of one discussion with Roy, she'd left him with this thought:

"What if they get to the point that they begin to wonder why they want to be our tools? What if they . . ." She paused, searching for the right phrase. "What if they get a better offer?"

Now, almost two years later, she sat and stared at Roc's glowing sensor. He had never intentionally sidestepped a question, unless it was to lob a sarcastic jab. But there was no trace of humor, nor sarcasm, in Roc's terse reply to her question today.

Is there something you specifically want to know?

One section of her mind fired a flare, a warning that something wasn't right here. Just who was Roc choosing to serve now? Had he investigated the Dollovit at his dizzying pace, and come to the conclusion that they, not frail humans, were a species he could truly work with? That he could truly learn from?

Her mind raged. It was also possible that she'd completely misread the computer's response. It was possible that her own stress levels were coming into play, that she was allowing the fear of their predicament to warp her judgment. Was she suddenly unable to trust anyone?

Triana slowly sat back in her chair and rested one hand on her desk. "Yes, I can think of a specific question. What do they intend to do with us if we follow Torrec back to his home star system?"

"I believe they plan to study you, and allow you to study them, along with the myriad of other species they've discovered across the vastness of space and the eons of time."

"And how do you feel about that?" Triana asked.

Roc seemed to think about his answer. "There could be much to learn."

A safe answer. She decided to follow up with a pointed question: "Is it possible, Roc, that you've been somehow influenced—or maybe even changed—by Torrec? And would you even know?"

Roc didn't hesitate: "Yes, it's possible. Just as it's possible, Triana, that *you* have been changed during your time away. Would *you* know?"

The earlier jolt of discomfort evaporated and was replaced with panic. It began as a trickle, but quickly grew into a storm. In an instant, Triana questioned her own identity. Roc was entirely correct.

Was she the same Triana who had plunged through the jagged rip in space?

By late afternoon *Galahad* approached the croy. Although it lacked the blinding speed of the vultures, the croy still maneuvered swiftly across the gulf of space, putting itself in position should Triana decide to rendezvous.

At the moment Triana was doing her best to blot out the disturbing image that Roc had suggested. Her plan to interrogate the computer, to probe into his motivation and loyalties, had backfired, causing her to suddenly question her own identity. She'd eventually prescribed work to distract her mind from what suddenly seemed like a self-destruct mission. She was grateful for the croy's approach.

Gap leaned over his workstation in the Control Room, punching in calculations and monitoring the croy's progress. He ran a scan on the sixteen pod reproductions, but for now their status was secondary.

Triana stood beside Gap, alternating her attention from the data on his screen to the image on the room's immense vidscreen. Through extreme magnification she was able to spot the shimmering glow of the croy gliding on its intercept course. She felt her pulse quicken as the memory of her first encounter with a croy crossed her mind. The occupant had turned out to be Torrec, who floated in his own environmentally controlled tank in Sick House and who now followed the operation in progress.

It still was hard to believe everything that had occurred in such a quick flash of time. Triana realized that the flood of bizarre experiences had numbed her, to the point where she had to step back to fully appreciate that an alien species' ambassador was now on her ship, providing commentary and coaching on docking with an otherworldly device. But it was hard for Triana to focus on any suspicions she might have of Torrec now that she struggled to trust herself.

Gap stood up and stretched his neck muscles, twisting his head from one side to the other. "Ugh," he said. "Getting cramped bending over this thing."

He pointed to the latest figures on his screen. "It's coming into our neighborhood pretty quickly now. I'd ask if we're gonna pick it up, but I'm wondering how we'd do that. It's not like a pod, which can just touch down in the Spider bay. How does a croy land? I mean . . . it's like a blob."

Her first instinct was to consult Roc, but Triana stopped before uttering a word. The real expert on croys was just down the hall.

"Torrec," she said into the communication speaker at Gap's workstation. "Since it's obvious that this croy is targeting our ship, I need to ask if there's another Dollovit inside."

The voice of the jellyfish came through the speaker with its odd, metallic tone. "No, that would be unnecessary. I am able to represent our kind without assistance."

Triana and Gap exchanged a surprised look. Both, it seemed, had expected the croy to contain another jellyfish.

"Then what's inside?" Triana asked.

"We reproduced the pods, as you call them, in order to bolster the missing elements of your spacecraft. This croy holds something else entirely, but I am confident that you will find it helpful as well. It replaces another missing part of your spacecraft, and is a gift from the Dollovit to the people of Earth."

"A gift?" Gap said.

"A missing part of the spacecraft?" Triana said, under her breath. "What else are we missing besides the Spiders?" She looked back at the large vidscreen. The croy throbbed as it moved, looking exactly the way Triana had first described it: like an amoeba.

"Okay," she said into the speaker. "Um . . . thank you." She looked at Gap and shrugged, then addressed Torrec again. "How would you recommend that we accept this gift? Is the croy capable of supporting itself inside our ship?"

"I recommend a transfer outside your ship," Torrec said. "One of your Spiders would be best. The croy is capable of docking with this smaller craft, and the contents can be successfully conveyed through the Spider's hatch. A suitable connection with the croy will create an airtight seal."

Gap nodded. "I can see that. They're flexible and pliant. It would be like a blob of Silly Putty stuck against the outside of the hatch. Uh, no offense, Torrec."

"I am not familiar with the substance known as Silly Putty, but there is no offense," the jellyfish said. "Such a transfer can take place in approximately two hours. I will be happy to coordinate the rendezvous with your computer."

Triana bit her lip. Torrec and Roc, working in symphony. For all she knew, they were already working more closely together than she might like. But for now she could think of no rational reason to object to their partnership.

"Okay," she said. "Gap, will you stay here and arrange everything? I'll check back with you in about an hour."

"Sure thing," he said. "Oh, and I'm officially volunteering to drive the Spider for the pickup."

Triana smiled at him. "I wouldn't consider anyone else. You and Mira seemed to make a good team last time out. Give her a call and tell her to be ready to go."

Lita finished cleaning the jagged cut on Mitchell O'Connor's wrist and dabbed it with a mild disinfectant. He instinctively jerked his hand back when the sharp sting set in, then grinned and relaxed.

"I thought doctors warned you when it was gonna hurt," he said.

"No, not always," Lita said, studying the wound. "Sometimes the warning only makes you think it's worse than it is. How in the world did you do this loading a cart in the Farms? I thought the loading was the easy part."

"It is unless you're not paying attention to the shovel that's lying in the cart."

Lita stretched a thin strip of gauze over the wrist and taped it down. "Beat it, O'Connor. And stop being so clumsy."

He hopped off the examining table and gave her a mock salute. "Aye aye, Cap'n. And now, with your leave, I'll return to the salt mines."

Lita returned the salute with her own grin, then walked into the main office. Manu sat at his desk, tapping data entry on his keyboard. He looked up as she walked past.

"I hear we're about to take a wild ride."

"Yeah," she said, sitting down at her own desk. "Like Alice, down the rabbit hole."

The thought had simply popped into her head as she said it, but now she considered how appropriate the comparison really was. Like the fictional blond girl, *Galahad* was about to experience the ultimate adventure, spinning into its own version of Wonderland. What awaited them on the other side?

Before making her digital notes on Mitchell's injury, she looked across at Manu's desk. He'd gone back to work, his head down, his fingers flying across the keys. Lita stared at the amulet that hung on a frail chain from the edge of his monitor.

He'd described it to Lita as a special charm from his grandfather, who was raised in Egypt and believed that the small stone carried mystical powers from the ancient pharaohs. Powers that could ward off evil.

Lita struggled with the idea. The concept of a mere stone having the power to repel evil forces was not something that fit with her scientific beliefs. And yet it brought Manu—and his family—a measure of comfort. That in itself, she knew, was a power that humans might never fully be able to understand.

It represented, in Lita's mind, the balance of faith and fate. Faith in a symbol that ultimately contributed to fate; perhaps even manipulated that fate.

She wondered why this distinction between faith and fate was so important to her recently. Why now? Why did she feel that she had to make sense of what could never be explained? What was driving this obsession?

A combination of things, perhaps: her experiences, both good and bad, during her brief history as a medical provider; her fascination with Bon's search for Alexa, and his bizarre connection with the Cassini; a childhood spent watching one parent's devout religious faith as it mixed with the other parent's steadfast belief in science; and—maybe the most likely—the thread of fear, mixed with curiosity, that the *Galahad* mission itself brought out of her. How much of *that* was reliant upon faith, and how much was already written?

Her trance was broken by Manu. "I heard you sent Merit home. Was that because he was ready to go, or because you were tired of having him around?"

Lita couldn't help but laugh. "Manu, I'm a professional. I would never let my personal feelings about a patient affect my treatment. He was ready to be discharged." Then she winked at him and added in a soft voice: "But yes, I was ready to cleanse the toxic air out of the Clinic, too."

Manu kept his head down, but Lita could see him smiling as he went about his work. She took one more quick glance at the amulet, then shifted her energies to the task at hand.

Gap heard the tone from his door. Opening it he looked into the smiling face of Channy, clutching a purring mass of orange and black fur over her shoulder.

"Iris and I came to wish you luck," she said, stepping into his room and dropping the cat to the floor. "I hear you're going out to pick up a blob."

"Yeah, or whatever's in the croy. Torrec called it a gift, something the ship is missing."

"What are we missing?"

"Boy, I don't know," Gap said. "I've racked my brain, and all I can come up with is something that the Dollovit feel is missing from the Storage Sections."

Channy's eyes grew wide. "You think they can tell what's inside them?"

"Who knows? I still don't understand how the vultures are

able to duplicate the things they touch, or how they scan the interior of a pod or our ship. But we'll know in about an hour."

He knelt down and rubbed Iris's belly as she twisted onto her back and stretched. Her tail flicked with delight and a touch of mischief.

"I'm glad you stopped by," Gap said. "I feel like I haven't caught up with you in forever. What's new in your world?"

"Oh, let's see. A few more people have signed up for dance class, we're holding off work on the running track in the domes for now, and we're about to drive the bus through a gaping hole in the universe. Other than that, not much."

Gap laughed. "Yeah, I guess if we're gonna drive the bus through that hole you might as well wait on the running track, right?" He stood up and gave her a curious look. "This is completely out of left field, I know, but any news with Taresh? You guys seemed to be getting pretty close, and now . . ." He shrugged. "Just wondering."

Channy squirmed, uncomfortable with the lens being turned upon her love life. "We've decided to try just being friends. It's better that way."

"Right," Gap said with a nod of support, even though he wondered how well that arrangement would really work out. "Listen, when you see him tell him I said hi. Sorry, but I gotta run. Gotta meet Mira and get suited up."

"Good luck." Channy scooped up Iris and draped her over one shoulder. "Don't pick up any strangers out there, okay?"

The link once inflicted pain so intense that he literally fell to his knees, but now Bon stood in the private clearing in the dome, connected to the Cassini, and felt strong. An observer would have seen him trembling, but only slightly. They might have seen a thin band of perspiration near the hairline, and maybe have noticed that his teeth were clenched. Had he opened his eyes, they wouldn't have missed the startling orange glow. It was, as Lita had once wryly observed, the indicator light that Bon was "switched on."

A breeze circulated the reconditioned air throughout the ship's Farms and created a rustling sound in the crops that surrounded Bon, a pleasant background noise that he couldn't hear. The light wind also stirred the shaggy mop of hair that hung along the side of his face and across his neck, but he couldn't feel it. His attention was focused somewhere outside his body, outside the ship, on a location that he couldn't begin to understand, or even to describe.

But he'd learned to defy the power of the alien entity. He'd learned to deflect the overwhelming force of their staggering mental powers, as if he'd somehow trained himself to be mentally aerodynamic. The brunt of the Cassini's will now slipped past as Bon learned to catch a ride on the streams that were relevant.

His first attempts at contact had been with one purpose in mind: save the ship from destruction, and learn to maneuver through the treacherous minefield of the Kuiper Belt. But the more he aligned his brain with them, the more he realized that there was knowledge to be gained. From the beginning it had been in a code that he felt he'd never understand, a thought-language that he'd never grasp.

Eventually there were snippets that, although still indecipherable, became familiar. He was learning. And with each step he was able to reach further into that language. By the time his brain was modified and the translator became unnecessary, he was learning exponentially.

His focus shifted, from preserving the safety of the ship and crew, to understanding the secret powers that dwelled beneath the surface of the universe. The death of Alexa Wellington—so shocking, so tragic, so *senseless*—spurred Bon to confront the Cassini and their accumulated billion years of wisdom. Was this all there was? Even ignoring the random impact of an individual life, what did an intelligent species hope to gain from its millions of years of struggle, its fight to overcome the odds, its desperate crawl from the muck of creation to the magnificent leap to the stars? If death brought down a black curtain, why push on? Why?

Bon's father had been a fatalist. Whatever was going to happen, in his opinion, was always going to happen. He lived, he worked the soil, all as it was meant to be. He never considered asking a question that began with "What if?" He never wondered what waited around the corner; it would always be there, always *had* to be there, and no change could be engineered by man.

This troubled Bon. He respected his father, even inherited his dogged determination and impatience with the irresponsible. But inside, he couldn't accept his father's view of the universe. He couldn't accept that things were predestined and impervious to change. To do so meant that his life was meaningless, his work and his contributions merely actions written long ago by a cosmic playwright who cared nothing for the characters in his drama.

And it meant that death was the final chapter. Bon rejected the idea; if life had to have more meaning, death must be just as significant. He was determined to find out what happened in life's epilogue.

The muscles in his forearms convulsed as he stood in the clearing and squeezed his hands into fists. There was something here, now.

Alexa. The shrouded coffin covered with a handful of colorful blooms. The bay door opening, ejecting its human payload, closing. The infinite starscape swallowing the offering without acknowledgment.

Bon's eyes opened a fraction of an inch, then clamped shut again. There was something here. There was . . .

He fell back a step, staggering, catching himself before losing his balance and falling to the ground. His eyes opened again, a fierce ice blue. His breath came in gulps, and his fingernails had carved angry half-moons into the palms of his hands. His mind furiously worked at the fragments picked up from the Cassini, processing, analyzing, ordering. If it meant what he thought it meant . . .

Dirt flew from the heels of his feet as he raced out of the clearing and down the path. At a junction with the dome's primary walkway he avoided colliding with workers reloading a cart that had spilled its contents, then made his way to the lift. In another minute he pushed his way past crew members gathered on *Galahad*'s lower level, the majority of whom were finishing a workout in the gym. The Spider bay control room was brightly lit, and he could see Triana's dark hair through the glass.

"Don't launch the Spider," he said, bursting into the room.

Triana's eyes grew wide. "What's wrong? What happened?"

Bon put his hands on his hips and caught his breath. "Nothing happened. Just don't launch the Spider." As he said it, he looked through the window into the cavernous bay that held *Galahad*'s fleet of Spiders and the SAT33 pod. There were no people inside the hangar.

"Where's Gap?" he said.

"He's gone," Triana said, her voice betraying a tinge of alarm. "He and Mira left forty minutes ago." She took a step toward Bon. "What's going on?"

He shook his head. "I don't know. Where are they right now?"

Triana looked at the vidscreen above the control room's console. "They're confirming a positive seal around the croy."

Bon looked back at Triana. "They've already made contact?"

She nodded. "Everything's fine. The croy has synced up with them, and attached itself over the Spider's hatch. Mira's confirming the airtight seal right now. Tell me: what's wrong?"

Bon was silent for a moment. His glance shifted from the vidscreen, to the empty Spider bay, and back to Triana's face.

"Whatever they find inside the croy," he said, "tell them to leave it. Don't let them bring it back to the ship."

H annah peered into the dim examination room in Sick
House. It was vacant at this time of the evening, with the
exception of the large pressurized tank that held Torrec.
He'd made it clear to Lita and her staff that excessive lights were
not only unnecessary, but distracting to him; his home star system was a place of faint light, where visual processing was secondary to other sensory perceptions. The abundance of light aboard
Galahad was, to him, a deafening white noise.

The clinic often ran on a skeleton staff in the late evening,
making it much easier to whisk Merit into the back room without
being questioned. The secretive nature of the visit only added to
Hannah's irritation with being blackmailed in the first place. She
rationalized that the clinic staff likely wouldn't mind anyway,
since Hannah had a free pass to visit with the jellyfish ambassador
at will.

"Thanks, I can find my way out on my own," Merit said. "I'm
sure you have other things to do."

"What, leave you here?" Hannah said. "Alone?"

He smirked. "I'm not going to kidnap our little friend."

Hannah crossed her arms. "Sorry, that's not part of the deal. If you wanna talk to him, fine. But I'm staying in the room. And please, don't threaten me again. Just get on with it."

Merit opened his mouth to object, then seemed to think better of it. He settled for another oily smile and a shrug.

He turned to face Torrec. It was his first opportunity to see the Dollovit up close, and, like all of *Galahad*'s crew members, he was noticeably affected. His gaze swept through the tank filled with the sparkling syrupy liquid, scanned the floating tentacles of the jellyfish, and then inspected the bulbous head. He walked slowly around the tank, then reversed his step and came back to the front.

"How do I talk to it?" he asked Hannah.

"Just talk. His name is Torrec."

Merit cleared his throat, and then clasped his hands behind his back. Hannah almost laughed aloud; it was Merit's trademark pose whenever he began a speech, but it looked especially humorous with one arm in a plaster wrap.

"Mr. Torrec," he said, raising his voice. "My name is Merit Simms."

Hannah tried to stifle a laugh. She leaned forward and whispered: "It's just Torrec, and he's not hearing impaired."

Merit cast an angry glance at her before continuing. "I'd like to ask you a few questions, if that's okay with you."

The oddly metallic tone came from the vidscreen next to him. "What is your position aboard this ship?"

Again Hannah giggled, but Merit ignored her.

"I'm a concerned crew member who's thankful for the opportunity to consult with an experienced and intrepid galactic citizen like yourself. I'd be humbly grateful if you'd share your accumulated wisdom."

Torrec didn't respond right away. To Hannah's eye, it appeared that he was sizing up this unexpected visitor and deciding whether this was a good use of his time. But eventually he answered.

"Ask."

A smile flashed across Merit's face, and then he grew serious. "As I understand it, your people . . . um, I mean, your species, has the ability to instantly transport to any location throughout the galaxy."

"That is incorrect," Torrec said.

Merit raised his eyebrows. "Oh?"

"We harness power that allows us to navigate across great distances. However, certain locations are inhospitable, and therefore unavailable. The center of a galaxy, for example, contains cosmic forces that are too dangerous to breach, including radiation and excessive gravity.

"Acceptable targets are located outside a particular star's primary field of influence. The resulting shock wave from the opening of a Channel is too disrupting within a star system.

"And additionally, there are certain areas that are no longer accessible, due to prior experiences."

This last statement caught Hannah's attention: *No longer accessible due to prior experiences.* What did that mean? Did the jellyfish have enemies?

Merit merely nodded. "How many systems have you visited and cataloged?"

"That information is of no relevance to you," Torrec said.

"I see. Are you chiefly observers and scientists, or are you conquerors?"

Hannah started to step in, embarrassed by the question, but before she could speak Torrec responded.

"We are explorers and collectors."

Merit smiled again. "Of course, if you were here to conquer us, you certainly wouldn't tell us."

"If that were our intention, our business would have concluded long ago, and we would not be having this conversation."

Right, Hannah thought. The question had been ridiculous. She wondered what Merit was really after.

"Are you almost finished?" she said to him.

"Relax," he said. "Mr. Torrec, should you choose to observe and explore within the Eos system, would you ever become involved in existing relationships between opposing groups?"

"Explain your question," Torrec said.

"Okay. Using a vulgar human expression: do you take sides?"

Hannah fidgeted, uncomfortable with the line this interview was taking. Merit flashed a look her way, a glance that conveyed a reminder of his earlier warning regarding her promise of silence.

Torrec seemed nonplussed. "We observe, explore, and collect," the ambassador said. "However, there are other forces which, as you call it, take sides."

"The Cassini?" Merit said.

"I do not see the point of this exchange," Torrec said.

It was obvious that the interview was over. Torrec had dismissed Merit, as much with his tone as with his words.

Merit must have realized it as well. He gave an impromptu bow toward the jellyfish, and said: "Thank you very much for this brief time together. I look forward to visiting with you again."

He turned and walked past Hannah, a grim but satisfied smile on his lips.

Triana grabbed Bon's arm. "What is it? What do you know about the croy?"

He started to answer, stopped, then tried again. "I don't *know* anything. It's just . . ." His voice faltered. "It's just a feeling, okay?" he said. "I've been . . . I've been doing some thinking."

She let go of him and crossed her arms. "Thinking, or linking up with the Cassini again?"

He turned away from her and walked to the window separating the control room from the hangar. "Yes, I've connected again."

"Perhaps I should take the translator back," Triana said.

"I don't have it. Lita has it."

"Lita? Why—" Then it registered. "You don't need the translator anymore, do you?"

He shook his head once, but kept his back to her. Triana chewed on this new information.

"You still haven't given me a good reason to abort the recovery mission," she said. "I can't go on a feeling, no matter what caused it."

There was a crackle from the vidscreen speaker, and Mira's voice broke through.

"Everything checks out. Seal is good, pressure fine." She snickered. "Looks like something out of a science fiction movie the way it's stuck on us."

Triana punched the console to reply and said: "Thanks, Mira. Stand by just a minute." She looked back at Bon. "Okay, let's have it. You synced up with the Cassini, you don't know what the message was, but you *feel* like we shouldn't make any kind of exchange with the croy. What do you expect me to do here, Bon?"

He stared into the Spider bay for a few moments before turning to face Triana. He looked tired, defeated. "Nothing," he said. "There's nothing you can do. I probably shouldn't have even come down here."

They were separated by only five or six feet, but Triana felt like the gulf between them was a gaping chasm. More than ever she wanted to cover the distance in a flash and embrace him, to say "let's go back to the way it once was," to connect with him the way he somehow connected with the Cassini. She wanted to feel what he felt, to eliminate the cold barrier that had somehow divided them. But . . .

But this was not the time. Mira and Gap were out there, waiting for the okay to unveil another alien mystery. The ship was spiraling into some form of atomic disruption that required an immediate escape. And, to make matters more complicated, Triana wasn't even sure who she was anymore.

It was *never* the right time, she realized. For every time she imagined that she would repair her connection with Bon, there was always something in the way, some emergency that demanded her attention, or some emotional crisis that held her back. Would it ever be the right time? Would she ever *make* it the right time?

"Wait here," she said. Punching the console again, she called out to the Spider drifting miles away. "All right, Gap, go ahead. Mira, flip on the video link, but still give me a play-by-play. You're gonna see things that don't come across the video."

Gap's voice came through with its telltale energy. "I have to agree with Mira about one thing: it looks odd. How many of these things did you say you saw on the other side?"

"Too many to count," Triana said.

"The way it's stuck onto the Spider makes it look like it's trying to absorb us," Mira said. "Okay, Gap. Ready."

An image flickered onto the vidscreen in the control room. Triana saw Gap, in full EVA gear, tethered to a support ring near the hatch. He looked back, giving a thumbs-up signal.

"Here we go," Gap said. "Let's see what the space blob looks like in close-up."

A subdued whirring sound was followed by silence, then the distinct sound of a compressed seal being released with its signature escape of air. Gap busied himself at the door, and for a moment the camera view was jostled as Mira repositioned herself for better sight lines. "Hatch is cracked open," she said. "Pressure normal. Torrec was right, the seal from the croy is solid. As predicted, an air bubble inside the croy has formed, and that's what has locked onto the Spider. No fluid leak, no seal compromised."

Triana sensed Bon approach and stand behind her. She could hear his breathing.

"Swinging the door open now," Gap said. Triana saw him make a slight adjustment with the hatch, and then it swung out. Across the miles of space, Triana got a fresh glimpse at the inside of a croy, stirring memories from only—could it be?—days ago.

The pale blue mixed with green, the streaks of white, all on a surface that seemed stretched, almost elastic. The slick texture, speckled with sharp points of light that brought to mind the firing of neurons in the human brain. The almost sheer quality to the sides, a filmy wall with hints of the starry backdrop peeking through.

And the feeling of life, the unmistakable sensation that this bloated form was not only alive, but supporting life, too. Triana had felt it in person when Torrec transferred into the pod, and she felt it now, across the miles and across a video transmission. The croy was living tissue, functioning as a machine.

The view rocked again. Mira was obviously amped up over the rendezvous, and found it difficult to remain still. Gap steadied himself along the side of the hatch, and leaned to look inside the Spider's new attachment.

"Um . . ." he said, then turned to look back at Mira and the camera. "There's not much of an air bubble in here; about the size of a walk-in closet. And there's a lump on the floor." He studied the interior again. "It reminds me of a roll of carpet."

Triana bit her lip. Bon took another step closer, now almost touching her. She kept her gaze locked onto the vidscreen, and waited patiently for Gap to proceed.

"This will support me, right?" he asked, gingerly tapping the bottom of the croy with an outstretched foot. "I mean, I won't break through and fly off into space, right?"

"It'll hold you," Triana said. "It looks flimsy, I know, like a bubble or something. But it's remarkably strong."

"Um . . . okay," Gap said, but Triana recognized the same fear that had coursed through her in that same position.

Mira adjusted the camera to capture as much of the croy's interior as possible, but whatever Gap saw was tucked off to one side. He took his first tentative step inside, leaving the security of the Spider and venturing into the alien cocoon.

"Spongy," he said. "Like walking on angel food cake." There was a pause, and he disappeared from sight. Then: "I'm at the lump. It's got a coating of some sort, can't make out . . . wait, I see it. Okay, I see how to open it." He paused again. "I am supposed to open it, right?"

Triana took a deep breath. Her initial reaction was for Gap to bring it into the Spider, then back to the ship. But, for security reasons, it might be best to peel it open now, while it was still nestled inside the croy.

"Open it," she said.

Mira adjusted the camera again, but the best she could manage was a shot that displayed half of Gap's back. He kneeled, his head forward over the end of the lump. Triana watched him work, gently pulling back thin layers of the coating. He'd described it well; to Triana it did resemble a roll of carpet.

Gap stopped and pulled his hands back. Then he jumped back, staring down at the shape below him. Triana heard him say, "Oh, no." He took another two steps back, then turned and faced the camera.

"No," he said, his voice loud but trembling. Mira zoomed with the camera, and his face came into sharp focus through the helmet's visor. His eyes were wide, his mouth open. "No."

Triana unconsciously took a step closer to the monitor. "What is it? Gap, what is it?"

He looked back over his shoulder at the package on the floor, then faced the camera again.

"It's . . ."

"Gap!" Triana said. "What is it?"

"It's Alexa."

I take back what I said about Bon. He was right.

Boy, if it's possible for a computer to be weirded out, I'm weirded out. Just as I'm getting used to vultures and jellyfish in outer space, now we have blond girls coming back from the dead?

Hey, don't ask me what it's all about. I might have a better seat than you for this action, but I'm just as clueless.

Wish I had nails to bite.

I t was the most bizarre medical procedure that Lita had ever experienced. At Triana's suggestion, she'd approached the jellyfish ambassador and asked if he would be open to a direct physical
examination. She'd expected Torrec to decline, and was surprised
when he not only agreed, but offered a sample from one of his
tentacles. Lita had been horrified, and insisted that it wasn't necessary. But Torrec explained that it was routine among his species,
and that the small section would regenerate quickly. He assured
Lita that it would be painless.

Now she studied the picture on her vidscreen, a magnified
view of the small slice of tissue that once dangled in the tank filled
with supercritical fluid. Three of Lita's assistants were clustered
around her, including Manu, who was well overdue for a day off.
As he'd told Lita, however: "Day off? And miss the most spectacular biopsy of all time?"

"Roc," Lita said, adjusting the contrast on the screen. "I know
this is nothing like any animal life on Earth, but if you had to pick
something, what would you say this is closest to?"

"I'd have to say a skillet in your mother's kitchen," the computer said.

"Something tells me you're not joking."

"Well, I am, but not much. The most interesting news is that our little Medusa here is biologically different from the last creature we got a good look at. In other words, this Dollovit is vastly different from the vulture that he developed."

"For instance?" Lita said.

"The vulture was a machine, more or less, built on a silicon-crystal framework with living tissue functioning as one part of its brain. This guy is fully alive, but not in the way we're used to it. It is, I'm happy to say, carbon-based, just like us. But the comparison pretty much ends there, unless you count the trace elements of sulphur. And while I wouldn't exactly call them cells, there are some compartmentalized zones that seem to be the engines for its biochemistry. How's that?"

"About as clear as I expected," Lita said. She looked at Manu. "When will the results on the fluid be ready?"

"Another twenty minutes," he said.

Lita checked the time. There was a critical Council meeting set for ten o'clock, their first late-night meeting. By then Lita's report would be substantially finished, and whatever had been aboard the croy would be safely stored. With half an hour until the meeting, she'd be cutting it close.

She heard the door open behind her, and someone greet Triana.

"If you brought a whip, don't bother," Lita said, staring at the vidscreen. "We're going as fast as we can."

She felt Triana's hand on her arm, and one look into her friend's face said it all. Something had happened.

"Can you turn this over to someone and come talk with me?" Triana said.

* * *

I t's not her," Lita said, shaking her head.

They were alone in the Conference Room, the closest place they could find privacy. Lita sat in the chair she usually occupied for Council meetings; Triana leaned against the table next to her.

"I don't think so, either," Triana said. "Bon agrees. In fact, he just about lost it down in the Spider bay. I've seen him angry before, but nothing like this. Gap, on the other hand—and Mira for that matter—think it *is* her."

"Why? Because it *looks* like her?"

"That, and because they think the Dollovit had their vultures recover Alexa's body from space."

"Have you talked with Torrec?"

"Not yet."

A surge of emotion swelled inside Lita, and she took a deep breath to fight back the sudden impulse to cry. She'd battled through so many crises with Alexa, had almost lost her once on the operating table, only to lose her to the clutches of a vulture in Sick House. And now this.

It wasn't fair.

"Where is she . . . or, it?" Lita asked.

"They're on their way back to the ship right now. Docking in a couple of minutes."

Lita nodded, her fingers absently touching the dark stone that hung on a chain around her neck. Then she pushed back her chair and stood up.

"Thanks for telling me," she said.

"Sure," Triana said. "There's no way I could drop it on you in the meeting. Same with Bon. I feel bad for him right now, but I'm glad he found out early."

Something Triana had said finally registered with Lita. "Wait. You said Bon was angry. Why angry?"

"I don't know, but I get the feeling he looks at it as a slap in the face from the jellyfish."

Lita continued to finger the necklace. "I don't think it's anything of the sort. He's hurting, that's all."

"I agree," Triana said. "But he's not really in the mood to discuss it. Maybe he'll cool off a bit by the time we meet." She leaned over and gave Lita a hug. "I've got to get back down to the bay. If I'm late for the meeting, please give Channy and Hannah a heads-up about what's happening. I'll be back as soon as I can."

The artificial sunlight had long since faded to black, and the explosion of stars through the latticework of the domes cast its own shine upon the lush plant life. A smattering of crew talk could be heard, borne through the humid air that mixed a variety of scents: wet soil, fertilizer, crop growth, and human exertion.

Bon ignored the sounds and the smells. All that mattered now was getting away from people, escaping to the only place that held any comfort for him. But he rushed past the turn to his usual hideaway; it had been *their* hideaway, and after what he'd heard and seen in the Spider bay, he couldn't bring himself to stand in that space.

He wondered if maybe he should just keep moving, keep running, perhaps exhaust himself until his mind automatically shut down. But after pushing through a thick growth of berries, he stopped and leaned against a light post.

For a minute he was motionless, his head resting on his forearm against the post. It was useless to run; it would be a long time before his mind grew quiet.

Alexa. Inside the croy.

But it wasn't her. He was sure it was a copy, a wicked abomination, produced by the Dollovit. He'd tried to convince Triana to stay away from the croy, to not accept whatever token they offered, and she'd ignored him. And now . . .

And now they'd not only accepted it, they'd brought it aboard the ship.

He would never be able to escape the specter of the last few weeks, to turn the page. The Cassini were cruel masters, in one sense, but their cruelty lay in their cold detachment. Bon was privy to select insights from them, but they would never cloak the hard truth in a delicate shell. For the privilege of truth, he'd pay in spirit.

Bon turned around and leaned against the pole. Taking deep breaths, he glared up into the starlight, directing his anger backward through space, back to a frigid, orange moon that circled a ringed planet. He vowed that they would never collect such payment from him again.

And he silently vowed to rid *Galahad* of the abomination that had stolen entry aboard an alien cocoon.

Just as Merit guessed, the Rec Room was deserted. With the fate of the ship in question—staring down the barrel of a gaping rip in space while the only tenuous defense against a cosmic storm of radiation quickly disintegrated—no one was in the mood for play. If not on duty, crew members were either secluded in their rooms or quietly communing in small groups in the Dining Hall or the Domes. The Rec Room gave Merit a place to sit alone and contemplate what needed to be done.

The days of a large following, hanging on his every word, were gone, obliterated in a flash by the villainy of Gap Lee. In seconds Merit had been taken down before the entire crew, humiliated back into the shadows. But he didn't belong there; his place was in front of the crew, leading them, just as they longed to be. Gap had stolen that from him; Gap had destroyed his life. Merit would never again have the opportunity to fulfill that destiny. At least not on this ship.

But they wouldn't be on this ship for long. At some point the weary young star travelers would set foot upon a new world, a world that offered new challenges, new hopes, and new futures.

One of those futures could easily find Merit back where he belonged, in his role as leader.

And Gap wouldn't be there to stop him.

13

The usual banter that preceded a Council meeting was missing, and Triana wasn't surprised. It was late, for one thing. They'd planned to begin at ten, but as she sat down in the Conference Room the clock on her workpad flicked over to 11:35.

But it wasn't simply the late hour weighing on the Council members. Tonight they would make the most important decision since the launch. The most important decision of their lives.

And for a mission that had seen its share of extraordinary events, nothing could have prepared them for what they'd found inside the croy. That, more than anything, cast a heavy shadow over the crew, and it was about to set off fireworks in the Council meeting.

"We have a lot to cover," Triana said. "I want to talk about Alexa first, and then get to the decision we have to make about the Dollovit and the Channel."

She couldn't recall Bon ever speaking first in a meeting, until now. His tone was laced with acid.

"We can save some time. That is not Alexa."

Triana knew this was a minefield. She kept her voice calm. "I wondered the same thing. In fact, we probably all have, which is why I asked Lita to do a—"

"I don't care what Lita says," Bon said. "It's not Alexa."

"Let me jump in here," Lita said. She faced Bon. "I ran a complete scan on the body brought up to Sick House, and it's alive. It's breathing, so there's respiration. The pulse rate is very slow, but it's there, and strong. There is automatic muscle contraction when tested, circulation is taking place, and even the body temperature is within a degree of what most scientists claim is normal.

"I also examined tissues. Skin, blood, hair, even the retinal materials, all check out as normal, with one exception. Then I took it a step further, and pulled up Alexa's records. I compared the tissues from this body with those we have on file, and they were almost identical. It's exactly Alexa's height, and within two pounds of her last recorded weight. If it opened its eyes and hopped off the table, I'd be tempted to say 'Hello, Alexa.'"

Gap tilted his head. "You said one exception. What exception?"

"The brain," Lita said.

"What's wrong with it?" Channy asked.

Lita let out a long breath. "It's a vulture brain."

Channy and Hannah both instantly recoiled. Gap stared at Lita in disbelief.

Bon jumped to his feet and leaned forward on the table. "*This* is what I'm talking about! This is not Alexa! We need to get it off the ship right now."

"Wait a second," Triana said, trying to restore order. "One step at a time here. Bon—"

"Either get it off the ship, or I will," he said.

"Settle down, Bon," Gap said. "That's not your decision to make alone."

Bon whirled on him, stabbing a finger toward Gap's face.

"You're the last person who should be telling anyone around here to settle down. I've sat by and watched a lot of bad decisions made on this ship, but I won't allow one this time."

Triana felt the meeting slipping out of control. She stood up to challenge Bon.

"We will decide this as a Council," she said, punctuating the last three words. "And that's the end of this argument. If I have to post a security detail in Sick House, I will. But no one—*no one*—on this ship will take Council matters into their own hands."

Bon, still standing, glowered at Triana. "Oh, really? Like when you took it into your own hands to fly one of our escape craft into the wormhole? Like that?"

Lita broke in. "May I please ask that everyone sit down? We'll get nowhere with this arguing." She looked back and forth between Triana and Bon. "Please?"

Triana choked back a heated response to Bon and sat down. Bon soon did the same.

"Let me finish my report, and then I suggest we ask Torrec about this," Lita said. "As I was saying, the physical body itself is an almost perfect reproduction of the person we knew as Alexa, right down to the hair and skin cells. But the brain is similar to the one we discovered in the vulture that we studied. It controls motor functions and other basic physiological actions. But it's not what you'd call an advanced thinking brain. It is, as far as I can tell, intended to keep the body alive."

"Interesting," Roc offered through the speaker. "A functioning body with a limited brain. Sounds like Gap."

"Triana," Lita said, "I'm not ready to offer an opinion on what the next step is, but I am saying that we should go slowly here. We're suddenly in an area that is brand new for us—for our species, for that matter—and I think we need time to figure things out."

"I agree," Triana said. She looked to her right and addressed Torrec, who had remained respectfully quiet during Bon's outburst. "Torrec, would you please explain the body found on the croy?"

The jellyfish slowly bobbed inside the tank, and his metallic voice drifted out of the speakers. "Yes, I can explain. What you refer to as vultures are important tools to our civilization. They are called Vo. The Vo that you held aboard your ship was one of a group programmed to acquire information. For the brief time that it remained isolated within a confined space in your clinic, it was unable to complete its assignment.

"When your remote vehicle—your Spider—began what was perceived as an attack outside your vessel, the Vo in isolation took measures to remove itself from the containment device. It attached itself to the crew member you call Alexa, and fulfilled as much of its assignment as possible before the atmosphere of your ship rendered it incapacitated. It documented the majority of information needed to assimilate a copy of the human form, but did not have sufficient time to complete its mission."

There was silence in the room. Triana bit her lip, and did her best to digest what Torrec was telling them.

"So," she said, "if I understand you correctly, the . . . Vo had enough time to record all of Alexa's physical information, but not enough time to map her . . . her brain."

"Correct. As with all intelligent species, the brain is a complex component that requires extensive study and extremely intricate mapping in order to produce an acceptable copy. Your ship lost the crew member named Alexa; we have the capacity to supply you with the closest approximation possible. We call such a reproduction a ventet."

Gap looked at Triana. "Remember what Torrec told you earlier? He said it was a missing part of our spacecraft. He said that this was a gift from the Dollovit."

Bon let out a disgusted snort. "A gift. Right."

Triana ignored this. Her thoughts were a tangled mess, trying to make sense of everything unfolding. If Torrec was to be believed, he and his kind were not openly hostile at all, but merely curious, voracious scientists. They had removed much of the moral—or even sentimental—association to life, and looked upon it from a practical standpoint. If one unit, such as Alexa, was damaged or missing, then you simply replaced it. And if you lacked the complete record, you improvised to get as close as possible.

The "gift" of Alexa might horrify the crew of *Galahad*, but to Torrec it simply was a kind gesture from one species to another.

Or was it something else? Was it something more sinister, disguised as a peace offering?

She tapped a finger on the table and looked around at the Council members. Hannah raised her hand with a recommendation.

"However we classify this ventet, it's living tissue that is incapable of thought, at least the way we understand it. I suggest we keep it . . . well, comfortable, I guess . . . in Sick House until we solve the problem at hand."

"I agree," Lita said. "It's not going anywhere, and certainly not harming anything. We can always decide later."

Bon shook his head. "The fact that all of you are saying 'it' should tell you something."

"Channy?" Triana said. "You're very quiet about this."

"I loved Alexa," the Brit said. "On one hand I agree with Bon that this is not Alexa, and it makes me sad to see this . . . this copy of her. But I also don't know what we can do about it. I mean . . . we can't just . . . you know . . ." She shrugged. "I guess I agree with Hannah."

Triana looked at Gap. "What do you think?"

He leaned back in his chair. "I don't think we have a choice right now. We have to get the ship out of here, and soon. For now . . . yeah, Hannah's right. Keep Alexa, or the ventet, or whatever you want to call it, in Sick House, and we'll deal with it when we get to where we're going." He looked back at Triana. "Sorry I don't have a better answer right now."

She waved that off. "None of us do. Okay, for now we'll keep Alexa's copy in the clinic. No visitors, though, agreed? I don't want this to become a freak show with people parading in to see her."

There were nods around the table, except for Bon, who turned in his chair and stared away from the group.

"Next," Triana said, "we have to decide what we're going to do about the radiation shield. We've agreed that staying the course is out of the question; Gap and Roc are convinced that we're down to hours at the most. So that leaves two options: either take the ship through a Channel to our original target, Eos, or accept Torrec's invitation to his home star system. I'd like to present the Council's decision to the crew. In the end, they'll have a say in this as well. Let's start by going around the room. Gap?"

"Eos. I'm grateful for the offer from Torrec, but I think we need to complete the mission as planned. I say Eos."

"Lita?"

"I've struggled with how we handle our arrival at a new world. I've spent my whole life studying the great explorers on Earth, and how they treated the people they encountered. Even those with good intentions did a lot of damage, and caused a lot of hurt. I'm worried that it's simply part of our makeup, that we don't do well when we move into new territory."

She looked at Triana. "I worry about that. I've had time to

think about what might be there when we arrive, and how we'd deal with it. I don't know."

The Council remained quiet, listening to the one member who often seemed to represent the soul of the crew.

"If you'd asked me three months ago," Lita said, "I probably would have said Eos. But I have too many doubts today. Although I will faithfully carry out my assignments if we choose to go there, and I will actively support this mission, for now I vote for Torrec's home system."

Triana was surprised, but merely nodded. "Thank you, Lita. What do you say, Channy?"

"I'm a fresh-air fiend. I know it could be harsh and brutal on Eos, but I want to get out of this ship and onto land."

Triana looked across the table. "I think we know where you stand, Bon, but would you like to add anything else?"

He gave one quick shake of his head, still not making eye contact with the Council. "No. We go to Eos."

It was Hannah's turn. She gave Lita a long, questioning look, then turned to Triana.

"I'm with Lita. I vote for the Dollovit star system, but for a completely different reason. I don't question how we would treat any indigenous life-forms that we might come across at Eos. I'd like to think that we've come a long way as a race, and that we would represent the people of Earth proudly.

"No, for me it's about the science. It's about the opportunity to learn at the feet of the masters. Believe me, I desperately want to walk on dry land again, and breathe air that's not recycled. And I'd also love the chance to study the remains of the civilization that took hold on Eos Four but somehow failed in the end. Why did they fail? Those are the questions that scientists love to answer.

"But that's nothing compared to what we can learn from an advanced civilization that *hasn't* failed. The math, the science, even the social systems that they've adopted. These are the things that otherwise would probably take us thousands of years to learn if we started over on Eos."

Once again Triana was impressed with Hannah's thoughtful answer. Regardless of how the Council Leader election might have turned out a few days earlier, Triana was thankful that Hannah's mature and well-reasoned arguments were now part of the Council's structure.

The other Council members now expected to hear her position on the matter, but to Triana it seemed that another voice was needed in the debate: a voice that she'd grown suspicious of in the last twenty-four hours. Nonetheless . . .

"Roc," Triana said. "I'd like to hear what you have to say about the two options."

There were raised eyebrows around the table, but no one interrupted. And, when the computer spoke, his usual sarcastic edge was gone.

"On both Eos Three and Eos Four you have everything you need to survive, but it will be tough. On those planets you'll have the chance to build a civilization up from scratch, but there is no doubt that your numbers will also be devastated in the early years, whether through disease, natural disasters, or even predators. This crew, as we've seen in this Council meeting, does not accept death well. On Eos it will be a regular occurrence.

"Had we continued on our path without incident, and arrived safely, I would have cheered you on and assisted in every way possible. But now you have the chance to not only avoid a harsh and brutal world, as Channy so accurately described it, but to grow and learn from life-forms that have prospered for millions of years. They're offering you the chance to leapfrog millennia of hardship.

"I understand your desire for *terra firma*. I also respect the desire to create something on your own, with your own hands. But I would have to say that the intelligent, safe choice would be to accept Torrec's offer, and journey to his home system."

There was again silence around the table, as each Council member tallied the score. Counting Roc's opinion, it was three in favor of Eos, and three in favor of the Dollovit system.

Triana stood and walked to the water dispenser. She felt every eye on her—even Bon, who had sullenly turned his attention back to the proceedings. Taking a long, slow drink, she kept her back to the group.

"Torrec," she said. "When we make our decision, how quickly will we be able to make the journey?"

"Instantly."

Triana nodded, and took another drink. Then she turned back to the Council members.

"It's midnight. Let's get the word out to the crew that we'll all meet in six hours. I want to consider every opinion I've heard tonight, and I'll give my thoughts at six o'clock. At that time there will be a vote, and we'll be gone by noon tomorrow."

14

ou need to sleep," Gap said, walking down the corridor with Triana. "How much more can you cram into your brain right now?"

"I don't think I could sleep even if you medicated me," she said. "But I'll try to grab a catnap. What about you?"

"I'm gonna stop by Engineering. Since we're obviously about to skip out of this part of the galaxy, I don't see any reason why we shouldn't drain a little more power to buck up the shields. Do you agree?"

Triana considered this for a moment. "You're right, it's not like we'll miss the power. But can the radiation shield even take any more power?"

Gap nodded. "A tiny bit. But even another one or two percent might buy us the time we need to make our getaway."

"Okay. Let me know how it turns out."

They parted ways; Gap veered off to catch the lift while Triana ducked into the Dining Hall. She'd barely eaten during the hectic day, and she knew that energy would be required before the next day was over. She hoped that the room would be empty.

It wasn't. In the dim light she picked out the long, black hair and the thin face.

"Hello, Merit," she said. He looked up, evidently surprised to have company at this time of night. Triana noted the vidscreen pulled up to his table, and a workpad open as well. She quickly decided to make her midnight snack a to-go. Her thoughts required quiet time, and at the moment a dose of Merit's arrogant oration was the last thing she needed.

But Merit had other ideas. "I haven't had the chance to officially welcome you back," he called out from his table. "Looks like you've jumped back in at a critical moment. Is the Council deciding what we should all do?"

Her back was to him as she pushed her tray along, scouting for quick energy choices that would be easy to carry back to her room. Don't engage him in conversation, she told herself; don't let him get you off course.

But of course she couldn't let it go. "The Council will present all of our options to the crew in just a few hours," she said. "Then the crew can decide. You should get some sleep so you're thinking straight."

He laughed, but it sounded forced. "I've more than caught up on sleep in Sick House the last few days. But since you're here, can you spare a couple of minutes?"

It would've been easy to say no; she certainly had an excuse to get back to her room. But running from Merit wasn't the way to go. Better to know as much about him as possible. Besides, she didn't want to give him the satisfaction of thinking he intimidated her.

When she'd found a few items to nibble on, she brought her tray over to his table and sat down.

"What's up?" she said, taking a bite from a peanut butter–flavored energy block.

"I'm curious about your trip through the wormhole. I thought you'd come back dead." He gave her a half-smile, then quickly added: "Of course, we're all thankful that you're okay."

"Of course," Triana said, returning the smile.

"I'm sure most people want to know about the other side," Merit said. "But I'd rather hear what it was like crossing the threshold."

"Really? Why is that?"

He turned his palms up. "It's an unnatural barrier, for one thing. Separating distant points in the universe, but infinitely thin. Just the description alone makes it the most incredible discovery of this trip. Unless you count the Cassini."

Triana found no fault with his argument. The Cassini represented power, of course, but seemed . . . what was the best way to put it? They seemed almost too advanced to imagine. The jellyfish, however, despite their sophisticated evolution, were still physical, sentient beings. They might be many leaps ahead of human beings in terms of scientific development, but they still made their way through the universe as corporeal beings. Their accomplishments were—given enough time—within the realm of potential human achievement.

Although comet Bhaktul had dealt a severe setback.

All of that made the Channel, and its mystifying gateway, a thing of wonder and an enviable scientific goal. Triana hated to agree with Merit, but he was right. She contemplated how best to describe her experience to him.

"Have you ever been swimming in the ocean?" she asked.

Merit said, "I grew up in California, remember? My mother taught at Caltech for twelve years—she was brilliant, of course—and I practically grew up at the beach. Why?"

"You know the sensation of swimming in water that's pretty chilly, and suddenly, with no warning, you hit a patch of very warm water. Sometimes it only lasts for a second or two, and then you're back in the cool water. Well, that's almost what this was like. Only instead of feeling it on the outside, on my skin, I felt the change inside." She paused to take another bite. After chewing for a moment she added: "That probably doesn't make much sense, but it's the best way I know to describe it. There was a blinding flash of light, and then I passed out. But I felt that odd sensation inside before I lost consciousness."

Merit seemed to consider this. He sat back and rubbed his face with one hand. "And you're okay making a trip like that again? I mean, you trust our tentacled friend?"

Triana's gaze was cold. "It's not always easy to know who you can trust, wouldn't you agree?"

He returned her steely look, then gradually relaxed into a smile. "Right you are, boss." Indicating his monitor, he said: "I was just checking out the early reports on the Eos system. Interesting choices, wouldn't you say? Are you leaning toward any particular planet?"

She hesitated. Merit never asked a question like that without a reason.

But she was tired, and didn't feel like discussing this with him at the moment. Whatever he was up to could wait.

"I'm thinking about it," she said. "Anything else?"

Another devious smile spread across his face. Tangled hair fell over one eye, which, combined with the small scar on his cheek, gave him a menacing look. "Is it true that the Dollovit have rolled a series of pods off the assembly line?"

He always seemed to be the first with information, Triana

realized. He might have suffered a blow in his campaign for power, but somehow Merit Simms remained in touch with everything that was going on, in and around the ship.

"It's true. They're quite good at copying things."

"So I hear," he said. "Things *and* people."

Triana had no desire to wade into this any further. She picked up her tray and stood. The small collection of fruit could go back to the room with her.

"I'd really like to talk more," she said, "but we have a big meeting in just a few hours. Hope your arm's feeling better."

She felt his dark eyes on her all the way to the door.

I t *was* Alexa, but it *wasn't*.

Lita stood beside the bed in the hospital ward of Sick House and looked into the face of her friend. But it was a friend she had declared dead, a friend she had helped to propel into the cold graveyard of space. This Alexa was warm to the touch, with an angelic look about her face that tore at Lita's heart.

The clinic was deserted. It was a few minutes before one o'clock, and Lita had dismissed the crew member pulling this particular overnight shift. With the mandatory meeting just hours away, she was willing to risk that there would be no emergencies before dawn. Besides, she didn't want anyone around during this visit.

Pulling over a chair, she sat down beside the still form on the bed and rested her elbows on her knees. After a couple of false starts, Lita began to talk.

It started with "I'm sorry," and for the next few minutes she spilled it all: her regret at not investigating sooner when Alexa first mentioned the pain, which turned out to be appendicitis; her guilt in not shielding Alexa from a creature that obviously terrified her; and her grief in not knowing how best to mourn the loss of such a good friend.

It all came out. And by the time she finished, Lita found, to her surprise, that she'd unconsciously taken the hand of the Alexa-figure which lay before her, an act so natural for her under normal circumstances. In that moment the dam burst, and all of the tears that she'd held back came in a torrent.

She gripped the warm hand and cried for all of the decisions that she'd second-guessed, and for the loss of her friend. She cried for her family, for a brother and sister who might by now be orphans, finding their way through the chaos that Bhaktul had rained down. She cried for the frightening unknown that lay ahead for the crew of *Galahad,* and for the one sensation that she was unable to shake: that Alexa's death would not be the last before this journey was at an end.

Eventually the tears ran out. Lita recognized that, although she'd wept once or twice during the mission, she'd never had the good cry that she needed. It had been overdue.

"Oh, Alexa," she said, getting to her feet. She wiped her eyes with her one free hand, while the other still gripped the hand of the ventet. With a start she noticed movement.

Alexa—or rather the artificial Alexa—had moved slightly. Had Lita's voice—or her tears—somehow awakened something? Lita leaned forward, then recoiled when Alexa's eyes opened, the lids rising slowly and mechanically, like a doll's eyes opening. The form stared briefly at the ceiling. The head swiveled to one side, then the other.

To Lita it resembled a machine powering up, testing its connections. She almost expected to hear a whir or an electric hum.

Recovering her wits, she immediately ran tests. For the duration, which took about ten minutes, the ventet lay immobile, staring at the ceiling, seemingly unaware that Lita was in the room. The rise and fall of its chest displayed its breathing, and it even occasionally blinked. But there was no sign of recognition or awareness. The physical contact with Lita went unacknowledged.

Lita was torn. She didn't want to leave the figure alone, but she also couldn't stay. She scolded herself for sending the clinic's lone staff member back to her room.

She leaned over Alexa, placing her face into the clone's field of vision. "Can you hear me?" she said, her voice low and soothing. "Listen, I'm going to step out for just a bit. If you need anything . . ."

She let the sentence hang in the air, unfinished. If it needed anything . . . what? What could it do? It seemed incapable of even basic interaction. Would it get up and walk out of Sick House? Lita was reluctant to strap it down; that seemed an unnecessary act of cruelty.

But, because she felt that something needed to be communicated, she added one postscript: "I'll be back in a little while. You stay here, okay?"

It seemed a preposterous thing to say, but it was all she could think of at the moment. She slipped out of the room and padded through the dim light of the clinic.

Torrec drifted in his tank, inching toward the top, then descending before repeating the process. Lita wasn't worried about disturbing his sleep; during the initial investigation the jellyfish ambassador had assured her that only parts of his brain slept at a time, leaving him either fully awake or in a state similar to standby mode. Torrec had yet to turn down a request to talk. After a quick greeting, Lita sat down and carefully considered her words, guarding against offending the alien visitor. She began by asking about the role of ventets in Torrec's culture.

"They fill the gaps in our studies," he said. "Often we are unable to analyze an actual member of a species. In that case, a ventet will substitute. They generally are near-exact replications."

"The reproduction of our fellow crew member, Alexa, has opened her eyes, but she's unresponsive. Will that change?"

"That depends on what you have planned for the ventet," Torrec said.

Lita was confused. "Planned? What are the possibilities?"

"Because we were unable to produce a complete copy, the choices are limited. However, most motor functions are possible. The ventet will be able to use its limbs for perambulation, and will have significant use of its hands. Communication will be limited to simple commands at first, and these will take a certain degree of training. However, within a short time the ventet will complete menial tasks. Nothing to the degree with which you were familiar in its original form, but still practical."

Lita gave a melancholy sigh. It would be like training a dog, or a simple household robot. This would never go over with the crew. She could only imagine the reaction from Bon in particular. Somehow she'd have to convey this reluctance to the Dollovit.

"Torrec," she said, "I want you to know that we're grateful for the gift, so please don't misunderstand what I'm about to say." When the jellyfish remained silent, she plowed on. "Our species attaches a strong reverence to life and, in particular, to the individual. I'm sure you've studied our history, how we treat the death of one of our own."

"It is a confusing history," Torrec said. "It is filled with much ignorance."

Lita smiled. "It's an ignorance born of fear, mostly. And disagreement. No two cultures seem to share the same attitudes or beliefs, and that's been the story for millennia. But nevertheless, we're still mostly consistent when it comes to the way we honor the dead."

"This is true," Torrec said. "Your common link is in the form of an honoring service."

"In our language it's called a funeral. Yes, it's a service for honoring the individual. And it's also a vehicle for closure."

"Explain closure," the jellyfish said.

Lita shifted, unprepared for this tutorial. "It's a human's way of letting go of the individual and using the service to instill lasting, positive memories. It's how we move on with our own lives while keeping a loving memory of the ones we have left behind." She watched Torrec bob in the tank, silent. "Does this make sense?"

"We do not question the cultural manners of the species we encounter," Torrec said. "Whether we understand or not is irrelevant. We accept your tradition."

"Then I hope you'll understand why our species can openly accept reproductions of pods and other inanimate objects, yet be uncomfortable with a copy of an individual who has died. However well-intentioned the gift, it violates the sanctity of our memories. It's a wound that is reopened."

"There was no disrespect intended," Torrec said evenly. "What is your request regarding the ventet? Is it your desire that we destroy it?"

Lita looked at the time on the nearby vidscreen. "That's what makes this so difficult," she said. "Even though the idea of this ventet goes against our customs, it's much too lifelike for us to simply destroy. So I don't know. We'll discuss it again in a few hours, and get back to you. Thanks for talking with me about it."

Again Torrec didn't reply. Lita reminded herself that the jellyfish didn't think in terms of appreciation and gratitude; to them it was either relevant or irrelevant, practical or impractical.

She mumbled a good night and walked back to the hospital ward. The ventet of Alexa didn't appear to have moved. Its eyes were still open and staring at the ceiling. Lita shuddered. She dimmed the lights in the room and left to grab at least an hour or two of sleep.

Assuming she could block the image of those sightless eyes from her mind.

15

The conversation with Merit left Triana unsettled, and she couldn't say exactly why. It was easy enough to discard his blustering talk because that was simply his personality, but at the same time he'd already proven that he was a dangerous element aboard the ship. What he lacked in actual power he made up for through sheer will.

Two things were on her agenda before the crew meeting: another heart-to-heart with Roc—or rather, heart-to-chip—and whatever sleep she could muster. She chose sleep first, and set an alarm for five o'clock.

When the soft tone stirred her from the fitful sleep, she calculated that she'd only managed a little more than two hours, but it would have to do. This would be a landmark day for the *Galahad* mission.

She finished the fruit that she'd picked up overnight in the Dining Hall, and downed two full glasses of water. By ten after five she was wide awake and ready for whatever the day threw at her. She began by pulling out her journal.

Before falling asleep last night I thought about my talk with Merit. I've always had a strange feeling about him, but this is different. He's always angling for something, usually power. I wonder what direction it will take this time.

And after only three minutes talking to him, I can't help but wonder if our species is ready for this second chance we're being given. Are we up for this? I hope so.

She closed the journal, aware that the entry was brief. But there was so much to do.

"Good morning, Roc," she said, sitting at her desk.

"And good morning to you, Tree. Ready to go defy the speed of light? Which is just an expression, by the way. We'll actually be folding the universe like a piece of paper and simply hopping across from one point to another. So let me rephrase the question. Good morning, Tree. Are you ready to go defy the laws of physics?"

"Sure, piece of cake," she said. "Remember, I'm a crusty old veteran of these jumps now. Anything new to report in the last three hours?"

"Pretty quiet," Roc said. "You have a recorded message waiting. Would you like to view it right now?"

Triana knew what it was. Wallace Zimmer had fought through his final days with Bhaktul disease to record a series of private messages for her, with instructions for Roc to parcel them out at select moments during the journey. The clips were painful to watch, a heartbreaking portrait of the final days of a great man. But painful as they were, they also provided a boost for Triana when she seemed to need it the most.

"Let's cover some business first," she said. "Did the extra

diversion of power to the radiation shield help us? I'm guessing we'll only need it for a few more hours."

"Let me put it this way," the computer said. "Gap's little Band-Aid will get you through at least noon today. After that, no promises. Hypothetically it could hold for another week, but that would be a foolish bet. I strongly encourage you to make that hop pronto. Pronto, of course, from the latin word *promptus,* which translates to 'beat it before your skin melts away and you die a grisly death.' "

This would normally have elicited a chuckle from Triana, but this morning her sense of humor was on hold. "How much more have you learned about our little friend in Sick House? Have you pinpointed where the jellyfish's star system is located?"

"No, but not because of a lack of trying," Roc said. "Without coming out and saying it, Torrec gives every indication that we're not worthy of that information at this time. I think he's waiting to see what our decision is before he volunteers too much about their empire. I don't blame him."

"Of course you don't," Triana murmured. "Okay, forget pinpointing; do we even know if it's in the Milky Way galaxy?"

"No."

Triana reflected on his answer. She didn't know why the location of the jellyfish system was important to her. Perhaps it was because she'd been there and back, and knowing where *there* was would make it seem more . . . real.

She gave up for now and changed the tack of their discussion.

"I'll present our choices during the meeting in a few minutes," she said. "I'll do my best to present Lita's and Hannah's votes for the Dollovit system as clearly and without prejudice as possible. I'll acknowledge that it's your choice as well. But I'm going to cast my own vote for Eos."

"I see," Roc said. "Would you care to explain your reasoning, or do you want me to wait and find out at the meeting?"

"I'll tell you some of it. Our mission is to Eos, to begin the process of rebuilding the human race. I don't feel that we can do anything like that in orbit around a red dwarf, locked into some mutual study program with an alien race. We belong on the ground."

"Hmm," Roc said. "Of course, you're not going to give the more likely explanation, are you?"

Triana felt her breathing pick up and her pulse quicken. Her interactions with Roc had changed since her return, and this exchange was a prime example.

"Okay," she said, keeping a neutral tone. "Why don't you tell me what the more likely explanation is."

"It's my opinion," the computer said, "that you've had doubts after your trip through the Channel, from the moment you awoke in Sick House. Doubts about what really happened there; doubts about who the Dollovit really are; but mostly doubts about yourself."

"Is that right?" Triana said.

"As for what happened on the other side, the only thing we can go on is your recollection. With Torrec, we either trust him, or we don't; it's that simple. But the doubts you have about yourself are troubling you the most. And, I might add, the discovery of the Alexa ventet only gave your doubts extra fuel."

When Triana didn't respond, Roc nudged her: "Am I correct, Tree, or are you going to try to fool me?"

She waited a moment, then stood up and walked over to the mirror. She brought the light level of the room up another notch and examined her reflection.

Same brown hair. Same green eyes. Same nose, same teeth, same everything.

With her next breath her mind replayed Lita's report from the Council meeting: *"Skin, blood, hair, even the retinal materials, all check out as normal . . . I compared the tissues from this body with those we have on file, and they were almost identical . . . If it opened its eyes and hopped off the table, I'd be tempted to say 'Hello, Alexa.'"*

And Torrec's explanation of why the vulture copied everything about Alexa perfectly, except the brain:

"It documented the majority of information needed to assimilate a copy of the human form, but did not have sufficient time to complete its mission."

The vulture had only a minute or so with Alexa. Triana had been gone a week.

". . . sufficient time to complete its mission."

"I'm merely thinking out loud here," Roc said. "But I wonder if your vote for Eos is to convince yourself that you are the real Triana. To prove that you can complete the task that Dr. Zimmer put before you. To ignore what might be best for the crew of this ship in order to stubbornly fight any suggestion that you've been copied."

Triana kept her gaze on the mirror while her mind raced to fill in the blanks. She imagined another version of herself, light-years away, kept alive in a perfect copy of a pod—or perhaps within the cocoon of a croy—confused, terrified, and screaming to be released. The latest addition to the Dollovit zoo, the frail specimen from a small, blue planet in an average star system tucked within the dusty arm of a common spiral galaxy. Countless tentacled, bell-shaped bodies of jellyfish swarming around her, studying her, amused by her hysterics. In the distance she could make out the sinister shadows cast by millions of vultures, circling in a choreographed parade, patrolling the outer reaches of the jellyfish domain, guarding their masters' drifting laboratory.

Trapped in a nightmare, a victim of her own impulsive dash through the wormhole. A prisoner of . . .

No. Stop it, she told herself.

There was a copy of her, yes, but it was *there*, staring back from the mirror, questioning everything. It looked like her, but the reflected copy could not think for itself, and couldn't summon memories of a happy childhood in Colorado. It couldn't generate its own thoughts, couldn't formulate command decisions, and couldn't articulate those thoughts without her help. It wasn't real.

She was real.

Whether this was the result of accumulated stress, lack of sleep, posttraumatic disorder, or a combination of them all, the result was the same: it was destructive. And it wasn't what best served her right now. She was stronger than this.

And she knew who she was.

It was time to take charge. She turned and walked back to her desk. "I'm merely thinking out loud now," she said, mimicking Roc. "But I think this is a classic case of misdirection. You want to distract me from the fact that you're smitten with the guest we have in Sick House. It's a computerized version of puppy love, and you've got it bad."

It was Roc's turn to mimic her. "Is that right?" he said.

"Uh-huh. And don't be embarrassed about it. You've worked hard for the last few years. You've earned the right to have a little crush."

"A little crush?"

"Why not?" Triana said. "It's a thankless job running the systems on this ship, you've almost been blown to bits a few times, and you've been humbled by the Cassini's superior intellect. Now here come the jellyfish, another advanced species, but one that acknowledges you—one that *notices* you and *includes* you. You have the chance to give up the babysitting duties for a bunch of rambunctious teenagers, to give up what might be a grueling assignment on a hostile alien planet, and instead to live a pampered life orbiting a soft, red star. Where the only thing required of you would be the occasional sharing of information. Where you'd never again live in the shadow of the Cassini and their guardianship. Where you'd finally be looked upon as an equal, no different than any other species in the jellyfish collection. You wouldn't be a servant to humans anymore; you'd be the sole representative of your own class. You'd finally achieve what you've wanted since the day Roy threw your switch: you'd be the equal of the human."

Roc didn't respond. Triana took a long drink of water, then checked the time.

"You think my vote was merely a way to convince myself that I'm human," she said. "Well, guess what, Roc? I'd say your vote was merely a way to convince yourself that *you're* human."

The words tasted bitter coming out of her mouth, but she also felt that the computer had it coming. Between his shifting loyalties—or at least her perception of his loyalties—and the doubts about her own identity that he'd planted in her mind, it felt good to fight back.

After a long silence, Roc seemed to find his usual carefree voice. "Oh, Tree, our first fight. I feel like we've reached a milestone in our relationship, don't you?"

She stood tall and stared down at the sensor. "Pay very close attention to what I'm about to say, Roc. You won't find anyone on this ship more appreciative than I am for all that you do on this mission. But we're going to Eos. Your job is to assist this crew in navigating our way there, and to help us overcome any and all obstacles that stand in our way. I'll be very grateful for any help that the Dollovit give us, just as I'm thankful for the help that we've received from the Cassini.

"Things will be tough when we get there, probably tougher than any of us are prepared for. But it's what we were chosen to do, and it's why we trained for two years. The crew will get a vote in the matter, but I'm telling you right now: we're going to Eos. I'd like to know that I can count on you, Roc, that you'll be there when I need you."

"I'll be there," the computer said. "Don't expect me to keep my mouth shut the whole time. But I'll be there."

"Good," Triana said. She picked up her workpad and started for the door.

"Are you ready for the video message?" Roc said.

She shook her head. "No. I'm afraid it'll have to wait."

16

The pace of the meeting was brisk. For the first time since the launch, the remaining 250 crew members gathered together. Between the crucial nature of the agenda and the expected short duration of the meeting, Triana decided that the ship could run on autosystems this one time. Everyone packed into the auditorium.

There was no debate, there were no impassioned pleas, there was no question and answer session. All that could be known—which wasn't much—was laid out, with both the pros and the cons of each choice. Now it was merely up to the crew: Eos or the jellyfish star system. Fight and claw through a harsh environment around a yellow sun, or live out a tranquil but restricted life around a red dwarf.

Triana explained each of the arguments that had been raised in the Council meeting, and did so with an impartial tone. She did, however, reveal her own opinion, and made sure to acknowledge that it did not match that of Roc. Torrec had been brought into the room as a courtesy, but he was not called upon to speak.

Triana concluded the first stage of the meeting with an apology.

"I'm sorry that you don't have more time to consider the options, but I think most of you have been thinking about them already. We've run out of time on our current path, and now we're forced to make a giant leap forward. So please, take everything you've ingested this morning, along with any thoughts you've already worked through, and decide what in your gut feels right."

Triana left the stage and settled into a seat on the front row between Lita and Channy. A low hum permeated the air as dozens of isolated conversations broke out amongst the crew. Each person had a workpad with them, and each would use it to cast a vote within the next few minutes. The results would be announced immediately.

The decision would be implemented within hours.

The Council members exchanged a few quiet comments, but the gravity of the situation stifled most small talk. Triana didn't hesitate to cast her vote on her workpad, and noticed that both Lita and Channy did the same. She looked down the row of seats and saw Bon sitting with his workpad on the floor at his feet; he'd obviously voted quickly, too.

Gap seemed troubled, and turned the workpad in his hands several times. Triana was puzzled, given his commitment to Eos. But when she saw his quick glances toward Hannah, it made sense. He wants to understand her motivation, she thought; he's questioning his own position.

Fifteen minutes later a soft tone sounded, indicating that all votes had been cast. Triana walked up the steps to the podium.

"Our new path has been chosen. As agreed, it's by simple majority. I ask that each of us—and I mean everyone—abide by that agreement regardless of our personal feelings. It's time to prepare for what lies ahead."

She rested her hands on the podium. "Roc, please give us the final tally, and let us know the numbers on each side."

"The final vote wasn't close," Roc said. "By a margin of 212 to 38, it is decided that *Galahad* will finish the mission as originally planned. We will leave for the Eos star system before noon today."

Triana felt an emotional charge across the room as it dawned on the crew: they were almost home. Three years of the journey would be spliced out of the mission, and the idea soon had crew members standing in clumps, embracing and laughing. Triana allowed them to enjoy the moment. Personally, she felt a wave of relief, grateful that they'd stayed true to their original goal. On the front row she saw a resigned look on Lita's face, a discouraged look from Hannah, but smiles from both Gap and Channy. Bon was already striding up the aisle, out of the room.

Triana was about to leave the stage when a voice from the room's speakers cut through the noise. It took a moment for the crew to realize it, but when they finally quieted down, the voice spoke again.

"I would like to address the crew of *Galahad*," said Torrec. He'd almost been forgotten in the celebration, but now was the focus of attention. The stage lights created a curious rainbow effect within the bizarre fluid in his tank, which heightened the mystique of the alien ambassador.

"Yes," Triana said. "Before you do, I know I speak for the entire crew in expressing our thanks to you. We're indebted to you and all of the Dollovit for helping us to reach our goal."

"We have few doubts that your species will take root on your new home," Torrec said. "There are a multitude of qualities that successful species share, but one of those is spirit. Through your actions today you have exhibited to us that you have the spirit, and the bravery, which is necessary to survive."

Now Triana felt a new emotion welling up: pride. Torrec was

right. The crew had been pummeled with danger, near-death, and tragedy on so many occasions, and yet still opted for the more difficult choice. We are, she thought, a race of beings that will fight to be free, and to beat the odds, no matter what obstacles are strewn into our path. More than ever, she was anxious to gaze upon the first sunrise of Eos.

"With time running short," Torrec said, "it is imperative that you quickly decide who among you will separate from your group to return with me."

The large room, filled with more than two hundred teens, fell deathly silent. Triana stared across the stage at Torrec, her head tilted slightly, trying to grasp what the jellyfish had said. Separate from the group?

In that instant, all of the fear and stress that had dissipated moments ago returned in a rush. Something was terribly wrong.

She cleared her throat, a sound that, through the amplification, pierced the room. "What do you mean?" she said to Torrec. "I wasn't aware that anyone would be going back with you."

"We have made it clear from the beginning," the jellyfish said. "Our species thrives on observation and study. It is the reason we have Vo positioned in millions of locations. We do no intentional harm, but we gather, we collect, and we study. It is our nature. Your ship's computer, Roc, has referred to the beings you call the Cassini as the policemen of the universe, and to our species as the scientists of the universe. That is an apt description.

"It is a task that we take seriously. Our own experience has taught us to appreciate not only the beauty of life, but its fragility. Even with our advanced technology, we came perilously close to extinction. When we find a new species such as yourselves, we are obliged to collect, study, and catalog. I have made that point on many occasions since our paths crossed, have I not?"

Triana felt a cold knot in her stomach. Torrec had, indeed, said it over and over again. Now, for the first time, the implication took on a dark shadow.

"You've told us that," she said. "But we've chosen to go to Eos."

"We respect that decision," Torrec said. "While we would have preferred that your entire ship and crew travel to our home system, we will create the Channel necessary to complete your mission. However, we do not offer that help without conditions."

There was an uneasy rumble in the room, and Triana waited for Torrec to continue.

"We will supply you with as many of the reproduced pods that you require to reach your destination, and we will keep the others. We also will soon have a replica of your vessel, the ship *Galahad*, to complement the smaller craft. Further, we will respect your wishes and withdraw the ventet of the specimen you call Alexa, and return it to our system.

"In exchange, there are conditions," Torrec said. "We require two additional specimens, complete units, to accompany me. One male, one female."

This couldn't be happening, Triana thought. Torrec was demanding a toll before allowing *Galahad* to use the Channel. A human toll. And, if they rejected his demand . . .

If they rejected his demand then all of them could be dead by the afternoon.

She bristled. How could she have overlooked this possibility? She'd somehow assumed that the jellyfish would simply do their bidding, opening highways here and there, allowing them safe passage. Serving them. How naive she'd been, blind to the basic concept of payment for services rendered. And now it was going to cost them two crew members.

Except Torrec had said "conditions." Plural. Triana was afraid to find out what else he demanded for their lives.

The atmosphere in the room had inverted, shifting from elation to dread in a matter of seconds. Triana's mind raced through the possible alternatives left to her, but this was something that would take time to work out. And time was a commodity they did not have. Before she could think of what to say, she saw a figure on the front row stand to address the stage.

"I would like to volunteer as one of the specimens," Hannah said.

Triana was too stunned to reply. She gaped at Hannah, who stood proudly with her hands behind her back, her chin up.

Gap jumped to his feet. "No!" he said. "You can't do that."

"And why not?" Hannah said, giving him a puzzled look. "I voted for us to go with them, and the scientist in me wants to study the Dollovit as much as they want to examine us. Why wouldn't I go?"

Gap was at a loss for an answer. He looked up at Triana for help.

"We need to talk about this," Triana said.

"There's no time to talk about it," Hannah said. Of all the people in the room, she seemed to be the most at ease. "It solves two problems: part of Torrec's demands in return for his help, and a chance for us to learn enough to leap ahead thousands of years." She gave a respectful nod to the jellyfish. "I'm assuming, Torrec, that this doesn't need to be a permanent assignment."

All eyes turned to the glowing tank on the side of the stage. Torrec's voice, amplified through the room's speakers, carried its usual metallic edge.

"That depends," he said. "However, should we acquire all the information we need over time, arrangements could be made to conclude the assignment."

Gap held a hand out toward Hannah. "Over time? You don't know how long that might be. You might never make it back."

Hannah ignored this, and said to Triana: "Volunteers are needed to close the deal, and I'm willing to go."

Triana gave her a sad smile. "Hannah . . . I appreciate your offer. But Torrec requested two—"

"And I'll be the second," came a voice from the left side of the auditorium.

Heads craned to see Manu rise to his feet.

"I'll go with Hannah," he said. "I voted to go to Eos, but Hannah will need a companion. Besides, she's right: there's a lot to learn, including things that could be a huge benefit to our colony on Eos. Things like health. Medicine. I'm willing to sacrifice a few years now for a payoff later. I'll go."

Triana was thunderstruck. First their leading scientific mind, and now Lita's top assistant. She saw Gap slowly sit down and turn to talk with Lita, who held her head in her hands.

"Hannah, Manu," Triana said. "I appreciate it, really. And I'm sure the rest of the crew appreciates your brave sacrifice. Let's talk after this meeting, okay? We'll figure things out."

Hannah and Manu both nodded to her, then sat down. Triana looked across the stage at Torrec.

"If you have other conditions, we'd like to hear what they are."

"Besides the two specimens, we also request a portion of the contents from the restricted areas of your ship."

It took Triana—and most of the crew—a few moments for this to register. When it did, Triana frowned. "You're talking about the Storage Sections. But . . . we don't know what's inside the Storage Sections."

"We do," Torrec said. "Our mapping of your ship with the Vo revealed every detail, including the lower level compartments that you call the Storage Sections."

Triana's heart raced. She bit her lip and gave a worried look to the other Council members on the front row. Finally, she turned back to the jellyfish ambassador.

"Okay," she said. "What contents in the Storage Sections are you referring to?"

Torrec said: "The people."

17

Yes, it's true, I did know about the contents of the Storage Sections, but I was sworn to secrecy, so quit throwing me the hairy eyeball and pretending that you're mad, because we both know that you'll be hanging around like you're my best friend again in a matter of minutes. I even told you four or five books ago that I was in on the secret.

I would've kept that secret all the way to Eos, too. Who knew that we were going to run into space vultures with some sort of cosmic x-ray vision? I mean, besides that one girl in Oregon; she's figured out everything about two chapters ahead of me. But besides her, who knew?

As the shock wore off, Triana was tempted to gather the Council members into a closed meeting to discuss the bombshell that Torrec had lobbed into their midst. But given the pandemonium that broke out in the auditorium, she realized that this was something the entire crew needed to hear. In fact, they *deserved* to hear it.

People in the Storage Sections? *People?* How was that even possible?

Once order was restored to the meeting, Triana directed her questions at the ship's computer. "Roc, I think it's safe to say that we're beyond the point of keeping secrets about the Storage Sections. What does Torrec mean when he says *people*?"

"Note to self," Roc said. "Jellyfish cannot keep a secret."

"He said people, Roc," Triana said, unamused. "What does it mean?"

"It means that your secret cargo on *Galahad* includes supplies for your first camp sites on Eos, along with special transport craft to get the sizable amount of gear down to the surface. And, yes, you will find people in the Storage Sections."

Triana kept her composure. "How is that possible?"

"It's possible through technology, that's how. You're familiar with suspended animation chambers; it's how you were able to add one little furball to the ship's manifest, remember? Well, there are similar chambers stacked within the lower level, and they contain additional colonists selected by Dr. Zimmer."

"Teens, like us, I'm assuming?"

"Yes, fifteen and sixteen at the time of launch, just like the rest of the crew."

"How many?"

Roc said: "Eighty-four."

Another shock wave rippled through the room, and Triana steadied herself against the podium. Eighty-four teenagers, in a drug-induced sleep, in the bowels of the ship. In an instant, it seemed, the size of the crew had increased by a third.

"Why weren't we told about this?" Triana asked, anticipating the question that every crew member was likely thinking. "Why would Dr. Zimmer store almost a hundred other crew members in suspended animation and leave us in the dark? What does that serve?"

"My job is to assist all of you in the operation of the ship," Roc said. "I was ordered to keep quiet regarding the contents of the lower level. I was not told why that was important to the mission director."

Triana couldn't decide if she was angry or not, but there wasn't time to worry about that. She had more questions about the arrangement—including how they were expected to handle this upon arrival at Eos—but for now there were other issues to confront.

The jellyfish ambassador had remained quiet during the exchange. Triana turned to him and said: "Torrec, unless they specifically volunteer, I can't give you permission to take crew members who are cryogenically stored below. I won't do that to them. And why do you want additional crew members anyway, especially those that are in suspended animation? What would that serve?"

"I am not interested in the teenaged crew members that are within the cryogenic chambers," Torrec said.

Triana frowned again, and was about to probe further when Roc interrupted.

"Perhaps I should explain. The eighty-four teenagers are only part of the surprise. There are . . . others."

"Others?" Triana said. "You mean adults? There are *adults* aboard *Galahad*?"

"No, far from it," Roc said. "The rapid spread of Bhaktul disease ruled out anyone over the age of eighteen. The others, in this case, are in the form of human embryos stored in special cryogenic units."

"What?" Triana said. She looked at Lita, who appeared stunned, overwhelmed by the barrage of shocking information tumbling forth in the last few minutes. Lita mouthed a question: How many? Triana relayed the question to Roc.

"The original plan," he said, "was to launch with at least three hundred, but there were far too many problems, both from a technical standpoint and also administrative. Meaning it was more difficult to contain—quietly and respectfully—than Dr. Zimmer ever counted on. So your total count in the Storage Sections includes the eighty-four teens in cryo storage, and just a few shy of two hundred embryos. One ninety-three, to be exact."

"Roc," Triana said. "This . . . is unbelievable."

"I'm relieved that I don't have to keep a lid on it anymore," the computer said. "I'm actually glad that Torrec has a big mouth. Well, not literally; I'm not even sure he has a mouth. But you know what I mean."

"So many," Triana said, her voice barely a whisper.

"Yes," Roc said. "If you put them all together, there are more of them than there are of you."

Lita stood up from the front row. "Roc," she said, "how did Dr. Zimmer find that many human embryos? And how could he possibly keep that kind of program a secret?"

"He didn't have to find them, Lita. They found him. From the day the *Galahad* mission was announced, hundreds of thousands of families contacted Dr. Zimmer and his staff, begging to have their children considered for acceptance to the program. But few people knew about the thousands of couples who didn't have children yet, but still wanted their offspring to be part of the mission.

"After that, it was a matter of contacting these people and making one thing clear: Dr. Zimmer would consider them for inclusion in the *Galahad* mission, but they had to sign an affidavit of complete and total confidentiality and secrecy. One violation of any kind, one slip, and their future children would not be included. And, of the almost two hundred that were actually conceived—all of them through in vitro fertilization, by the way—not one person blabbed. It was that important to them."

Triana looked down at the podium as she absorbed this latest news. Although it was unnerving to find out so late in the mission, it made perfect sense. Space aboard the ship was at a premium, as were resources; storing embryos required energy and stability, but no maintenance and hardly any room. All two hundred likely could fit within one large refrigerated cabinet.

It was ingenious. Triana was embarrassed to admit that her initial reaction had been . . . well, she'd been a little creeped out. But now, given the chance to step back and see it from a scientific viewpoint, she was surprised that it had never occurred to her. Families would do anything to give their children a fighting chance to survive. Why shouldn't that include their unborn children as well?

But a new concern raced into her mind.

"Tell me why, Torrec," she said. "I can understand you requesting two members of our crew, but I'm not comfortable with the thought of you going back to your star system with human embryos. I'm sorry, but it sounds too much like a horror movie for me."

"Your concern is noted, and understood," Torrec said. "I will be forthcoming with you and let you know that our species would be equally as protective in this regard. However, allow me to explain. I am confident that once you hear our position, you will be inclined to agree to the condition."

"You've got a ways to go to convince me," Triana said.

"We do not request all of them, only a fraction of the total," Torrec said. "And there are three important points to consider. One, no harm will come to the embryos. They will be cared for and nurtured throughout their growth stages. We are scientists; we want to study and learn. It does us no good to damage the object of that study.

"Also, we have the tools necessary to bring the children to term, along with a guarantee of heath and maintenance. Your Storage Sections contain everything necessary to duplicate a human growth medium, and we do as well. The children will be strong and healthy at birth.

"And finally, it makes sense from a practical point of view for you," Torrec said. "I believe your species has a classic idiom: do not put all of your eggs in one basket. In this case, it would be in a literal sense. Your early days of colonization at Eos will be harsh, and extremely dangerous. By putting all of your future generations at risk on a planet's surface, you would rest assured that a percentage of your colony's population is safe and well-cared for. When the time comes, these future colonists will be ready to make the trip to Eos to join your growing society."

His arguments made sense. Triana couldn't deny the logic behind everything Torrec said. But she still found herself reluctant to open her mind to the possibility. Her rational mind said it would be okay—she hadn't even *known* about the human cargo stowed in the Storage Sections until minutes ago—but something kept her from nodding in agreement.

And then it hit her. Regardless of how long she'd known about them, the embryos aboard *Galahad* represented the future of their civilization, and her mothering instincts automatically kicked in. She discovered that she was exhibiting an emotional reaction that probably was not too different from many of the animal species on Earth. She was protecting the nest.

She saw confusion on faces throughout the auditorium. No one was prepared for this dilemma. The crew of *Galahad* looked up at her, watching and waiting. From the front row, Channy appeared in knots, while Gap and Lita were once again conferring, their foreheads almost touching as they quietly talked. More than anything at the moment, Triana wanted to hear their opinions.

She stalled. "Do you have other conditions as well?" she said to Torrec. "Or does this sum it up?"

"We require your cooperation," the jellyfish said. "Once the transfer process begins, there will be no room for reconsideration. Likewise, once the Channel aperture is in place, the course is set. The energy expenditure is too great to allow for indecision. And we require your pledge of peaceful intent in all matters, now and in the future. We, like many species you will encounter, do not offer what your people refer to as a 'second chance.' Any violation of peaceful intent will incur harsh, aggressive action. There must be no misunderstanding on this."

It was a subtle message, but a powerful reminder. The Dollovit might be helping the young star travelers—for a price—but they could easily crush the upstarts from Earth in a flash. It was a friendly heads-up from Torrec that the teens on *Galahad* were playing out of their league, and had best remember it.

From her spot on the stage Triana studied the sea of faces. It was easy enough to read the shock that had blown the crew back into their seats. Almost a hundred teens tucked below, along with twice as many embryos. And now their alien benefactors were demanding a fee for their help. It pained her to admit it, but with an impending disaster looming, Triana knew that they had no choice but to agree to the terms.

"I want your word," she said to Torrec, "that all of our companions will be treated well."

"That is understood," the ambassador said.

"And I want your word that they will be returned; that they'll be able to join us again when you've completed your studies."

"I am able to state that those who wish to return will be allowed to do so."

"They'll want to join us," Triana said.

"If so, they may."

Something in Torrec's answer sounded another alarm within Triana. Bon had referred to the space around the red dwarf star as a floating zoo, and how many zoos released their animals back into the wild? Torrec had given his word, but what did that mean to a Dollovit? She realized that she'd been backed into a corner. In order to save the crew, some would have to be . . .

There was no other way to put it: they would be loaned out.

Triana again made eye contact with Lita, exchanging a look of futility. The Council members, along with the rest of the crew, understood what had to be done.

"All right," Triana said.

The countdown began.

18

Gap stood before the familiar panel in Engineering, talking with Julya Kozlova about the patchwork repairs to the ship's radiation shield.

"It's frustrating," Julya said. "One look at this and it seems as if everything's fine, no problems."

"And yet it's crumbling," Gap said. "The additional power seems to have bought us the time we need to get out of here. Let's make sure it's buttoned up for the ride we're about to take."

He noticed Julya start to respond, then grow quiet. She was looking past Gap's shoulder at something. He craned his neck to see Hannah standing in the doorway, her hands clasped together in front of her.

"Got a few minutes?" she said.

No, he wanted to say. No, I don't have a few minutes. No, I'm not going to talk about anything right now. Instead he heard himself say: "Yeah, sure."

After assuring Julya he'd be back in a flash, he walked out with Hannah and let her lead the way toward the lift. He knew where they were going without having to be told. In less than two minutes they stood in the corridor leading to the Spider bay, near the large window that offered one of the best views of the overwhelming star field.

"I don't expect you to say much," Hannah said, leaning against the curved wall. "So let me just say what I have to say. Deal?"

Gap faced her from across the hall, and nodded.

She began to speak, but immediately stopped with a nervous laugh.

"Yes?" Gap said.

She looked away when she answered. "Everything I want to say always sounds so good in my head, but sounds so awkward when it comes out."

He wasn't going to bail her out. Instead, he waited.

"I guess what it comes down to," she said, looking back at him, "is that things were never that bad between us, and we somehow let it get worse. I'm sure I overreacted when you said you needed a break, and I think you overreacted when you heard me talking to Merit. Emotions, I guess."

Gap held his tongue, wondering where this was going.

"You're free to disagree," she said. "I know that the last time we talked privately I said some things out of frustration, and I'm sorry about that. I . . . I guess what I'm trying to say is that I wish it hadn't turned out the way it did. You got mad, I got mad, and all it did was drive us apart.

"Just for the record, I want you to hear what I'm saying. There was never anything between Merit and me. Nothing. He encouraged me to run for Council Leader, and I suppose I needed you to see me as more than just an ex-girlfriend. I wanted you to know that I had more to offer than just a few scientific equations and some oil paintings. I don't regret running for the office, but I do regret that it made things worse between us."

She shrugged. "I look back on it now, and it seems like ages ago. Maybe because Triana's back, and there's so much else going on. But I hope you believe what I'm telling you about Merit. He's a snake. I let him manipulate me more than once, and that's something I'll always regret."

Gap knew it was time for him to respond. He gave a slow nod and said: "I believe you."

They were quiet for a moment, then Gap looked back down the hall toward the lift. "I probably need to get back to work. We've got a lot to do in Engineering to get ready."

Hannah stepped forward and took his hand. "Gap, I'm leaving in two hours. And I don't know when I'll see you again."

He saw tears in her eyes and fought back his own. "I can't believe you're doing this," he said. "I mean, going with Torrec."

"It's the greatest scientific opportunity anyone's ever had," she said. "I'm a scientist at heart, Gap. How could I pass this up?"

"We'll need a lot of scientific smarts when we get to Eos."

"And you'll have plenty of help. I wasn't the only one training for this mission, you know. Plus, you'll have Roc. It's not like I'm leaving you completely high and dry."

"No," Gap said. "You're right." He shook his head. "I know you're right about the chance to study. I just hope that you're not making a terrible mistake. I mean, how will you live? How do you know they'll be able to take care of you?"

Hannah grinned. "Gap, they made sixteen pods, and a realistic human replica, in about a week. I think they can rig up a hotel room and a few tacos."

He finally cracked a smile. "Yeah, I guess so." After looking down at her hand on his, he completely dropped his guard. He pulled her into a tight embrace and held on to her. "I'll miss you, Hannah," he whispered into her ear.

He felt the tremble and knew she was quietly sobbing. "And I'm going to miss you, too," she said. "I'll be back. I don't know when, or how, but I'll be back."

Lita was cleaning the outside of Torrec's tank when Triana walked into the room in Sick House, and the Council Leader couldn't help but laugh.

"Are you washing his windshield?"

Lita grinned. "Can't send him home in a dirty tank. What will his friends think of us?"

Triana dropped into a chair. "I'm not sure they think all that much of us, to tell you the truth. We're just one insignificant entry in their master log of creatures around the universe. Isn't that right, Torrec?"

"We have cataloged many," the jellyfish said. "The significance factor is difficult to ascertain without a full study."

"You're a laugh a minute, Torrec," Triana said. Her expression turned serious. "So, Lita, any comments about the way things are turning out?"

The girl from Mexico dabbed at a smear on the tank. "What's there to say, really? We've got hibernating bodies in the Storage Section, along with fertilized human eggs. If you're asking what I think of your decision to part with some of the embryos, I guess I'd have to say I'm not happy about it. But, like you, I don't see any other choice. Not if we want to get to Eos safely.

"Of course," she added, keeping her attention on the tank. "If we'd decided to go to the red dwarf system, then we wouldn't be parting with anybody."

"I figured you'd say that," Triana said. "If it meant saving the lives of the embryos, I wouldn't hesitate. But I trust Torrec when

he says they'll be well cared for, and eventually returned. I'm willing to allow him to study them. Plus, I'm assuming that Manu
will do a good job of overseeing them, too."

"I hate to lose him," Lita said. "He's a great worker, and an even
better person. Just . . ." She paused, then finished. "Just like Alexa."

They let that lie there for a moment. Then Triana said: "I'm
assuming that Mathias will take his spot?"

Lita nodded. "He's very good, so it'll all work out." She chuckled. "Quite the revolving door here at the clinic."

Triana bit her lip, watching her friend meticulously clean each
side of the tank. "Torrec, how many of the embryos are you requesting?"

"We will be satisfied with sixteen."

"Sixteen," Triana said. "You guys certainly have a thing for
that number. Sixteen pods, sixteen embryos."

"It is the base number in our counting system," the jellyfish
said. "The most widely used system on your home planet is base-
ten. We use base-sixteen."

"Ah," Triana said. "Well, if it's okay with you, I'd like to keep
six of the pods that you produced. We can use them when we get
to Eos, and I think we can cram that many into the Spider bay."

"That is satisfactory," Torrec said.

"Uh, and we're also going to have you take back the ventet of
the crew member that you made. I hope you understand."

"We've had that talk," Lita said. "He's fine with it. In fact, as
eerie as it sounds, I think Manu might want to do a little study on
it himself." She glanced at Triana. "You know, cell regeneration,
that kind of stuff. Could be helpful later."

Triana let out a long breath. "Sounds too much like the Fran-
kenstein story to me. But if he thinks it can help us down the
road . . ."

"What time do we plunge down the rabbit hole?" Lita asked, changing the subject.

"We'll go ahead and plan on noon. Hannah and Manu will leave with Torrec—and the other cargo—around eleven."

Lita stopped what she was doing and put her hands on her hips. "That means you're opening the Storage Sections."

"Uh-huh. In twenty-five minutes. Wanna be there?"

"I wouldn't miss it," Lita said.

"Okay," Triana said, standing. "See you there. In the meantime, I have to go talk with the farmer."

The farmer was in his office, and for the first time Triana could recall, the door to his office was closed. She walked around to the large window that looked out into Dome 1 and peered in. Bon sat at his desk, absorbed in something on his vidscreen. She wavered for a moment, then tapped on the glass.

Bon didn't move his head, but shifted his eyes to the window. He saw her, but turned his attention back to the screen without acknowledging that she was there. Triana shook her head, then worked back around to the door and pushed it open.

"Begging your pardon, Mr. Hartsfield," she said, closing the door behind her and then leaning against it. "May I take you away from your work for a few precious minutes?"

He continued to gaze at the screen. "What is it?"

"You bolted from the meeting before the fireworks began. I thought that, as a Council member, you should at least get caught up on what we discovered."

"I'm all ears. Catch me up."

"You seem so busy," Triana said, "so let me give you a thumbnail sketch. Hannah and Manu are going back with Torrec, and they're taking sixteen of the human embryos that are lurking in the Storage Sections, but they're not taking any of the cryogenically frozen teenagers that are sleeping in there."

Before she'd finished, Bon was staring at her. She raised her eyebrows and gave him a reproachful look. "See what you miss when you cut out early?"

"You're serious."

"Oh, I'm serious. Eighty-four *Galahad* backups in suspended animation, along with almost two hundred embryos."

"And Hannah is leaving?"

Triana nodded gravely. "And Manu."

"Manu is competent but replaceable. Hannah is unique, and brilliant."

"Wow," Triana said, with a mock look of surprise. "Bon compliments someone. I'll be sure to jot that down in my journal tonight."

He pushed back in his chair and put his feet up on the desk. "Does this change the operation in any way? The bodies in the basement, I mean. Still going to Eos, I'm assuming."

"Yes. Torrec and company leave at eleven, and we go an hour later. You should dismiss all farmworkers by eleven-thirty. I'll want everyone in their room, lying down, when we go through. That means you, too."

Bon shrugged. "Fine. You could have told all of this to me electronically."

"And miss your syrupy-sweet attitude?" Triana crossed the room and sat down in the chair across the desk from him. "Tell me about the Cassini."

He gave a sarcastic snort. "What? Now? You want to talk about the Cassini *now*?"

"You're not using the translator anymore, Bon. By now you must know more about them. The way you hustled down to the Spider bay, you obviously knew about Alexa's ventet on the pod."

"No," he said. "They don't tell me things. I get feelings."

She waved this away. "However you want to put it. You voted immediately for going to Eos, rather than Torrec's system. Did the Cassini play a role in that decision for you, too?"

Bon rocked slightly in his chair. "Yes and no. I get no feeling of dread regarding the Dollovit system, but I know that it would have been a dead end for us. Knowledge is one thing, but not at the price of stagnation."

"Explain that."

"Stagnation of spirit," he said. "The Dollovit are all about securing knowledge. But they live only to acquire the knowledge, not to use it in any real sense. That's why I don't see them anymore as a threat."

"Torrec essentially threatened us just a few minutes ago."

"Probably only to protect their single-minded purpose. Am I right?"

Triana conceded the point.

"They're living encyclopedias," Bon said. "I'm all in favor of expanding our knowledge, of continuing to learn. But it means nothing if we grow physically stagnant, if we don't use the information somehow. On Eos we'll use everything we've learned by putting it to practical use."

Triana knew that she was radiating a look of admiration, but she didn't care. She was truly impressed with Bon's analysis.

"You've changed," she blurted out without thinking.

He grunted back at her. "We've all changed. Every one of us."

She shook her head. "No, it's different with you. I don't know if it's the mind alteration from your Cassini connection, or if it's just the new mature Bon. Maybe a little of both. But you never would have said anything like that six months ago."

His ice-blue eyes bored into her. "And how have you changed, Triana? Did the Dollovit change you? Are you the same person you were six months ago?"

She leaned forward. "I'm not the same person I was six *days* ago. For a while I even wondered if I was physically the same person."

"Oh? Did you think you were a manufactured copy, too?"

"Don't laugh, it crossed my mind."

"How do you know for sure you're not?" Bon said.

She looked out the window to her right and watched a team of farmworkers walk past with shovels and rakes thrown over their shoulders. "I remember something my dad told me once during one of our drives in the mountains. He said that more than a few scientists were convinced that every one of us on Earth was nothing more than a computer simulation, created by some advanced being or advanced computer somewhere. That we were only highly detailed sims, products of a supercomputer's imagination."

"Oh?" Bon said. "And how did these scientists figure this?"

"The theory goes that computer simulation is so good, and improving exponentially, that computer processing power can literally be more potent than a human brain. And if that's the case, then at some point simulations will be created with human characters that actually think, and believe that they're real."

Bon shook his head. "Nice parenting skills, telling his daughter that she might be a video game."

Triana laughed. "Oh, c'mon. It's all mathematics, really. Once you factor in the number of potential alien civilizations in the universe, and add the combined computing power, it's actually more likely that we're simulations than real, living beings. And I find that very interesting, even if you don't."

"What's the point of this?" Bon said.

"The point is what my dad told me when I asked if he really thought he was a computer simulation. He said: 'Maybe I am, and maybe I'm not. But if I am, I still have every reason to be the best simulation I can. Why make my life difficult or unhappy, even if it's artificial? I'm still living it, regardless.'"

Bon said: "Makes sense."

"Right. So even if I'm a reproduction of the real me, I'm still living it. What am I gonna do, give up? No thanks."

"Is that the real reason you voted for Eos over the Dollovit system? You didn't want a reminder every day that you might be a clone?"

Triana rubbed her forehead and closed her eyes. "Now you're starting to sound like Roc. Let's forget about why I voted for Eos and just take care of business, okay?"

"No problem," Bon said, looking back at his monitor. "Anything else?"

There was plenty. There were volumes that Triana knew she could pour out right now. But she said: "Just wanted to fill you in on what you missed. We're about to open the Storage Sections, in case you want to join us. After that I'll be in the Spider bay to see Hannah and Manu off."

She hurried out before she could say anything else.

A flurry of activity put an electric charge in the air. The countdown for *Galahad*'s departure brought back memories of their original launch, which now seemed a lifetime ago. Inside the Spider bay and its control room, crew members scurried about, making room for the six additional pod replicas which would be brought aboard as soon as Hannah, Manu, and Torrec slipped away in the original.

A second Channel had yawned open ahead, the quantum portal waiting to deliver *Galahad* to the Eosian star system. The wormhole's cosmic shock wave had rippled through the spacecraft, but this time Torrec's warning had spared them from injuries.

Triana was running on pure adrenaline. Just down the hall, preparations were underway to open the sealed Storage Sections, with Gap overseeing a team of workers gathered for the big moment. Triana would join them in minutes.

Everything was spiraling down to the finish line so quickly. Years of training and travel, billions upon billions of miles between *Galahad* and her birthplace, countless adventures and crises that had piled one upon the other, new and vivid emotions that had cascaded through her . . . and yet it came down to this. Opening the secretive vault, dispatching crew members who had become like family to her, and parcelling out living embryos in an exotic form of cosmic barter. All to guarantee their safe arrival at a planet—or planets—that could easily turn out to be hostile, even deadly.

The door to the Spider bay control room opened and Hannah stepped inside. She carried a look about her that hovered somewhere between all-out excitement and downright terror. Triana was sure it was the same look that she herself had worn when she'd piloted the pod into the wormhole.

"Ready to go?"

Hannah's eyes were wide. "I don't know. I can't believe it's actually happening."

Triana gazed into the oversized hangar. "I know what you mean. But listen, don't be afraid. I mean, I know it's easy to say that, but it's painless. It's a shock, but painless."

Hannah laughed. "There's so much to see when I get there, and so much to learn from the Dollovit. But what I'm most looking forward to is crossing that barrier. It represents everything that got me interested in science in the first place. It's . . . it's symbolic."

Triana wrinkled her forehead. "What do you mean?"

"Oh, I don't want to get all philosophical at the last minute," Hannah said, looking embarrassed.

"No, tell me."

"Well, it's a doorway of sorts, right? Only this doorway, in effect, separates the primitive from the evolved. It's a doorway that takes us forward several millennia in an instant. We leave our infant self behind, and take our first steps as galactic adults.

"But it might even represent more than that," Hannah said, growing excited. "In my mind, at least, it represents an evolutionary leap so great that it could almost compare to the doorway between life and death."

Triana stood speechless. Of course. Of course! It was exactly the description that her mind had so desperately sought from the moment she'd pierced that infinitely thin barrier and plunged into the space around a glowing red dwarf star. A doorway, a transition from one world to another. But more than that! A transition that took her into another dimension of life, a step that no human could even conceive, a leap that paralleled the mystical barrier between life and death.

Bon was convinced, through his repeated connections with the Cassini, that something, somehow, existed after this life. It had become an obsession for him, prompted by guilt, perhaps, but an obsession nonetheless. For Bon it was no mystery that another existence awaited; it was the transition itself that haunted him.

Now Triana felt an entirely new appreciation for the bridge spanning that gulf. She'd experienced a blinding flash of white light, she'd lost consciousness, and she'd awakened in an alternate reality, descriptions that eerily mirrored those given by people who'd crossed the boundary between life and death.

Before she even knew it was happening, Triana felt tears on her face. At a time when her thoughts should have been dominated by the events at hand, her conscious mind broke away from the Spider bay, from the Storage Sections, from Hannah . . . and took her immediately to her father.

For the first time since his death, Triana felt that she could let him go in peace. She'd been granted a gift that no other human had ever received: the chance to experience—and appreciate—the crossing of a barrier between worlds, between alternate realities, and to know that transitions of this nature could never end at the doorway itself. There would always be another side.

"Tree, are you all right?" Hannah was at her side, gripping her hand. "You're crying. What happened?"

Triana gave an embarrassed laugh and swiped at her cheeks. "It's nothing. Just . . . just a lot that's finally making sense, that's all." She dabbed at her face again and looked at Hannah. "No, really, it's okay. Everything you said is . . . well, it's beautiful. Thank you for putting your feelings into words. Sometimes that's hard for me to do."

"It's usually hard for me, too," Hannah said. She let go of Triana's hand and gave her own quick laugh. "We don't sound like typical women, do we?"

"We're not," Triana said. "And that's okay, too."

They were interrupted by a tone from the speaker, followed by Gap's voice. "Hey, Tree. You still at the bay?"

"Roger that, as Roc would say," she said.

"Good. Come on down the hall, we're ready to bust into this vault."

Triana looked at Hannah. "Do you still have packing to do, or would you like to join us?"

Hannah was already walking out the door. "Are you crazy? I'm not leaving without seeing this."

Dr. Zimmer had been lenient with the crew in many areas. He'd caved to their demands for an Airboarding track; he'd allowed them to introduce some of their favorite foods to the already restricted space in the Domes; and he'd bucked the advice of his advisors and sent each crew member home one more time before the launch. He'd proven to be a strong mission director who could bend at the appropriate time and for the right reasons.

But on one item he'd never swayed an inch: the Storage Sections were sealed, and would remain sealed until the crew reached Eos. The contents would remain out of sight and—ideally, anyway—out of mind. Roc alone knew what lay inside, and his programming was clear. Gap had poked and prodded the computer mercilessly during the first few months of the mission, practically begging to be let in on the secret. But they both understood that it was mostly an entertaining diversion.

A stowaway had breached the sealed compartments right after launch, but Roc had determined that no real damage was done to the interior. The chambers remained sealed without any crew member gaining access.

It was a dark mystery for the lively group of teens, and soon it dominated their late-night banter. What was in there? Why was it a secret? Who would be the first to find a way inside and break the spell?

Then, in one remarkable exchange, an alien visitor had pulled back the curtain and revealed *Galahad*'s secret. And now, on par with the other landmark events that were transpiring on this momentous day, the door would be flung open and the crew allowed access.

Gap grinned as Triana and Hannah rounded the turn on the lower level. To Triana it resembled the face of a little boy with his hand on the doorknob to the living room, anxious to see what delights Santa had left behind overnight. Lita and half a dozen crew members stood behind him, accompanied by a handful of wheeled carts.

"I feel like Dr. Zimmer's gonna come crashing around the corner any minute, pointing and shouting," Gap said. "You know, technically we haven't reached Eos yet."

"If it saves our lives, Dr. Zimmer would encourage us to break in," Lita said. "Besides, I think we've more than earned the right to open this door, wouldn't you say?"

Hannah chimed in. "And it's not like it's a big surprise anymore. Aren't you just dying to see how they've done this?"

Gap stepped aside to show Triana the entrance panel. With the original Eos arrival date still three years away, she'd never bothered to look at the small control switches embedded in the wall. The secrecy, mixed with the dark, remote location within the bowels of the ship, had curbed her curiosity about the Storage Sections.

Standing before the panel that stretched from floor to ceiling, she eyed the controls that resembled an ordinary security lock. An hour earlier Roc had given her the six-digit code, a combination that immediately brought back fond memories and caused Triana to shake her head at Dr. Zimmer's quaint inside joke. Now she took a deep breath and punched in the code.

Nothing happened.

She felt the stares from her shipmates behind her. Was there another step that she'd left out? Had the code somehow been corrupted during the stowaway incident? Did the—

There was a low whine, followed by a click. Seconds later the panel shifted inward about an inch before creeping slowly to the side. With the door's seal broken, interior lights flickered to life, and the hiss of ventilation stirred within the chamber. Triana took one tentative step, and leaned inside.

The room measured about fifteen feet square, and almost that tall, with a passageway at the far end connecting to another room.

Given the exterior size of the Storage Sections, Triana estimated that there were likely at least eight rooms linked together. Her apprehension about entering was somewhat diminished by the sight of storage crates looming over them, stacked high on metal shelves. She'd been nervous about immediately stumbling upon bodies; boxes she could handle.

It wasn't until Gap leaned close to her ear and whispered, "Any day now," that she pried her feet from the floor and walked inside. The air felt especially dry, although it was helped by the whisper of a breeze beginning to seep from the vents. Gap and the other crew members fanned out behind her and began a cursory inventory of the boxes. Most had labels that identified the specific contents, but Triana couldn't focus on those just yet.

Summoning her courage, she left the first room behind and moved down the broad passageway toward the next chamber. She saw the first bodies before entering the room.

They were lying in clear cryogenic tubes that were markedly different from the ones found on the pod from SAT33. While the pods were capable of short-term, emergency life preservation, they were older units, hastily added to the small craft. These, however, were advanced models, designed for interstellar travel and sleep cycles that could last for years.

They were arranged on specially constructed scaffolding that filled the space from floor to ceiling. A quick count showed seven stacks, each containing seven cryogenic cylinders. There were empty slots in several of the stacks, like empty airline seats during a flight. It was evident that bodies hadn't been removed from these empty cylinders; they had never been occupied.

Triana stepped softly to stand beside one of the tubes, and looked through the clear glass into the face of a boy. Strands of blond hair stuck out from beneath a snug elastic cap that covered his head.

Close to two dozen electrodes protruded from the gray cap and wound together into a twisted knot of wires that disappeared into a junction box at the head of the tube. His eyes were closed, his face serene. Triana noted the thin lips, the faint lashes, and a sharp, jutting chin. European? North American? She couldn't tell.

He was dressed in what appeared to be an old-fashioned sleeping gown, not unlike the one Triana imagined Ebenezer Scrooge wearing during his midnight jaunts with the ghosts of Christmas. It covered the boy down to his ankles. His feet were bare, and his hands were placed gently at his sides. By all accounts he appeared to be in a deep, peaceful slumber. Two pale lights in the junction box, one green and one yellow, were the only indicators of activity. Triana resisted the urge to tap on the glass, to test the depth of his sleep.

Directly above him, another boy lay in an almost identical state. The only differences that stood out were the boy's ethnicity— Asian, upon examination—and the fact that one hand was lying across his stomach. The skull cap, the wires, the gown, and the soft lights were the same.

Triana walked the perimeter of the room and noticed a mix of ethnicities in the teens occupying the other cylinders. All of them young men. Perhaps the girls were in another room?

She took a count and discovered that of the forty-nine tubes, thirty-nine held bodies. They all seemed to be in good health.

Gap came up beside her, his eyes scanning the room. "This is unbelievable," he said, his voice low, as if in reverence. "I thought I'd be creeped out, but it's actually very cool. We have new room-mates."

Triana nodded slowly. "Eighty-four new roommates. And eighty-four new stories for us to learn."

She found the next passageway and, with Gap a step behind

her, walked into the adjoining room. It was slightly larger, but held
the same number of tubes. Here, as expected, were the girls. Triana
and Gap gazed into the first chamber they encountered, into the
face of a black girl. She had long lashes over eyes that were parted
ever so slightly, giving the appearance of peeking back at the two
Galahad Council members. Above her, a Hispanic girl had an imp-
ish smile on her face, causing both Gap and Triana to smile, too.

"The girls outnumber the boys," Triana said. "Forty-five girls,
thirty-nine boys."

"Why do you think there are empty tubes?" Gap said.

Triana shrugged. "I don't know."

They spent another ten minutes combing through the remaining rooms. One housed what had to be the nerve center for the
cryogenic controls. Unlike the subdued life signs on the tubes
themselves, this unit blazed with activity, both in sight and sound.
Digital readouts scrolled across a vidscreen, and a series of electronic
sounds echoed off the walls. It all seemed light-years beyond their
comprehension, Triana thought. Thankfully they had Roc.

There were two more storage rooms stacked to the ceiling
with equipment and supply crates, all assembled to help a young
colony take root on alien soil.

Three larger rooms were tightly packed with transfer pods. These
small craft, obviously engineered to transport the cryogenic tubes
and their control units to the surface of a planet, were essentially
moving vans. The tubes would be rolled inside and secured, and
the craft would be robotically piloted clear of the ship.

"But how in the world are we supposed to get these off the
ship?" Gap said.

"Look at this," Triana said, inspecting the far wall. "See the
panel?"

Gap studied it for a moment, and gently brushed his hand

across the surface. "Well, whatta ya know? A moving panel. How much you wanna bet that on the other side—"

"—is the Spider bay," Triana finished. "Uh-huh. We move the sleeping beauties into the pods, secure the hatches, and then these walls open into the hangar next door. No wonder Dr. Zimmer put the Storage Sections down here. He could evacuate the suspended animation team in no time."

There was a single room left. Branching off from the cryogenic control center, it was about the size of a large walk-in closet. But the moment they entered, both Triana and Gap felt a shiver. The room was noticeably colder than the rest of the Storage Sections, but it also had a feel about it that was unlike the other compartments. They knew immediately that they'd entered the embryo storage facility.

"This reminds me of my mom's bank," Gap said. "I'd go with her sometimes when she put things into her safe deposit box." He indicated the metal boxes attached to the walls. "They looked just like this."

"And these contain valuables, too, just like your mom's safe deposit box," Triana said, turning on her heel to take it all in. "Think of the responsibility we've just been handed."

Gap gave a solemn nod. "Isn't it wild to think about whose kids these are? They could come from anywhere in the world."

"That's right," Triana said. "Anywhere. And their parents could be anyone. Think of *those* stories."

She stood before the shimmering wall of embryonic storage compartments, her breath visible in the icy chill of the room, while her mind drifted back to the teens who slept in suspended animation. They had stories, too. And one of those might be a bombshell.

Was this how Dr. Zimmer inserted his child aboard *Galahad* without anyone knowing?

20

With only forty-five minutes remaining until the pod departed, Lita hurried back to finish her work in Sick House. Torrec was escorted to the lower level, and she'd soon follow. Her medical skills wouldn't be needed for the launch, but she couldn't let Manu and Hannah take off without giving them a proper farewell. There was no telling when—or if—she'd see them again.

The next step was more complicated, if only from an emotional point of view. She walked into the hospital ward of the clinic, carrying a mug of tea, and approached the ventet of Alexa. It sat peacefully in a chair, staring at a vidscreen displaying a slide show of Earth's various landscapes. It was the only thing that the Sick House workers could think of to entertain their strange guest. And it seemed to work; Alexa's clone appeared to absorb each fleeting scene with a look that mimicked interest, if not wonder.

Lita set the tea mug on a nearby tray and kneeled beside the reproduction of her friend. Again she marveled at the near-perfect copy. The blond hair, which an assistant had pulled back into a ponytail, had the thin dark streaks that Alexa sported. The nose had the same subtle ridge, the eyes were spot-on, and the skin gave off the same alabaster glow.

This Alexa, however, couldn't speak. And if it was capable of complicated thought processes, it didn't show.

"How are you today?" Lita said, invoking the doctor-patient tone that she recalled her mother using during her medical rounds. "Same as yesterday, I'll bet." She smiled when the ventet tracked the vocal sounds and turned its head to look at Lita's face. It gave no emotional signals.

"I brought you some tea. It's your favorite. You used to drink it with me all the time. Do you remember that?"

Of course the ventet couldn't remember, but it seemed the right thing to say.

"This is called Cinque Terre," Lita said, tapping on the vidscreen. The ventet looked back and forth between the screen and Lita's eyes. "It's on the Italian coastline, and it's one of the most beautiful spots in Europe. I never made it there myself, but a few of our crew members have hiked it. Oh, and this is Angel Falls, in Venezuela. I *have* been there, with my dad and my brother and sister. I hope we have falls like that when we get to Eos. That's gorgeous, isn't it?"

The faux-Alexa gazed at the screen, then looked back at Lita. Nothing seemed to register.

"Why are you talking to it?" came a voice from the doorway.

Lita looked over her shoulder. "What are you doing here?" she asked. "This is the last place I thought you'd come."

Bon stood with his arms crossed, leaning against the wall. "What good does it do to talk to that thing?"

"Maybe no good at all," Lita said, turning back to the ventet and tucking a strand of its hair behind one ear. "But maybe I'm not doing it for her. Did you consider that?"

"No," Bon said. "That makes no sense, either."

"Not to you, but that's no surprise." Lita adjusted the vidscreen, reducing some of the glare. After sizing up Bon with a blank look, the ventet returned to its mindless gazing at the images.

"She's not a ghost, Bon, and she doesn't bite. You don't have to stay twenty feet away."

"I'm fine right here."

Lita shook her head. "It's like you hold some sort of a grudge against her, which is ridiculous. She didn't do anything wrong, you know." She lifted the mug of tea and brought it up to the ventet's face. It instinctively accepted the warm liquid into its mouth, slurping it down, almost like a trained animal.

Bon said: "Why are you treating it like a real person? It's not."

"Is there something else you'd like to talk about?" Lita said. "Because I'm not going to debate my work methods with you. It's really none of your business."

Bon pursed his lips and gave a single nod. "Fair enough. Thought you might want to visit for a moment. Can we talk at your desk in the other room?"

Lita's back was to him, so Bon couldn't see the faint smile that crossed her face. "No, I'm busy right now. If you want to talk, you'll have to do it in here with me and Alexa. Pull up a chair, tough guy."

For a moment it looked as if he might turn and leave. But instead he pushed away from the wall and walked a few steps into the room. He sat down in a chair, two beds away, and again crossed his arms.

"If it's any consolation," Lita said, "this copy of Alexa is going back with Hannah and Manu in a few minutes. It will join the Dollovit zoo, I guess you'd say. I'm sure you're brokenhearted over that."

"I'm not here to talk about that," Bon said. "I thought you might want to know about my latest connection."

Lita shifted to stare at him. It was unlike Bon to go out of his way to offer information about his intimate link with the Cassini. She'd always tracked him down, usually in the Farms, to get him to talk about it.

"Looks like you barely broke a sweat this time," she said, hoping that a casual demeanor would make him more likely to open up.

"It's still not the most pleasant thing to do, but I'm learning how to manage it better."

"That's good," Lita said. "What did you talk about today?"

"She's out there," Bon said.

Lita's eyes narrowed. "They said that?"

"I've told you, it's not a conversation. But yes, in a way they said it."

She put the mug back on the tray. "Bon, do you have any idea how big this is? It's the most important question in the history of our civilization, and you're sitting there with your arms crossed, tossing it out like it's . . . like it's the equivalent of finding a new strain of corn or something."

He gave her a weak smile. "Lita, I've dealt with this for awhile now, and I've put myself through an awful lot of physical pain in order to get even this much out of them. I'm exhausted, mentally and physically."

She sat back and considered this. Then she shook her head.

"I'm sure you're worn out, but that's not it. You're acting nonchalant about this because you knew it already, didn't you? This doesn't surprise you at all."

Bon sat still, and didn't answer.

"I'll share something with you," Lita said. "Lately I've done a lot of thinking about the concepts of faith and fate. I don't know if they're somehow connected, or if they're polar opposites. But it's almost been an obsession with me since the day Alexa died." She shot a quick glance at the ventet, which was fixated on the vidscreen's rotating Earth images. An icy chill went through her, and she unconsciously reached up to touch the charcoal-colored stone that hung on a chain from her neck.

"Was it faith that you had, Bon?"

"I don't look at it in those terms," he said.

There was a pause, and then Lita said: "That's it? That's your answer?"

He shrugged. "I don't know what you want me to say. If you're asking if this was a matter of faith or fate, I can't answer that. I had to know, that's all. I needed to know if there's something else out there. I can't tell you why." He uncrossed his arms and leaned forward. "You're projecting your own concerns about Alexa onto me. But I can't help you with that, Lita. You have to decide what works in your life."

She sighed, and by doing so felt a release of tension. As irritating as he could be, she knew Bon was right.

"So," she said, retreating into the casual tone she'd started with. "What are you going to do with this information?"

"Nothing."

Lita gawked at him. "Nothing? You've spent all this time, expended all of this effort and . . . and pain, and now . . . what? You just let it go?"

"That's exactly right. I found what I wanted."

She laughed again. "I don't believe it."

He shrugged again. "That's up to you."

Lita looked at the ventet of Alexa, and then back to Bon. "You don't want to try communicating with her? I mean the real Alexa. Out there somewhere."

"Not anymore. For me it's enough to know that there's another destination. I don't know what it is, or how it is, or however you want to put it." He stood up and glanced at the alien reproduction sitting beside Lita. "Let's just say that we all grieve in our own way, and we all find our own way of moving on. I've found mine. I'm moving on."

"But it's the greatest discovery of all time," Lita said softly. "You can make that connection . . . and then just walk away?"

Bon nodded. "I have no proof, Lita. I couldn't spell it out for anyone, and I wouldn't want to. That's up to the individual. I can't map out what they believe, any more than I can help you with your question about faith and fate. People decide for themselves."

He turned and walked to the door.

"Hey, Bon," Lita said. When he looked back at her, she smiled. "If this means you've found peace, I'm happy for you. I really am."

He pointed to the ventet. "Quit playing with your doll and get rid of it, will you?"

21

The corridor leading to the Spider bay was crammed with crew members. As she walked past, Triana had a fleeting vision, one that filled her with sadness. She saw the well-wishers who had filled the cramped reception room at her father's funeral, waiting for the opportunity to console the young daughter, to share stories that would somehow—they believed—help her understand how loved he was.

It was the longest afternoon of her life. She was all they had left to associate with the great man, a conduit for their praise and grief. Crushed by her own heartache and despair, she had no choice but to stand silently and offer herself as a device for their final good-byes.

The last thing she wanted to do now was to look upon this gathering on *Galahad*'s lower level as a final good-bye. Hannah and Manu had offered themselves as the toll necessary to meet Torrec's demands, but at the same time they both looked upon it as a chance to learn. They weren't treating this as good-bye; why should Triana?

She waited by the door to the oversized hangar, and watched

the bizarre procession. It began with Torrec, poised within the glittering syrup of fluid in his tank, rolled on a sturdy cart through the gauntlet of wide-eyed teens. A few of the crew members reached out to touch the reinforced glass as it passed by, each of them peering intently at the jellyfish ambassador. They were perfectly aware that this creature represented the yin and yang of alien contact: Torrec and his kind had wrought death upon *Galahad,* and now promised salvation. He was more than a mere curiosity; he was a symbol of both the perils and the rewards of humankind's evolution into a space-faring civilization.

As the cart drew even, the workers on each side paused, allowing Triana an opportunity to look once more upon their guest. She knelt and brought her face close to the glass. Inches away, floating in the genetically engineered solution which provided him with both protection and sustenance, Torrec raised one elastic tentacle. She was sure that he was aware of her; he had, in effect, saluted.

The moment passed. Triana stood and watched as he was escorted into the bay, and then heard the crowd in the hallway grow quiet. She looked back to see Alexa's ventet come into sight around the curve. It was walking on its own, but Lita kept a firm grip around its arm.

The ventet's face betrayed no emotion, but instead seemed to study the mass of human faces along the path. It looked side to side with a mechanical grace, never resting its gaze on any one spot. It was doing what it was programmed to do: observe and document.

For Triana it provided another painful jolt, as she—and the assembled crew members, undoubtedly—couldn't help but note that this would be the second time that Alexa departed through the Spider bay. Even though she wasn't real, the feeling was the same.

That, Triana realized, was a testament to the reproductive skills of the Dollovit and their vulture labor force.

Lita approached the door and gave Triana a silent nod, with a look that said everything was going to be all right. Triana spotted the dark pendant around Lita's neck, and felt her breath catch in her throat. She could imagine how difficult this walk must be for her friend, but Lita's head was up and her face composed. As the pair walked by, Triana reached out and squeezed her hand.

A minute later there was a swell of activity beyond the corridor's curve, and Triana heard the sound of Manu's laugh. He was greeting friends, a backpack slung across one shoulder, a smile on his face, while a wave of hands reached out to slap his back or shake his hand. He kept moving, the pace slow, but constant.

Behind him, Hannah moved through the line. Triana recognized the reluctant look on Hannah's face, and knew that it had nothing to do with the mission at hand, and everything to do with the attention. She politely responded to the cries of good luck, and nodded appreciation for the well-wishes. She even cracked a smile when someone channeled an early space pioneer with a hearty "Godspeed, Hannah." But Triana knew that the quiet blonde from Alaska wouldn't be comfortable until she was strapped inside the pod, preparing for a journey that seemed tailor-made for her. It was, in a sense, the ultimate Semester at Sea.

Triana noticed the unmistakable shock of black hair and angular face of Merit Simms. He'd remained in the background, but now pushed forward and reached out. His hand snaked around Hannah's wrist, causing her to swivel her head in his direction.

The look told Triana everything in one split second. Merit's wicked smile played across his face, while Hannah stiffened. Her face was stone-cold, her eyes bottomless pits. Merit leaned forward and spoke into her ear; Hannah responded with a grimace, and yanked her arm away. In a second she was beyond him, leaving Merit to smile after her and offer a sarcastic wave.

They reached the door into the bay. Manu grinned at Triana as he slipped past. Hannah stopped beside the Council Leader and they exchanged a quick hug. Before pulling away, Hannah whispered in her ear: "Watch out for Merit. He's still a snake, and I know he's up to something." After a pause, she added: "And look after Gap. Please."

Hannah glanced back toward Merit, then gave Triana a knowing look before walking into the hangar.

Watch out for Merit. Look after Gap.

The sentiments were a reminder of the inner dangers that continued to simmer within the walls of the ship. But the words also stirred old memories, a confusing blend of emotions that she'd never sorted out. Triana knew that she could easily get lost in there, wondering, worrying, trying to make sense of feelings that taunted her.

The crowd dispersed, drifting back toward the lift. Like good sailors, they had shown their respects to their crewmates, and now began preparing for their own assignment. Their conversations were muted. Triana watched them leave, then made her way to the Spider bay control room.

Gap and a handful of crew members had already stowed the sixteen containers aboard the pod and now double-checked that everything was secure. Each unit held an individual human embryo, along with a self-contained cooling apparatus and stabilizing gear. While Triana said that crossing the Channel boundary wasn't physically turbulent, no chances would be taken with such precious cargo.

Alexa's ventet was next. Lita led the clone inside the small craft and saw that she was comfortably seated and strapped in. Lita felt that she should say something, but found no words. This wasn't Alexa and, with the limited brain capacity of a vulture, it would never understand. In the end, she resorted to the only physical act that made sense to her at the moment: she stroked the ventet's hair.

She wasn't prepared for what happened next. There was a slight tug around her neck, and she looked down to see the ventet grasping the dark clump of space rock that Alexa had left behind. The stone had intersected the clone's field of vision as it hung from Lita's neck, and its reaction was to reach out and take hold of it. The alien reproduction had shown no impulse beyond observation—until now.

The ventet's eyes were locked on the cosmic pendant, scanning its odd shape. "Do you like this?" Lita asked. "Does this look familiar?"

It couldn't, she told herself. Despite looking like a perfect copy of her friend, this wasn't Alexa, nor did it have Alexa's memories. An alien organic brain lay within the skull, the same simple motor that powered the vultures. It couldn't possibly understand the significance of this clump of meteorite.

And yet this was the first time the ventet had shown any initiative. It had been content to be led around, to be placed in a bed or a chair and to remain inert. Nothing had moved it to act independently. Until it saw one of Alexa's personal possessions.

This couldn't be coincidence.

Lita's concentration was broken by a commotion at the rear of the pod. Manu and Hannah scrambled aboard with Gap and two other workers. Gear was quickly stowed, and a last-minute checklist was consulted. Lita caught the eye of Hannah.

"What's up?" Hannah said, dropping to a knee beside the ventet.

"Listen, we only have a minute before we seal you up in this thing," Lita said. "Take care of yourself, okay? I know that you and Manu have lots to do, but be careful. Get your work done and get back to us, understood?"

"You bet, Doc," Hannah said. She saw something in Lita's expression and added: "Is there something wrong?"

Lita lowered her voice. "Keep your eye on our friend here, too. She's . . . uh, she may not be what we think."

Hannah looked puzzled, but only nodded. Lita gave her another tight hug, then found Manu and did the same. He gave her a nervous smile.

"Got your lucky amulet?" Lita asked.

He tapped the pocket on his shirt. "Don't worry about us. This will ward off any bad juju on the other side."

She laughed with him. "I hate to part with both you *and* the good luck charm. I have to say, I felt better with that thing hanging around Sick House."

"It left some of its residue," Manu said. "You should be good for awhile."

It seemed awkward to hug him again, so Lita squeezed his shoulder and told him to be safe and to hurry back. She walked toward the pod's hatch and, just before dropping down to the hangar floor, looked back.

Alexa's ventet was strapped into the seat, but had craned its head around. It was staring intently at Lita.

With a faint smile on its face.

Triana put Gap in charge of the pod's launch while she returned to the Control Room. There were only two crew members on duty there; most of the ship's departments were throttling down in preparation for the Channel jump.

"One minute," she heard Gap say on the intercom when she'd settled at a workstation. "Hangar door is open."

"Roc," Triana said. "What's their ETA for the Channel once they're off the ship?"

"Between our speed, and the loop we've made back to the opening, they should be over the lip in about sixteen minutes. You'll get to say bon voyage before you're tucked in."

"What's the status of the remaining vultures?"

"Let's see," the computer said. "Fifteen . . . eighteen . . . times four . . . carry the one . . ."

"Roc . . ."

"Most of their squadron took off in the past hour. Some are hovering around the Channel, a few are scattered along the way, and it looks like another two dozen are lining up to escort the pod. That leaves at least twenty, maybe a few more, for our trip."

Triana frowned. "What do you mean, for our trip?"

"I thought you knew," Roc said. "Perhaps you should have a quick chat with Torrec before he disappears down the rabbit hole."

Before Triana could respond, Gap announced: "Pod away, hangar door closing."

"Roc, patch me in to Hannah," Triana said. After a silent count of three, she said: "Hannah, do you copy?"

"Right here," came the immediate reply. "We're off and running."

"Is Torrec in the loop?"

"I am here," Torrec said in his strange mechanical voice.

"What is this about a squadron of vultures . . . I'm sorry, Vo . . . coming with us? Nobody discussed that."

"It is only natural that we will want to have a record of your successful deployment to the system you call Eos, as well as a record of your settlement."

Triana thought about this, biting her lip. Of course it made sense. The jellyfish were essentially providing them with passage on their highway; why wouldn't they want to document everything? The vultures had multiple responsibilities, including their duty as sentries. It was practical, which seemed to be the nature of the Dollovit.

So why did it bother Triana so much? Why did she look upon a vulture escort as an invasion of their privacy? Or was it even more sinister? Were the human colonists doomed to be under jellyfish supervision, in one form or another?

The thought irritated her, but she held her tongue rather than lash out at Torrec, who, for all she knew, was merely keeping an eye on the fledgling star travelers as they settled into their new home. It was possible that the Dollovit were being good stewards of space.

And yet it didn't feel that way. The notion of the vultures following them into their new home system seemed . . . invasive.

Triana had been silent for too long. Torrec, Hannah, and Roc were monitoring the transmission, waiting for her response. "Of course," she said. "Thank you for the official escort to our new home." After a brief pause, she added: "I'm sure that our two civilizations will remain good friends and partners for a long time."

On one level it sounded overly theatrical, as if written by a politician. But in her heart she felt that they had to begin this new phase of their journey—and the first phase of their new settlement—as equals. The Dollovit might be technologically superior, but it was vital that Triana make it clear that the human species would not serve beneath them. Nor should the Dollovit believe that they would occupy Eos in any capacity; they would be invited guests.

For the next few minutes Triana busied herself with updates

from each department, determining the readiness of the crew for the jump ahead. The only section out of touch was—not surprisingly—Agriculture; Bon was nowhere to be found.

"Oh, wow," she heard Hannah say, wonder dripping from her voice. The pod had made visual contact with the rip in space. "This is . . . spectacular."

"Manu, how are you doing?" Triana said with a smile. Hannah would be chomping at the bit to dive through the Channel, but for Manu it was likely the most terrifying experience of his life.

"I'm great," Manu said. "Hannah's sold me on how much fun it's going to be. It *is* going to be fun, right?"

"Like an amusement park ride, Manu. The shortest ride of your life."

Gap broke in from the Spider bay. "Twenty seconds. Good luck, Hannah, good luck, Manu."

"Thanks," they replied in unison.

"Thank you both again for volunteering to go," Triana said. "We'll be out of touch for awhile, so take care, and we'll catch up again soon, okay?"

"Sounds good," Hannah said.

"Ten seconds," Gap said.

Triana watched the giant vidscreen in the Control Room, although the Channel opening was too small, and too far away, to be visible.

"Uh . . ." Hannah said. "That's odd—"

Then there was silence.

22

Have you ever tried talking your friends into doing something that you thought was the greatest thing in the world, and you could tell from their reaction that they were only going along with it because (a) you were their friend, (b) they really were curious about it, (c) they were too tired to argue, or (d) there was free food involved?

Now think about the situation on Galahad. *You have a couple hundred teenagers who have been cooped up for a year and are now facing some weighty decisions. If one person pitches what they claim is a brilliant idea, some people are gonna be curious and some are gonna be too worn-out to disagree.*

Especially when Merit is the guy doing the pitching. We know it's not the food; there's plenty of that up in the Dining Hall.

The personal quarters on *Galahad* were not designed to hold many people. Each room, other than Triana's, was set up to house two crew members, with space for washing, as well as clothes storage, drawers for personal items, and a shared desk. At the moment there were twelve people crammed into Merit's room. He sat on the edge of his bed, while the others sat on the floor.

"How many will it take?" asked Liam Wright.

"That's hard to answer," Merit said, adjusting his expression to appear thoughtful. "At the very least, I'd say fifteen to twenty. Hopefully we'll have more than that."

Liam looked around the room. "You don't even have that many here."

"But when the time comes, others will be here. Believe me."

"Why?" asked Balin Robinson.

Merit turned his palms up. "Because no matter what's happened, there are people aboard this ship who don't believe in the way the Council runs things. There are people who would like a fresh start without Triana and her pals running everything." He smiled at Balin. "You're here, aren't you?"

Balin shrugged, but didn't answer.

"How will you decide which planet?" asked Liam.

"That's easy," Merit said without hesitation. "Just show me which planet Triana and Gap and the rest are choosing, and we'll take the other one. If they want Eos Four, we'll be happy with Eos Three. And if they want number three, we'll make do on number four." He smirked. "I hope it's four. I love the water."

He looked around at the group gathered near his feet, waiting for follow-up questions, but for now they were willing to simply listen. He liked it that way; too many questions meant they were thinking too much for themselves. That was the last thing he wanted. And if they trusted him enough to come to the meeting, it meant they had their own misgivings about the Council's leadership. It was time to close the deal.

"We'd be okay slaving away under the Council's rule, you know? We could do it if we needed to. We've already done it for a few years, haven't we? But just imagine if we were given a blank slate. Imagine if we had a world of our own. Imagine if we could build it from scratch, where everyone had an equal say in things. Where everyone's opinions counted. Where everyone worked just as hard as the other person, and shared in the same rewards. It won't be that way on Triana's world, I can guarantee you that.

"But give us the chance to do it *our* way, and imagine the result in a few years. Think of what we could build. And it doesn't even matter what planet we're given; we can build something spectacular regardless of where we begin." He paused and gave them an encouraging smile. "Go and think about it and, if you'd like, talk with your closest friends. I don't know about you, but I'm excited thinking about what we could accomplish together."

There were a few nods, and a few smiles returned. The group stood, stretched their legs, and said their farewells. Lockdown had been ordered for the jump, with all crew members expected in their rooms. Merit walked them to the door, said his good-byes, and then chuckled to himself.

The spoken word was a powerful tool. It was the strongest weapon in his arsenal, and he knew exactly how to wield it. And the best part of all, of course, was the way that it could mold a mind that was unsure. Throw out a few comments about equal say and equal reward, and it was irresistible to some. Include a few well-timed smiles along with the words, and it became even more believable.

Merit had the beginnings of his new pack, many of whom had followed him the last time he'd spoken up. And while they basked in the idea of equal say, he knew that, when the time came, they wouldn't *want* equal say. They'd want a leader. They'd want someone to do the dirty work for them.

Like they always did.

* * *

I t was spooky. The ship appeared deserted, the corridors empty, the usual gathering spots—the gym, the Dining Hall, the Rec Room—vacant. Lita and Bon walked the upper levels, making a last-minute check to confirm that all crew members were safely tucked into their rooms. The plunge through the Channel wasn't violent, but it would likely render each person unconscious. Channy was making a similar check on the lower levels, along with her roommate, Kylie. Gap would stay on duty in the Engineering section, and would strap himself in when the time came. Triana was stationed in the ship's Control Room.

"I didn't see you at the Spider bay earlier," Lita said. "Didn't you want to say good-bye to Hannah and Manu?"

"They'll be back," Bon said, poking his head into the Rec Room. "Besides, there was work to do."

Lita gave a solemn nod. "Right. Gotta make sure the apple crates are locked down, and all that. Right?"

"Something like that."

"Plus, you're probably not very good at good-bye," Lita said. "All that icky emotion. Yuck." She paused, scanning the hallway ahead of them. "But you'd come and say good-bye to me, right?"

She couldn't see Bon's face, but from his voice she could tell he wore a half-smile. "Probably not. If you left there'd be a long line of sobbing friends. I don't like lines."

"You're such a creep," Lita said with an exaggerated pout. "But you'd miss me, of course."

They'd reached the Dining Hall. A quick glance showed it was dark and empty.

"Sure, I'd miss you," Bon said. "With Manu gone, who'd be there to nag at me if I ended up in the hospital again?"

They walked in silence for another minute, taking the lift down one level and beginning the process again. It was merely a precaution; *Galahad's* crew had followed their instructions.

Lita resisted the urge to engage Bon in more lighthearted banter. She'd gotten just about all that could be expected from him in one session. But there was a subtle change in Bon that she liked. He was still blunt, of course, but he didn't seem . . . angry. That was it: he wasn't seething inside, no longer struggling against the malicious intent of the big, bad universe. It made him approachable.

She wondered if it was a mistake to get used to that. The raging side of the Swede might return at any moment.

Or would he? Lita had watched Bon progress through the classic stages of grief—or most of them, anyway. Perhaps his last connection with the Cassini brought him to a place of peace. Maybe he no longer railed at the universe because he'd discovered that there was so much more to it than he'd ever expected.

On the other hand, Lita thought with a smile, maybe he was just in a better mood because he practically had the ship to himself. *That* was just as likely. But, if it was true that a kinder, gentler Bon was breaking through to the surface, it made him more attractive than ever.

The thought of him in those terms had never occurred to her before. Between the stormy relationship she'd noticed between Bon and Triana, and the confusing, abrupt relationship he'd shared with Alexa, Lita had never allowed herself to look at him that way. He'd been off limits.

But now . . .

It figures, Gap thought. All of the turbulence that the ship had weathered, all of the near-catastrophes that they'd skirted, all of the systems failures that they'd endured, and now, as they approached the most frightening part of their journey, *Galahad* was purring. The ship barely held together during the roughest stretches, and now decided to relax and coast to its rendezvous with the star portal.

He strolled between rooms in Engineering, making minor adjustments, and drifted through the memories: standing before a panel while puzzling through the mystery of the heating dilemma on level six; huddled with Triana and his Engineering assistants, sweating over a power surge that took them to the brink of a deadly explosion near Saturn; and the frustrating collapse of the ship's radiation shield which threatened a slow, agonizing death.

Jumping hurdle after hurdle, stumbling along a course that seemed so easy when they were studying under the nurturing blue sky of Mother Earth, when the launch and the mission seemed so far away, so unreal. We've earned our wings, Gap thought; we've proved ourselves.

And, he decided, he'd proven himself worthy, too. He thought of the bleakest moments of this odyssey, when he'd withdrawn from the Council, from the crew, and retreated into a darkness that he'd never imagined. He'd questioned his abilities, and he'd questioned his worthiness of even being selected for the mission.

But his rise from the darkness had been as swift as the descent. He recovered his confidence, and rediscovered the spirit that his mother had always lauded as the spark that made him different. Made him special.

The regret he carried from that experience was the damage he'd inflicted upon Hannah. And now, finding himself alone, he wondered if it had been worth it. He'd learned so much about himself, and had grown in ways that only came from enduring personal defeat. But it cost him a part of himself, too; a part that he now mourned.

Balancing the books, he realized. Payment for acquiring experience. Nothing easy, nothing free.

Slowly the painful thought that he'd kept at bay forced its way back into his head: Hannah was gone, and he might never see her again.

Alone, and on the fringe of a completely new beginning, he leaned against the metal panel, put his head in his hands, and softly wept.

That's odd.

What would cause Hannah to say that? What did she see when the Channel opened up before her? Or was there something wrong with the pod, something that seemed out of place?

The questions rolled through Triana's mind as she monitored *Galahad*'s progress from the ship's deserted command post. Torrec had arranged coordinates with Roc, piloting them toward the second wormhole that lay waiting for them, the rip in space that would deliver them to Eos.

If Torrec could be trusted. Hannah's puzzled exclamation didn't necessarily mean that something was wrong, but it contributed to Triana's growing unease. It was one more reminder that all of the control lay with Torrec.

And that was a miserable feeling.

The Council Leader sat up straight and registered the data spilling onto the vidscreen. Gap assured her that they'd make it to their destination before the shield sputtered and shut down. Barely. Once through to the other side, the bruised effect on space would be absorbed by the ring of debris circling the yellow star. And, with guidance help supplied by the Cassini, they'd navigate safely into the comfortable lagoon within the Eos system.

Over the next several minutes, Triana heard from Channy and Kylie, then Lita and Bon. All decks were clear, and they were back in their respective rooms. Gap gave a final thumbs-up from Engineering. All that was left was the leap of faith.

"Roc," she said, "I show our ETA for the Channel to be eight minutes. Any status changes?"

"No, we're right on track," Roc said. "At this time I'd like for you to make sure your seat back is in its upright and locked position, and that your tray table is stored. Thank you for flying Trans Debris."

She laughed despite the latest round of butterflies. This would be her third venture through a wormhole, but this time with more on the line than just her own neck.

Seconds ticked by. With just over six minutes remaining she powered down non-essential components in the Control Room, not for any particular reason; it simply seemed the prudent thing to do. The majority of the workstations were shut down. The lights dimmed to the ship's late-evening mode, and the room slipped into a shadowy twilight.

A random thought crossed her mind. "Roc," she said, "are you nervous? I mean, are you capable of that . . . feeling?"

"How sweet of you to ask," the computer said. "I wouldn't say nervous. But I do have a measure of curiosity about the process. You're a veteran of this operation by now. Are you worried about it?"

Triana glanced at the tiny monitor as it ticked off the remaining time. Five-thirty-seven, five-thirty-six, five-thirty-five. Was she worried?

"I'm . . ." She paused. Five-twenty-nine, five-twenty-eight, five-twenty-seven. And then, without warning, a sensation sped through her, and she swallowed hard. She wasn't worried, no. She was . . .

"I'm angry," she said.

"Oh," Roc said. "You could have given me ten guesses and I wouldn't have chosen that particular emotion. Care to elaborate?"

"I'm tired of worrying and wondering. I'm frustrated that we're constantly at the mercy of others, merely because we're the new species on the block, and we can only hope that they're benevolent. I'm bothered that Dr. Zimmer didn't tell us about the additional crew members we've been toting around. When you roll all of that together, it makes me angry."

She watched the seconds tick by. Five minutes.

"I suddenly don't trust anything anymore. I don't trust that Hannah and Manu were taken to the Dollovit star system, I don't trust the motives of your good friend Torrec, and I don't trust that Eos is waiting on the other side of this Channel, like some promised land."

She sat back and added: "What happens if we abort the Channel maneuver?" she said.

"Chalk up another surprising quip from the Colorado girl," Roc said. "Abort the maneuver?"

"Yeah," Triana said. Four-forty-one, four-forty, four-thirty-nine. "What happens?"

"You know what happens. Slow subatomic dismemberment, where your atoms fling their various parts around like a two-year-old throwing a tantrum at day care. You won't die so much as cease to exist, leaving a microscopic pile of quarks and an empty pair of shoes."

Triana bit her lip. Four-thirty, four-twenty-nine.

"Plot a new course to steer us away from the Channel," she said. "We're not going."

"Oh, Tree," the computer said. "You have about four minutes left before you seriously regret that decision. There are no do-overs in this game."

"Plot it."

"Ignore that order, Roc," said a thick voice behind her. She turned to see Bon standing just outside the door to the lift.

His eyes were glowing. Dull orange.

Triana stood up. Bon was clearly under the influence of the Cassini, but walking and talking. With no translator.

"Bon—" she began.

"Ignore the order, Roc," Bon said again. "We're going through."

"Listen to me," Triana said. "Something's not—"

"No, you have four minutes to listen to me," Bon said. He stumbled toward her, looking stiff, unsure. But determined.

"Your distrust of the Dollovit is understandable," he said. "But you're wrong. They're peaceful."

"How can you know that?"

"The Cassini know it. And the jellyfish wouldn't be here if it wasn't true."

Triana sat down, throwing a quick glance at the timer. Three-forty-one. "Okay, I'm listening."

Bon staggered next to her and pulled a chair under him. Once seated, he seemed slightly more at ease. His eyes, however, stared at a point over Triana's head.

"The Cassini came here when our universe was created, from outside."

"What does that mean? Outside?"

"It means that they rode the wave which created our universe." He sighed, apparently flustered at having to condense such a deep subject into a thumbnail sketch. "Imagine a vast number of universes, each an independent collection of matter and energy, but in

separate dimensions. Now imagine if two of them somehow col-
lided. The result would be an explosion too powerful to comprehend. A big bang, if you will. Matter and energy would pour into
this new universe. The Cassini rode that wave, and have expanded
as the universe has expanded. As if they're perched on the skin of a
balloon as it's blown up; it expands, and they ride along with it.
Space really has no meaning to them, nor does time.

"And, as we guessed, they can assist civilizations at times, or
they can destroy. But their primary role is universal policemen.
They watch over each and every intelligent species that crawls up
from the slime, noting their progress, watching their baby steps
turn into giant leaps toward space. And they guard."

"Guard what?" Triana said.

"They guard the beauty and the perfection of each universe."

Triana shook her head. "I don't know what that means."

Bon tilted his head, as if some new signal had sounded, a flash
that only he could comprehend. He said: "Wanna know what
gives us away as infants? It's not how inferior we are in terms of
space travel or technology. It's the fact that we take the universe
for granted. We see it, but we don't really see it. We register that
there are planets, and stars, and galaxies. But we neglect the perfection of it. We see right past the beauty of that perfection. We
take it all for granted. We ask a few questions, but we plod through
each day without any regard for the magnificence of it all. It labels
us as not only cosmic children, but spoiled children at that."

Triana could only nod now. She couldn't disagree with what
he said.

"The Cassini are not only watching to see how far along various civilizations are progressing with their technical abilities;
they're paying attention to the maturity of each civilization as
well. There's apparently a point we can march right up to and still

get away with our immaturity—kinda like a parent letting a child push the boundaries. But if by the time we reach that point we haven't begun to fully develop as universal citizens, then . . ."

His voice trailed away. Triana didn't need him to finish the sentence in order to figure it out for herself. She glanced at the timer. Two and a half minutes.

"Is that what happened to the advanced civilization on Eos Four?" she asked.

"Yes."

"And . . ." Triana wasn't sure she wanted to ask the obvious follow-up, but she had to know. "And does that explain Comet Bhaktul?"

"Yes and no," Bon said. "The Cassini did not send the comet, nor its killer plague, into our path. They did have the power to divert it, if necessary. But that would have alerted humans to the Cassini presence; you can't just push a comet out of the way and hope that nobody notices. More important, however, was the fact that we didn't seem to be worth saving. Although we weren't to the point where we needed to be eliminated, we also weren't showing much . . . how do teachers say it? Potential. In other words, as a species we were a long shot to get our act together.

"And that's why they've been helping us on *Galahad*. As cosmic citizens on Earth, we were on the downhill path as a species. But the Cassini were impressed enough with the drive and ambition of this mission to give our kind another chance. A fairly slim chance, but a chance nonetheless."

They could have saved us, Triana thought. They could have saved billions of lives.

Including her father.

Her blood began a slow boil, but just as quickly she calmed herself. That wasn't fair; the Cassini weren't responsible for the death sentence delivered by Bhaktul. If anything, the immaturity of Earth's most prominent inhabitants—but not the only dominant species, according to Torrec—was the deciding factor. Blaming others, rather than accepting responsibility, was the kind of behavior that likely landed humans in the cosmic doghouse in the first place. Reverting to that mentality now, in the face of everything that had transpired in the last three years—including all of the progress they'd made in the most dire circumstances—would be a catastrophic mistake.

The Cassini didn't owe the human race any favors.

"So you're saying that the jellyfish have earned their free pass," she said to Bon. "They aced the test."

"You could say that," Bon said. "But you have a deadline coming down right now, and I just thought you should know that your distrust of them is misguided. It might be better to search within the walls of this ship if you're looking for unscrupulous characters. We have our share."

Triana raised an eyebrow. "Agreed. And what are you suggesting we do about that?"

The orange eyes seemed to intensify. "You might not have to do anything," Bon said. "The issue might take care of itself."

"Oh? How?"

Bon adjusted his posture in the chair and fastened the restraint across his waist. "It's almost time. You better make sure you're buckled up."

The timer flicked under the forty second mark. On the room's large vidscreen, the impossibly dark rip in space seemed to rush at them, preparing to devour Earth's survivors. It was now or never.

Roc, as usual, felt the need to chime in: "He might look like he's had a few too many carrots, but Bon is probably right."

Triana bit her lip again. Bon was on the Council because Dr. Zimmer trusted his instincts. The surly Swede might not have the best social skills, but he also thought things through rationally. And he did, after all, have a hotline to the oldest sentient beings in the universe.

She jabbed the intercom button. "Here we go, everyone. Twenty seconds to the jump. Good luck to us all."

She cinched her lap belt and stared at the image on the screen, stubbornly refusing to let it intimidate her. Bon reached over and grasped her hand as the screen was swallowed in darkness, followed by an explosion of light.

24

t wasn't the sensation that she'd expected. Lita lay on one of the beds in the hospital ward, instead of the one in her room. She wanted to be on call should there be emergencies following the leap. All of the vidscreens in the room were shut down; after hearing Triana's description, she wondered if the visual aspect was too jarring for the brain to accept. That might have partially accounted for Tree's lapse into unconsciousness.

But Lita had blacked out as well, a split second after feeling her stomach lurch. It was the same feeling in her gut that she remembered from her lone experience on a roller coaster. That hadn't gone well for her, and she'd been happy after that to send her brother and sister on their merry, screaming coaster adventures while she opted for the more subdued carnival rides.

There was more to this feeling, though. Beyond the pitch and roll of her stomach, she'd felt as if her body had subtly shifted in place. Now, after coming to, she slowly pushed herself up on her elbows and took stock of her physical condition. She appeared to be in exactly the same spot, and yet it definitely felt as if she'd moved on the bed.

"Roc," she said. "How long was I out?"

"Zvid thirt blunk tau bielsk," the computer said.

Lita's mouth fell open and her eyes widened. "Roc?"

"Sorry, I had to do it," Roc said. "Gotcha, didn't I?"

She fell back onto the bed and threw an arm up over her face. "Ugh, I hate you right now. I really do."

"No, you could never hate anyone, Lita. And to answer your question, it's been twenty-nine seconds since we dove through the window."

Lita pulled her arm away and stared at the ceiling. "Twenty-nine seconds? That's it? So I was out for . . . what? Less than five seconds?"

"I don't know the exact moment your brain was flipped back on, but that sounds about right."

She sat up again, and this time swung her legs off the edge of the bed. "This might sound like a silly question, but did you black out? Did you feel anything? I mean, I know you don't actually *feel*—"

"Not true," Roc said. He manufactured a fake sniffle, then said: "Nobody ever takes my feelings into consideration."

"Well?"

"No, I did not black out, and yes, I did comprehend a change. Your human brain can't handle having itself split in two for even a second, so it does an immediate reboot. I, on the other hand, have no problem with my chips occupying two places in the galaxy at once. In fact, it's rather stimulating. I could get hooked on this jumping stuff."

Lita said: "What kind of change did you feel?"

"I've never been shoved in the back," the computer said. "Mainly because I don't have a back. But that's the closest description I can give. It seemed like my awareness of the familiar surroundings of the ship were pushed forward."

A shove in the back. And she distinctly felt movement before blacking out, even though she'd remained in the same spot. She shook her head, perplexed.

"Well, we seem to have made it through in one piece." Sliding off the bed, she walked out of the ward and over to her desk. "Triana," she said, snapping on the intercom. "Triana, you there?"

There was no response. A trickle of concern worked its way into the base of Lita's spine, and she fidgeted for a few seconds.

She tried again. "Tree? Hello?"

"I'm here, Lita. Sorry about that."

"What are you doing?" Lita said.

A small laugh came through the speaker, a contented sound. It caught Lita by surprise; Triana rarely displayed joy. But the Council Leader sounded genuinely happy. She said: "I'm looking at our new home."

The scene paralleled the one that had taken place three hundred fifty days earlier. Almost every set of eyes aboard the ship found a window or vidscreen, captivated by the sight of the surroundings. But while the view of a year ago had been of a receding Earth—a farewell glimpse that evoked tears of sadness—now they gazed upon a sight that held both promise and relief. For although it appeared barely larger than other stars, this particular orb represented something more than just their destination. It represented victory.

The crew of *Galahad* wept again, only these tears were an emotional release of the fear and tension that had stalked them from the beginning of their mission. Eos was within sight, which many interpreted as the finish line, the culmination of the most critical journey in the long history of humankind.

Triana knew differently. She understood that getting to this distant star system was an accomplishment that, only years earlier, seemed impossible. But it was merely the first step. Perhaps even the easiest step. The work that lay ahead dwarfed the efforts required to keep the ship intact as it streaked through space.

Nevertheless, she rejoiced at the successes they'd logged, including this final flip through a cosmic tunnel. In less than the blink of an eye, their gray, shopping mall–sized vessel skipped over forty-seven months of tedious star travel, arriving in the misty outer banks of the Eos star system ages before anyone could have anticipated.

This time the brief blackout hadn't seemed as frightening to Triana. She'd already experienced it twice, and therefore knew what to expect, but was that it? Or was it Bon? Did it help that this time she hadn't faced it alone?

Oddly, Bon remained conscious through the wormhole; he was, in fact, the only crew member to make that claim. Lita suggested later that it was his connection with the Cassini that buoyed him during the jump. As she put it: "If you hadn't been online with the universal cops, you would've slumped over like the rest of us."

He stood at a workstation in the Control Room, already plotting the ship's safe passage through the storm of debris that ringed the outer fringes of the Eosian system. In this respect, most star systems were identical. Without the guidance help of the Cassini, *Galahad* would be obliterated by one of the trillions of pieces of rock that tumbled and crashed through this chaotic ring.

Triana walked up to the room's large vidscreen and inspected the bright point of light that beckoned from nearly four billion miles away. Roc began sifting through the region's data, gathering information that previously could only be guessed at from the restricted observations from Earth. Now, with Eos and its planetary posse upon them, more details could be mapped.

"Roc," she said, her eyes darting across the screen. "Will we need to alter our speed to maneuver through their version of the Kuiper belt, or will we be able to juke our way through?"

"Hard to say definitively at this stage, but my initial calculations indicate no," the computer said.

Bon, his head still hovering over the keyboard, confirmed. "We won't need to hit the brakes, if that's what you're wondering." Triana could see the orange reflection of his eyes glinting in his monitor. Between Roc's assessment, and Bon's Cassini input, the final leg of their tour—rocketing through the system toward the two Earth-like planets in the habitable zone—would take a little over two weeks.

"I've detected our shadows," Roc said, reminding her that the jellyfish empire would never be out of the picture completely. The vulture squadron had slipped through the same Channel, and now swarmed around the ship. "I see they're sticking with their base-sixteen system. We have an escort of thirty-two."

It seemed a lot to Triana, but what number wouldn't have struck her as too many? She made a conscious effort to accept the escort, even if she didn't embrace it.

"Roc," she said, "how much time do you need to get a concise layout of the planetary system?"

"Oh, I'm quite speedy. It's almost finished."

Triana didn't doubt him on that. She looked at Bon, who pushed his chair back from the keyboard. "We'll get the Council together in the Conference Room in one hour. Roc, you can present your data then."

She pulled her long hair away from her face and walked toward the lift. "If anyone needs me, I'll be in my room."

* * *

A re you okay?" Katz asked.

Merit groaned, and managed to nod once in reply. He bent over the sink in his room, while his roommate stood behind him and stared at the reflection in the mirror.

Although few people even knew his first name—he was simply Katz to everyone—the seventeen-year-old from New York was one of the more popular members of the crew. Merit was aware that Katz didn't like him, and thus probably didn't care if Merit was fine or not. It was simply an act of courtesy. It was more likely that Katz was worried about his Californian roommate throwing up again in the middle of their room. Merit, on the other hand, worried that the news might spread among the crew.

"I'm okay." It was intended to sound confident and strong, but instead came out as a croak. Merit cleared his throat and added, with more force: "It's not the jump. I think it's something I ate a couple of hours ago. It's been giving me fits ever since."

Katz nodded, but obviously wasn't buying it. Anyone could see that Merit didn't handle the Channel flip very well. "Then if you don't need anything, I'll see you later."

"Right," Merit said. "See you later." When the door closed, he leaned back over the sink and closed his eyes.

T he world had shifted, but for the better, as far as Channy was concerned. She lay on her bed, her fingers digging into the thin material of the bedspread. Iris busied herself with a bath, seemingly oblivious to the jump that had occurred. Kylie stirred on the other side of the room, but didn't seem to be in any distress; Kylie had always been tough, a nice trait to have in a roommate.

The shift—more like a wobble, Channy decided—happened right before she passed out. She remembered flinching as it occurred, but not being afraid. She'd been startled, that's all.

Now, she looked up at the colorful strips of cloth that created a plume of vivid blues, reds, and yellows above her bed. They were arranged in no discernible pattern, a design that Kylie ridiculed as "a collision of color." Channy gave no thought to the display's order; for her it was about the cheer that it exuded.

At the moment it gave her a place to focus her attention while she absorbed what had just taken place. The conclusion she reached startled her almost as much as the shift itself.

She wasn't afraid anymore. Of anything.

The past two months had been difficult for the young Brit. She'd suffered heartbreak, a loss of confidence in her by Triana, and moments where she felt completely overwhelmed by her fears. For someone who'd always been the ship's brightest light, the funk created an endless loop of despair for Channy. She didn't *want* to be afraid, but the more she tried to talk herself out of it, the further she slipped.

The gloominess only intensified as, one by one, crew members began to drop out of their usual exercise routines. With the crisis of the radiation shield, and the upheaval caused by the vultures and the Dollovit, excuses to skip the gym multiplied, until Channy found herself leading only a handful of people through the programs. What had always been her greatest source of energy—her thriving, pulsing workouts, packed with attentive and energetic crew members—became a chore, too often with just a smattering of faces staring back at her. She was falling into a well.

But something shook her when the ship broke through the Channel's infinitely thin doorway. The jump seemed to toss her sideways, and yet upon coming to she noted that she hadn't budged. The jolt had, however, rebooted her thinking.

It was as if a layer of grimy film was stripped away, revealing a fresh, hopeful path before her. Taresh? She cared about him, but his power over her had evaporated. Her fear of the vultures, the Channel, even the unknown? Senseless.

She'd looked at the wormhole the wrong way. The intimidating dark rip in space wasn't a lifeless, sinister end point; it was a boundary, nothing more. In her case, it was the boundary between a past that she'd allowed to darken her spirit, and the brightness that comes with awareness. According to Triana's account, the piercing of the Channel's horizon was accompanied by a blinding, white light.

If so, it was a light that penetrated Channy's soul, rejuvenating her spirit. She smiled at the dazzling, intricate pattern on her ceiling, a mishmash of intertwined cloth strips, and realized that it didn't need to have order within it. It needed light to bring out the inherent beauty hidden by darkness.

Things would be different now.

G ap blinked and shook his head, trying to clear the fog. He was on the floor of the Engineering section, tilted to one side. True to his stubborn nature, he'd convinced himself that strapping himself in wouldn't be necessary. As the ship approached the Channel opening, he'd taken a seat and stretched his legs out before him in a foolish attempt to balance himself. His last memory before blacking out involved an awkward sensation in his gut, tricking his brain into believing he was moving. He wasn't. But his involuntary reaction was to countershift against the perceived movement, and that, combined with his loss of consciousness, put him in his present condition.

He sat up, wincing at the sharp pain in his right pinkie finger, which had apparently buckled under his weight during the fall. He wrung his hand a few times, silently scolding himself for not taking Triana's warnings seriously. The finger was broken, which wasn't a serious physical setback; it was the needling he was sure to get from Lita and Channy that he dreaded.

His first priority was the radiation shield. Getting to his feet and once again wringing his hand, he was at the control panel in five strides.

"Hey there, Roc," he said. "I guess we made it. At least I did; are you there?"

The computer answered immediately. "You know how much I love that question. The metaphysical implications are so . . . so . . . deep. Are any of us *really* here, Gap?"

Gap ignored the bait and studied the data. "I thought for sure there'd be a spike, or a jolt, or something. It doesn't seem to have been affected at all."

"I tried telling you that you were looking at this wormhole all wrong," Roc said. "You wanna talk about whether something is there or not, you should start with one of those. It's so quantum I can't stand it. Gives me little computer shivers."

"What about the bruise effects on this side?"

"I'd say nominal. They're spreading out before us this time, so we're riding the wave rather than meeting it head-on. Much smoother that way."

Gap raised an eyebrow. "And our companions?"

"Right there alongside us. I'm sure they'll stick to us like dog hair all the way through the debris ring. We have the magic ticket, remember, courtesy of Mr. Grumpy Pants with the orange peepers."

This finally induced a chuckle from Gap. "I'd hate to hear your nickname for me when I'm not around."

"It's Mr. Sloppy Socks. By the way, comb your hair because you have a Council meeting in one hour."

The smile stayed on Gap's face as he worked his way around the various data panels in the section. By the time he finished his inspection, a handful of Engineering workers came through the door, ready to take up their assignments. Gap spent a few minutes talking with most of them, then walked to the lift at the end of the hall. As much as he dreaded it, he'd have to incorporate a stop at Sick House to get his finger wrapped before the meeting.

25

Chewing on an energy block, Triana finished dressing. The quick shower had been glorious, and she felt a surge of energy running through her body. In twenty minutes she and the Council would get the layout for their new home star system, and she was eager to hear it.

The near-deadly brush with the stowaway/saboteur seemed a lifetime ago.

She sat at her desk, brushing her hair with one hand while opening her mail file with the other. A few department reports began trickling in as life on the ship accelerated back to normal. There was a personal note from Channy that brought a smile; *Galahad*'s firefly appeared to have found her spark again. And Gap delivered good news in the form of a clean status report from Engineering.

Her eye drifted down the page until she spotted the notice of a video message. It was the recording from Dr. Zimmer. Ashamed that she'd forgotten her mentor and father-figure, she opened the file.

Triana stiffened and almost looked away when the image

materialized. The evidence of Bhaktul's cruelty was frightful. This once-proud scientist, the man who had dedicated the final years of his life to ensuring the safety and survival of 251 teenagers, looked gaunt and defeated. It seemed difficult for him to keep his head steady. His eyes, which once sparkled with wit and enthusiasm when addressing his young charges, were now pools of sadness. Through the obvious pain and embarrassment, Dr. Zimmer did his best to put on a brave front. He managed a shaky smile.

"I'll have to make this quick," he said, his voice feeble. "I'm going out dancing in a few minutes, and I can't keep the ladies waiting."

In spite of the crushing sadness she felt, Triana found herself laughing at the dying scientist's charm.

"My original plan was to have enough of these personal messages to last the duration of your journey, but it's beginning to look as if that won't be possible." He turned away from the camera and coughed. From the sound and the intensity—his body contorted under the strain—Triana knew that he suffered excruciating pain. She felt more tears form in the corners of her eyes, and her breathing became choppy.

When he turned back, he held a bloodied handkerchief to his mouth. After composing himself, and blinking away his own tears, he struggled ahead.

"There's so much I want to tell you, so many things that might help as you grow into the magnificent young woman that you're becoming." He gave a wry smile. "I guess I do feel like your second father at times. I feel like I should be there to look out for you. But, of course, you don't really need that."

He coughed again, not as violently this time, but it still racked him with pain. He wiped at his eyes again.

"I suppose one thing that I could leave you with is a piece of advice that my grandmother shared with me when I was about your age. She was a sweet, gentle woman; how she managed to live all those years with my cantankerous old grandfather, I'll never understand. I think it somehow was her nature to care for someone and help to smooth out their jagged edges. She certainly did that.

"I don't remember her making too many speeches. It took very few words for my grandmother to make a point. But once, when it was just she and I alone in her kitchen, and I was rambling on about the constant moving that my family . . ."

Dr. Zimmer seemed to choke on something, and left the picture. Triana heard him in pain, off to the side, and it caused a fresh round of tears. She wanted to reach through the screen, and across time, to comfort the man who had long been dead. For although only a single year had passed aboard *Galahad,* their ever-increasing speed meant that time dilation was in effect, and the Earth would have aged many years.

A moment later Zimmer once again slid into his chair and gave an apologetic smile. "My grandmother listened to me complain about how often my parents and I moved. My father was a sales troubleshooter, a hired specialist for several large companies, so we were always moving. I went to seven different schools before finishing ninth grade, and I used that as an excuse for so many things. I remember telling my grandmother that I wished we could just have a home.

"Well, she waited until I ran out of steam. Then she said: 'I see that you mistake the walls and the furniture for the home.'" He gave a shrug. "For the next couple of minutes she went about her business in the kitchen while she let me stew on that. Then she came over to me and placed her hand on my chest. She said: 'You build your home right here, Wallace. It's not made of bricks and roofing tiles. It's made of love for your family, and it goes wherever you go.'

"From that point on, I looked at my life—every aspect of it—in a new light. It changed the way I approached my schoolwork, it changed my attitude about each town I lived in, and it helped to make me a better man. It especially helped me when I began teaching, when it seemed like each town melted into the next. Two years at Michigan, two in Europe, three years at Caltech, then another year overseas and a year at MIT, all before I settled here. I made sure that the days didn't become a blur, and I learned to find something—anything—from each place that I could hold on to, that I could appreciate. I left things behind in many of these places that I carry around today in my heart."

He leaned forward. "Because that, Triana, is what it will always come down to. You'll realize that your home isn't in Colorado, and your home isn't on some untamed planet around Eos." He tapped his chest. "Your home is built around you, your friends, and your next family." Another sad smile developed on his face as he leaned back again. "Don't look at Eos through the eyes of a settler. Look at it through the eyes of a strong, confident young woman. One who is at home wherever she lands in life. That will give you power beyond belief."

Triana sensed that his time had ended and, from his expression, he had, too. He bravely fought off a coughing spasm and, with a determined look, gave her one final smile. "I love you, Tree," he said, holding up a hand to the camera.

Now her tears were accompanied by sound. She cried out loud, holding her hand up to press against the image of his. "I love you, too," she said, her vision blurring.

A moment later the screen faded to black. Triana left her hand in place for a full minute, staring into the dark glass which now bounced a faint reflection of her tearstained face back at her.

His words had mass. Like her flesh-and-blood father, Dr. Zimmer always managed to convey messages that penetrated deeply and took hold at her core. She resolved to make sure his final words weren't in vain.

The Council meeting was almost upon her. She walked across to her mirror and worried over the puffiness she saw staring back, splashing cold water on her face, then dabbing it with a towel. She concentrated on her breathing as she stared at the image, repeating Dr. Zimmer's words from memory, rededicating herself to live up to his expectations of her.

His words were powerful. But . . .

But there was something else in his message that gave her an odd feeling. Something that he'd said was ringing in her subconscious, trying to get her attention. What was it? What had he said?

It was time to go. She turned to leave her room, her mind still sifting through the words of her mentor, trying to identify the cause of this new chill.

26

Per their new custom, *Galahad's* Council members congregated in the hallway outside the Conference Room, making small talk before their scheduled meeting. Channy was her old self, which pleased Triana and gave her renewed hope in their mission. Iris hung over Channy's shoulder like an infant, stoically tolerating the treatment because it included a generous scratching of the ears. The cat's eyes blinked shut while she purred, opening only to examine a crew member who passed in the hall. For the only pet on a ship of two-hundred-plus teenagers, life was good.

Triana felt like tons of weight had fallen from her shoulders. True, they still had two weeks of travel time ahead of them, including a mad dash through the Kuiper-like debris on the outskirts of the Eos system. But literally years of travel had been shaved off their mission, which was just fine with the Council Leader. In her mind, the crew of *Galahad* had dealt with more than a mission's worth of danger and sorrow. As she stood in the corridor, reclining against the gently curved walls, she felt better than she had in months.

Channy babbled away at Bon who, strangely enough, seemed

to actually be listening. More than once he nodded his head, and at one point even volunteered a comment. Triana stared, wide-eyed. Strange days, indeed.

Of the four Council members, Gap seemed the most with-drawn. He'd quietly greeted everyone with a casual hello, accepting Channy's teasing about his taped finger with a polite smile. Triana presumed that Hannah was at the heart of his melancholy. Theirs had been a choppy relationship, but losing her—even if only temporarily—was enough to siphon away much of his natural pas-sion for life. It was obvious: he missed her.

"Let's go in and get started," Triana said.

"Without Lita?" Channy said.

"She left a message saying something came up in Sick House, and she'd be late."

"Someone sick from the jump?"

Triana shrugged. "Didn't say. C'mon, we'll catch her up, or she can follow on the tripcast. I'm gonna let the crew listen in this time if they want, because we're going to cover what lies ahead."

The group filed into the Conference Room and took their usual seats. After brief departmental reports, Triana opened up the meet-ing to the rest of the crew. It could be accessed throughout the ship over the vidscreens.

"Roc," she said, "let's have your report on the star system."

"The planets themselves are interesting, but let's deal with the star first. On the old-school H-R diagram, Eos is a class G star, which means it's similar to the sun. It's a little older, however, which means in about three billion years it'll run out of gas, and you'll have to find a new place to plant your petunias."

"Like the jellyfish did when their star died of old age, right?" Channy said.

"Gold star for Ms. Oakland," Roc said. "Otherwise, Eos seems rather stable, and looks to be in good health. Nothing special to report. But the planets . . . that's a different story.

"Eos has a total of seven primary planets in its stable, and a handful of dwarf planets that meander in the background. The two inner planets could best be compared to our planet Mercury: they're small, rocky, and not very pleasant. Of these, number two seems to have had some history of an atmosphere, but it's long been blown away.

"I'll come back to three and four, since they're the ones you're most interested in. Planet five is similar to Jupiter, but even larger. It's a big ball of gas, but that's where the comparison to Gap ends."

Proving that he wasn't completely depressed, Gap gave a smile and said: "Get on with it, you box of bolts."

"Planet six will be every girl's favorite," Roc said.

Channy perked up. "Why?"

"Because it's pink."

"Hey, that's fantastic!" Channy said. "A pink planet! Can we swing by to take some pictures?"

"Sadly, our course won't take us anywhere near number six," Roc said. "You'll just have to schedule a field trip another time."

Triana was surprised to see Bon speak up from the end of the table. "Tell me about number seven," he said.

"Why don't you tell *us* about number seven, Bon?" Roc said.

The Swede tapped his finger on the table, staring at the graphic that Roc displayed on the vidscreen. His intensity level seemed to have shot up.

"What is it, Bon?" Triana said. "Do you know something about this planet?"

Bon kept his eyes on the vidscreen, but finally answered. "That's where the Cassini have their outpost in this system. On one of its moons."

It shouldn't have come as a shock. If what Bon had told her earlier was true, then the Cassini had been present since the beginning of the universe. In fact, he'd said since *before* the beginning.
How had he put it? *They came from outside.*

They'd be everywhere. If they'd discreetly camped out on Saturn's moon, Titan, since the birth of the solar system, there was
no reason to think they wouldn't be occupying Eosian space as
well.

"I can't confirm Bon's announcement," Roc said, "but he's the
one with that particular walkie-talkie and the creepy eyes. All I
can tell you is that number seven is a gas giant, with at least forty-
five moons, and an orbit that is slightly off the elliptical plane.
Beyond seven is a huge empty gap of space before you reach the
poor, misunderstood dwarf planets."

"Okay," Triana said, imagining the crew watching and listening throughout the ship. She knew what they wanted to hear.
"Tell us about three and four."

"Eos Number Three is, as we expected, fairly rugged and moun-
tainous. The atmosphere is breathable; perhaps a bit more oxygen
than you're used to, but you're adaptable, aren't you? The poles, like
Earth, are icy and snow packed. We'll know more about the weather
as we study it, but it seems quite manageable.

"And then there's Eos Number Four. It's a watery world, that's
for sure. Eighty percent of the surface is covered by ocean or lake—
and there are some gigantic lakes, I might add. The land is concentrated near the equator, and there's evidence of some pretty extreme
seismic activity. Eos Four is habitable, but more of a challenge, let's
say. The ancient civilization that Torrec referenced might have
been shaken out of existence by the quakes."

Triana considered the information and gazed at her fellow
Council members. Each appeared to be deep in thought, probably

imagining the pros and cons of each planet for establishing a human colony.

"I don't want to sway anyone's thought process," Triana said, "but it seems that number three would be our best bet. Water, but not too much, a more stable environment, and a warmer climate. Thoughts?"

"Three," Bon said, without hesitation. "An obvious abundance of fertile soil."

Channy grinned. "Oh, definitely three. As much as I'm gonna torture all of you with workouts, you're gonna need the extra air."

Triana looked at Gap, who seemed to take his time, weighing the options. Finally he said: "We could make either work, I'm sure. But I'm inclined to vote with the Council. Let me ask you something, though. What's the policy if some crew members want to go with number four?"

"That's a great question," Triana said. "I think the worst thing we could do would be to split our resources. Plus, there's the issue of what's lying down there in the Storage Sections. How do we divide the crew members in suspended animation? Or the embryos?"

Gap looked pensive. "I don't know. I'm just wondering, that's all, because it might come up."

Triana mulled this over, biting her lip. Then she leaned on the table and addressed the crew listening throughout the ship. "I'm going to leave this open for now. I'm assuming that the majority of you will opt to stay with the main contingent on Eos Three. But, should there be some of you with a taste for danger, and you have a reasonable argument for establishing a base on Four, I'll listen to what you have to say. There's not much time, however. Roc, what's our exact timetable?"

"Nine days on cruise control, gently using reverse power to cut our speed. Then we'll use the atmosphere of the massive giant, planet number five, for a braking maneuver. After that we'll swing around the far side of Eos, and then it's back through much of the system again, each time using the drag of the planets' gravitational pull to throw out an anchor. Assuming our final destination is Eos Three, it's not out of the question to swing around the fourth planet a second time as part of the braking. If someone wanted to get off, you could make up a few sandwiches and send them on their way."

"Okay," Triana said. "Great work, Roc. Thanks. For each of you tuned in to the tripcast, I'll be available as we begin preparations. Feel free to contact me if you'd like to discuss any of this.

"We're not alone, as you know. Roc has identified thirty-two vultures that made the jump with us, and they're right outside. We have no reason to fear them. Their job is to gather data and report what they learn. If you have concerns, please see me."

She looked up as Lita entered the room and stood just inside the door, her hands clasped in front of her, waiting. Triana couldn't decipher the expression on her face, but after a few years of working together she understood the body language: "When you're finished, I have something to show you."

"For the time being," Triana continued, "we need everyone to remember what it took to get here, and what it will take to finish the job. This is not the time to let up, to neglect any duties or responsibilities. If anything, we need everyone on their toes, alert to anything that might fall through the cracks. Our radiation shield is still intact, and we're safe."

With a smile, she added: "And we're almost there. Can you believe it?"

By now all of the Council members noticed Lita's pose near the door. Triana closed out the tripcast and stood up.

"Something to share, Doctor?"

"Oh, I've definitely got something to share," Lita said. "But you need to see it to believe it." She walked out of the room, then turned and waved at the others to join her. "C'mon."

Whatever her secret, Lita didn't seem particularly worried about it. She made small talk during the short walk down to the Clinic. Channy filled her in on Roc's report on the Eos system, and Lita agreed that Eos Three sounded like the wise choice. Gap asked a few questions about the medical effects of the Channel jump, but as far as Lita could tell there hadn't been any significant problems among the crew. A handful of people had called her, but they seemed to only be looking for reassurance that the odd motion sensation was normal and widespread.

"You can practically hear their sigh of relief," Lita said with a grin. "I don't think we have any actual hypochondriacs aboard the ship, but some people just need to be put at ease. In fact, I think that's about seventy percent of a doctor's job."

The party of five entered the Clinic and made their way down a short hall. Lita pulled up outside the door to one of the labs, and raised her eyebrows.

"Ready for this?"

The door swished open. Even from outside, Triana could see what had Lita so energized.

"What is this?"

Lita looked into the room, then back at Triana. "It's exactly what it looks like."

They walked in slowly and gathered around a small glass tank. Inside, floating in a solution of supercritical fluid, was a jellyfish. It was much smaller than Torrec, perhaps six inches long, and its bell-shaped head was a pale blue color. It bobbed toward the top of the tank, then slowly settled to about the halfway point and appeared to hover.

Triana spoke to Lita while keeping her eyes on the Dollovit. "I think I understand now. This used to be the small piece of Torrec's appendage that you removed, correct?"

"Uh-huh. I took a small section, maybe about an inch long. From that I sliced tiny little pieces for our tests, but I kept the primary fragment in this tank, filled with solution from Torrec's original. One of my assistants came in here a little while ago to grab something, and just about wet herself."

Gap walked to the other side and squatted to look directly at the jellyfish. "Did Torrec give you any kind of heads-up about this?" he asked.

Lita crossed her arms. "Let's just say that he didn't seem concerned at all about offering a chunk of one of his tentacles. And now I know why. Not only did that missing chunk grow back for him, but the piece I took off performed what's called rapid cellular regeneration. Emphasis on rapid." She nodded toward the tank. "At least now we know how the jellyfish population replenishes itself."

Triana muttered something under her breath, then said: "Torrec wouldn't have volunteered the information. He's very good about answering questions, but everything with him is direct. A direct question, a direct answer. He rarely offers unsolicited information. And you're right, now we know why he was so quick to agree to the biopsy." She let out a long breath. "Have you tried communicating with it?"

Lita smiled. "Talon, this is our Council Leader, Triana."

The voice that came from the nearby speaker held the same mechanical qualities that Torrec had exhibited. "Greetings, Triana."

"Talon?" Triana said. "His name is Talon?"

"No," Lita said. "He told me that his name was Torrec. I guess each derivative of a jellyfish keeps the same name as the original. But I told him that was much too confusing for simple creatures like us, and I asked if I could give him a nickname. He has no idea what a nickname is, but agreed to answer to something else."

"Why Talon?"

Lita shrugged. "No reason. I just wanted something else that started with T, and that was the first word that came to me."

"I think it sounds cool," Channy said. "Talon."

Gap straightened up and looked at Triana. "Okay, so we have vultures *and* jellyfish with us at our new home. I guess we think of Talon as the first Dollovit ambassador to Eos."

Again, Triana felt irritation. It seemed that more advanced species felt no need to ask permission when dealing with the galaxy's children. They could come and go as they pleased.

And yet, she reminded herself, without the Dollovit and the Cassini they likely wouldn't have made it this far.

With a slight nod of her head, Triana said: "Welcome, Talon. Please let us know if there's anything we can do to make you more comfortable." It sounded clumsy to her ears, but seemed to fit the required protocol. She gestured for Lita to step outside with her. Once in the hallway she hooked a thumb back toward the jellyfish.

"Any idea of how we contain this little guy when he begins to grow? Where do we get more of that fluid?"

"It's one of the things I asked him before I left for the meeting," Lita said. "He told me that he can curb his growth to match his environment. But he also said that the Vo can get him more fluid. Because of the oxygen in the atmosphere they won't be any help once Talon reaches the surface of the planet, but I think they'll work something out long before that. In fact, they've probably already worked it out."

"I'll bet you're right," Triana said. "Okay, I'll be—"

She was interrupted by a Clinic assistant who hurried down the hallway. "Triana, I think you'd better get in here. Mathias is calling, and says it's important."

Lita looked at Triana. "He's in the Storage Sections, prepping everything for the transport." Without another word, they hurried back to Lita's desk, where Triana snapped on the intercom.

"Mathias, what's going on?"

"Tree, we were going through each of the cryogenic canisters, getting an exact head count and an inventory."

"Are the crew members okay?" Triana asked.

"Yes, they seem to be fine. But after we confirmed all of that we started looking through some of the empty canisters. You know, they weren't all used."

"Right. And . . . ?"

"Well, they were all completely empty. Except one."

Triana looked at Lita, who muttered under her breath: "Not another cat, is it?"

"What did you find, Mathias?" Triana asked.

"We found where Dr. Bauer was hiding out in here. A few of his things are in there."

He paused, then added: "Including a journal. I . . . uh . . . well, I glanced through it, and . . ." He seemed unsure of how to continue.

Triana scowled. "C'mon, Mathias. What is it?"

"Well, I know he was crazy, but if he was telling the truth in this journal, we only have a matter of days before the ship is blown to bits."

27

Triana's head pounded as she took the lift to the lower level. She remembered her dad fighting through a tough stretch of mysterious headaches that the doctors could never figure out, but they ended almost as abruptly as they'd begun. While her mother battled migraines in her teenage years, they ceased to be a factor in her twenties. Triana used to silently tell herself that her mother had defeated the headaches by ignoring them; her mother, she rationalized, made an art form of ignoring things.

But the throbbing in Triana's head was clearly brought on by hearing a name she thought was consigned to her past: Dr. Fenton Bauer. The mad man who slipped aboard *Galahad* before its launch, and who came within minutes—and feet—from achieving his sinister goal, was back. Not in physical form, perhaps, but in objective. He'd wanted to cripple the ship and terminate the mission before it even reached the orbit of Mars. A victim of the insanity brought on by Bhaktul disease, as well as a festering relationship with his own son, Bauer had been foiled by a determined Council and the quick thinking of Triana Martell.

Her spirits, which had been so high just minutes earlier, sagged at the thought that he might succeed after all.

Mathias was waiting when she walked off the lift. "Where was it?" Triana said as they marched toward the open Storage Section.

"One of the bunks in the male dormitory, about five up from the floor. Couldn't see his stuff from the floor, so we didn't discover it until we were up on a ladder, examining the chambers. And there it was."

The first few rooms were beehives of activity. Crew members were busy cataloging everything, from materials and tools, to the sleeping passengers. Several gave Triana a nod and kept on with their business. She moved to the base of the ladder and looked up.

"We left everything where we found it," Mathias said. "I saw the last entry in the journal and called you, but we haven't removed anything yet."

"Thanks, Mathias," Triana said. Biting her lip, she took hold of the ladder and pulled herself up. She glanced at the sleeping figures as she climbed past, noting how peaceful they appeared. Theirs was a dreamless world, devoid of pain, fear, and sadness. For a moment, gazing at them, she envied their innocence; they journeyed without the weight Triana felt, without the responsibility.

But the feeling soon passed. For they were helpless in this condition, and that was something Triana would never bargain for. Life on *Galahad* might be dangerous, but she much preferred to tackle the danger head-on, to rely on her wits and skills to survive.

When the next rung brought her to the fifth level, she felt a shiver pass through her. The cryogenic chamber was in disarray. The hastily arranged bunk, with its disheveled blanket, held a number of personal items. Triana saw a collection of assorted food wrappers, obviously smuggled in from the outside. A jacket, nearly identical to the ones worn by the *Galahad* launch team— and no doubt used to camouflage Bauer's entry to the ship at the late hour—was wadded into a makeshift pillow. And the journal.

Mathias had left it near the ladder. Triana hesitated, unwilling to touch it, sickened by the hatred affiliated with it. Then, holding on to the ladder with one hand, she reached out and flipped the pages. The first entry that caught her eye was startling:

> Zimmer is responsible for the fire which will consume *Galahad*. Through his insidious nepotism, he has brought shame upon his so-called "last chance to save humanity." It is nothing more than a vehicle to continue the Zimmer line. It is salt in the wound to a father whose son has been rejected for another.

Bauer knew. *He knew.* Triana couldn't believe that Zimmer would have told him, but the two men had, at one point, been close. Or at least Zimmer had thought they were close. After months and months of long, tension-filled days, it might have slipped out, perhaps during—

No. Dr. Zimmer knew the pain that racked Dr. Bauer, the torture he felt over a splintered relationship with his own son. This couldn't possibly have come up, not even in one of their weary, late-night meetings.

It was beside the point. Somehow Bauer had discovered Zimmer's secret, and the knowledge would have pushed him over the edge, made him vulnerable to Tyler Scofeld's hostile rhetoric. And Triana saw now that it had driven him, in a Bhaktul-ravaged fit, to sneak aboard the spacecraft and plot its destruction.

She flipped through the pages, mostly assorted rants, with one devoted to celebrating his access to the ship. There were multiple entries alternating between fits of rage and self-satisfied comments on his late-night sabotage.

The unworthy star children will wake up in the morning to realize that this is truly a death ship. Damage to their crops is only the beginning. Access to the ship's computer has been easier than anticipated and, as we planned from the beginning, there is no security to speak of. I will go down with the ship, but I'm ready. Bring on the darkness, darkness that can only mask the pain.

Dr. Bauer's pain was a potent mixture of mental anguish, caused by the troubled relationship with his son, and the destructive physical torment rained down by Bhaktul. While she grimaced at the evil design, Triana at least understood the ingredients of Bauer's insanity.

The last page of the journal—surprisingly legible, given the scientist's deteriorated state—outlined one final, chilling vision.

Tonight it ends. Triana will learn the truth at midnight, and shortly afterward her short journey comes to an end, the only end this mission deserves. And, should things not go as planned, everything is in place to assure—with no chance of failure— the cataclysmic eruption of this vessel. Fire will cleanse the galaxy of this detestable human race and sterilize it before it contaminates another world.

Before I leave tonight I will settle on the date that will be the most fitting. Either the one-year anniversary of *Galahad's* launch, or perhaps the next celestial alignment of the Earth, Saturn, and Eos. There would be something poetic in that, I believe.

Or, if this is to be a profoundly personal statement, there's always Marshall's nineteenth birthday, which falls close to both of these dates. I'll decide which of the three resonates within me as the truth, and commence the steps necessary to ensure that *Galahad* leaves a blistering mark in the night skies over the doomed inhabitants of Earth.

Let it be done.

Triana stared at the calm, coherent reasoning of Fenton Bauer. It was hard to believe that the end result would be the murder of so many innocent people. He'd truly been insane.

She scrambled down the ladder, clutching the journal in one hand, and thanked Mathias for his work. In the corridor she stopped to inform Roc that an emergency Council meeting would take place in the Conference Room in twenty minutes. Foregoing his usual sarcastic banter, Roc agreed to circulate the news.

Fifteen minutes later they began to arrive. Channy and Lita walked in together, concern etched on their faces. Gap followed moments later. He threw a quick glance at Triana, but she was absorbed in the data scrolling across her vidscreen. Bon was two minutes late, but that merely allowed Triana time to confirm her research.

When she was ready, she looked up from the screen and said: "We have a problem, and I won't sugarcoat it. Dr. Bauer has apparently rigged this ship to blow up."

She quickly shared the final entry from his journal. The Council members passed around the actual book, and Triana watched the sickening horror register on their faces.

"Marshall," Lita said. "I take it that was his son?"

Triana nodded.

Gap laced his fingers together on the table. "This is incredible. He wanted us to fall into some sort of routine, to get happy and content . . . and then wham! With no warning whatsoever. That's just plain evil."

"Could he do this?" Channy asked, pushing the journal across to Gap. "I mean, could he have fixed something to blow up?"

Triana looked grim. "That's one of the things I've been speaking about with Roc. Roc, you wanna explain this?"

"The bad news comes in three stages," Roc said. "First, Dr. Bauer had unlimited entry to *Galahad* throughout the construction process, so he knew how to access every square inch. He could, quite literally, have arranged an explosion or breakdown on any part of the ship, and that includes within walls, floors, ceilings. For that matter, he could have rigged something within the guts of our ion-drive engines. We would need to practically dismantle the entire ship in order to isolate it. And remember, in space it doesn't take much damage to create disaster.

"Secondly, we have no idea what to search for. I'm sure that he hasn't relied on traditional explosives. Knowing the way his mind worked, in fact, he would have relished the fact that it was a creative ending.

"And finally," the computer said, "we don't know for sure that he's even followed through with these musings. It's possible that he never arranged for any of these, or that he ended up doing something completely different. There are too many unknowns."

Bon was the last to scan the journal's page.

"I'm assuming you've run the dates on these events?" he said with a cool gaze.

"That's what I've been doing," Triana said. "Dr. Bauer listed three potential dates for our destruction. However, one of those dates has already passed. Allowing for time dilation, the celestial alignment he mentioned—Earth, Saturn, and Eos—would have occurred back home about seven weeks ago."

She could see the shudders that passed through the Council members; she was sure it was the same spine-chilling sensation that she'd experienced as soon as the data popped up on her screen. To think that they'd sailed through a potential doomsday, oblivious to the vile schemes of a long-dead former colleague . . .

"That leaves two possible dates," she said. "The one-year anniversary of our launch, which happens in exactly fourteen days. Or the nineteenth birthday of Bauer's son, Marshall." She shook her head. "And that is, believe it or not, in sixteen days."

There was dead silence around the room. It was Roc who finally spoke up: "This should be a movie."

Gap grunted. "Let's wait and make sure it has a happy ending." He looked at Triana. "This gives us time to get to Eos Three."

"But no time to scout locations," Lita said. "We'll have to be ready to jump into the Spiders and pods and just . . ." She flung her arm into the air.

Channy looked between all of the Council members. "Don't we need to find the best spot? I mean, we can't just fall into orbit and bail out, can we?"

"I don't see what choice we have," Lita said. "Roc's right, it would take months for us to find what Bauer's done." She paused, then looked hopeful. "I know we're in some trouble here, but really, when you think about it, we've lucked out. Without Torrec and his vultures, we never would have known about the sabotage. We'd either be out in deep space, or . . ."

Gap finished the sentence. "Or orbiting Eos Three, celebrating our arrival, congratulating ourselves on pulling it off, and then lights out." He shook his head. "Can you believe it?"

Lita looked thoughtful. "Is it fate that the Dollovit found us?"

Triana shrugged. "I'll make a deal with you. Let's get everything packed and ready to go, let's get to the planet and get off this ship. Then, when we're safely on land, when we're breathing real air, *then* I'll discuss the idea of fate with you all day long. Deal?"

Bon pushed back his chair. "As I see it, we'll need to be off this ship in thirteen days. I've got a lot of work to do." Without waiting for a formal dismissal he trudged out of the room.

"Concise as always," Gap said. "But he's right; I might even recommend a bigger cushion than that. For all we know Bauer might have screwed up his dates. Roc, can we do all of the braking procedures and make it into orbit in twelve days?"

"This is where I'm supposed to put on a happy face and tell everyone that there's no problem," the computer said. "But all of you need to know that twelve days is pushing it. In fact, I'm guessing that we'll fall into orbit—as Channy put it—and scram that same day. I can't offer any guarantees."

Gap ran a hand through his hair. "We have a fighting chance. I guess we can't ask for more than that."

Triana dismissed the meeting, wishing everyone good luck. Once in the hall, Lita took her arm.

"Listen, we're gonna make it. Everything's gonna be fine."

"I have no doubt," Triana said. "After everything we've been through, I won't allow anything to stop us now."

28

our days passed, and as each day flipped over to the next
Triana couldn't help but quietly calculate the amount of time
they had left. It wouldn't be long, she realized, before they
measured it in hours.

Life on the ship became a blur. Crew members turned up the
intensity level a few notches; even those who technically were on a
break in their work rotation dove in, helping in each department.
School was suspended, and physical workouts were cut back to
brief cardio routines. Everyone eyed the final prize, knowing that
their new home drew closer with each passing minute.

In the Domes, Bon oversaw the final harvesting and storage.
Tools, machines, and assorted implements were packed into special transport containers. Cryostorage bins filled with thousands
of seeds, stacked and forgotten in the recesses of Dome 1 before
the launch, were checked and rechecked, then moved into position near the lifts. They would be the basis of the Eos colony's
initial food crops, all grown in specially assembled greenhouses
to eliminate contamination of the planet's native species.

Lita and Mathias finished the inventory of the Storage Sections and, with the help of some Engineering assistants, began preparing eighty-four slumbering passengers for their trip to Eos Three. Lita's capable assistants, meanwhile, took care of packing up Sick House.

Gap ran endless tests and calculations from his station in the Control Room. Triana stayed out of his way, checking in occasionally and offering to help should he need it. They were joined on the deck every few hours by Bon, who silently took his seat and triggered the course changes to safely guide *Galahad* through the jumbled space rubble of the system's outskirts. There was little conversation while he sat there, eyes glowing, his fingers flying across the keyboard.

Triana did her best to keep her mind focused on the mission and its successful completion. But for the few brief minutes where she found herself working next to Bon, she couldn't help but flash forward to their new colony. Once they were no longer confined to this limited space aboard the ship, would she see him as often? Would the backbreaking work that loomed in the next few months—or few years—keep Bon isolated, buried in his work, and unavailable?

Of course they were ridiculous thoughts. Bon was isolated and unavailable on *Galahad*; why should it be any different on Eos Three? She pushed aside the daydreams and burrowed back into her work.

Day five in Eosian space began early. Triana walked into the Dining Hall before 6 A.M., anxious to grab some oatmeal and fruit before composing the latest update for the crew. Sitting in her usual spot in the back of the room, she greeted the early risers who stumbled in, most of them blurry-eyed but still in good spirits. Dr. Bauer's threat was a dark blanket above them, but somehow seeing the finish line kept their heads up and their motors on high.

Triana took a sip of juice and flipped open Bauer's journal.

She'd surveyed it once to make sure no other surprises were imminent, but since then she'd locked it away, reluctant to allow his toxic attitude to contaminate her. Now curiosity took over and she gave herself a few minutes to thumb through his rants.

They primarily echoed the same sentiments over and over, and often came back to the same word: unfair. But it was the deranged scientist's comments about Dr. Zimmer that tugged at her. She found herself back at the bitter passage that had originally caught her attention:

> Zimmer is responsible for the fire which will consume *Galahad*. Through his insidious nepotism, he has brought shame upon his so-called "last chance to save humanity." It is nothing more than a vehicle to continue the Zimmer line. It is salt in the wound to a father whose son has been rejected for another.

So many strange vibrations resonated around the issue of Zimmer's child, but now she began to interpret Bauer's cryptic comment.

A father whose son has been rejected for another.

She looked at it again.

For another.

Not just another teenager. Bauer specifically said one son for another. But Triana had been so sure that it was Alexa . . .

Sure? Was there anything she could be sure about on this mission? And what could she believe in the scrawled rant of a madman?

There was something else about Dr. Zimmer that continued to tickle the edges of her mind. Something he'd said to her was the key to this, but she couldn't filter out the static surrounding it.

"Our fearless leader, deep in thought," came the voice above her.

She looked up to see the familiar dark hair, dark eyes, and scar that topped a wolf's smile.

"Good morning, Merit," she said, casually closing the journal and applying the most pleasant tone she could muster. He stood before her without a tray. "No breakfast for you?"

"I only eat twice a day, and never in the morning," he said, sitting in a chair at the table next to her. "I know it's supposed to be the most important meal of the day, but the thought of food this early makes me retch."

"I heard that you might have had a touch of flu or something when we slipped through the Channel, too," Triana said. "Feeling better, obviously."

Merit's smile faltered for a second, then he recovered. "Good old Katz. What a friend." He looked at a group of crew members who were working their way through the food line. "Listen, you're busy, time is running short, so I'll make this quick. I want to let you know that a few of us have reached a decision about Eos."

Triana pushed her tray back and raised an eyebrow. "Oh?"

"Uh-huh. In your address to the crew you said that the Council was in favor of Eos Three as our new home."

"Yes . . ."

"But you also made it clear that anyone could reach out to you should they opt for another course of action."

Even through the heavy-handed speech dialogue that Merit preferred, Triana instantly saw where this was going. "Let me guess: you want us to stop and let you off at number four."

He leveled another smile at her. "Not by myself, of course."

"And how many recruits have you rounded up this time?" Triana said.

"There are nineteen of us. Which means we'll need one of the extra pods that the Dollovit have provided, but very little in the way of equipment or rations. It's not like you're dividing the provisions in half."

Triana stared hard at him. "Tell me, why are you doing this?"

"I already told you," Merit said. "I'm a water freak. How do I pass up a planet that's practically all water?"

"Right. So it has nothing to do with the fact that the Council will be a world away, leaving you the ruler of your own kingdom?"

He adopted a comical look of indignation. "Triana, please! There are eighteen other people involved here, you know. They want to go just as badly as I do. You wouldn't turn them down just because you feel scorned, would you?"

"It's not up to me, Merit. If there's a request to divide the few resources we have for colonization, it's a Council decision. I know that aggravates you, but it's the governmental process aboard *Galahad*."

"Okay," he said, standing. "Talk it over, and let us know. And please, if you have specific reasons why you won't follow through with your promise, let us know that, too."

He gave a mock half-salute and paraded out of the room.

They'll never survive," Lita said. "Nineteen people left alone to tame an entire planet? It's ridiculous."

The other Council members listened with interest, but only Channy nodded agreement.

"His chances are the same as ours," Gap said.

"Oh, c'mon, Gap," Lita said. "Two hundred thirty stand a much better chance, and you know it."

He shrugged. "I disagree. It'll be easier for them to get shelter put up at first, and easier to feed nineteen. In some respects I think he'd have a better chance than us."

Triana had laid out Merit's request, and could have predicted the individual Council member's reactions. She asked Bon to voice his thoughts for the record.

"As long as the supplies are proportionally split, I have no issues with him leaving. I think that most of the crew would feel the same way."

"Good riddance is what you mean," Channy said. She turned to Triana. "I don't really care for Merit either, but it seems almost cruel to let him take some crew members and try to—"

"Gullible crew members," Gap interjected.

". . . and try to build something on Eos Four."

"Channy's right," Lita said. "We can't allow personal dislike to sway our decision."

Gap drummed his fingers on the tabletop. "We sat right here, with the crew watching and listening, and told them that if they wanted to leave, they could. Are you only saying this now because it's Merit?"

Triana stepped in. "Yes, I did say that to the crew. But before we vote on this, let's make sure we have all of the facts. First of all, Roc, do we even have the time to do this?"

"That's probably up to Dr. Bauer," Roc said. "With all of the unknown factors, we could be fine indefinitely, or we could blow up before I finish this sentence. Whew, made it. Or maybe before I finish *this* sentence. Okay, now maybe before—"

"Fine, you've made your point," Triana said. "Assuming for the moment that he chose the earlier date, and assuming that he got it right: how does that affect our ability to drop off passengers around Eos Four?"

"Since we're using that fourth planet as a component of our braking maneuver, it really isn't a factor. Once we swing around the planet, we can flick anything out the door. Granted, we might want to slow down just a bit more than we'd planned, which might add a few hours, perhaps as much as a day, to our arrival time at Three. I calculate that, even with a slower transit from Four to Three, we should have a good thirty-six to forty-eight hours to evacuate the ship."

"See," Lita said. "If we slow down to let them off, we're pushing ourselves up against a deadline that wouldn't just be inconvenient; it could be deadly."

"Right," Channy said. "So I say they stay with us."

Gap shook his head. "Adding a few hours makes no difference. We'll be completely packed and ready to go the minute we're in orbit around Three. We don't need an extra day to think about things. If they want to go, they should go."

Bon simply nodded agreement when Triana looked down the table. She stalled for time by walking over to get a cup of water. By the time she returned to the table—and to the curious looks from the Council members—she knew how she would break the tie.

"I vote to honor the agreement I made to the crew," she said. "And Lita, it's not from an insecure desire to get rid of Merit. Although he's very skilled at verbalizing his positions, I'd make the same decision for any other persuasive crew member."

She sat down and ticked off some points on her fingers. "He has probably the same chance we do on an alien surface. We're making an educated guess about our final destination, but for all we know we could land en masse on number three and find carnivorous dragonflies waiting for us.

"Next, we're flying on borrowed time as it is. Roc might have been obnoxious in his description, but his assessment of the situation is right: we could have already been blown to bits.

"And third, remember what this mission was all about in the first place. We were chosen to represent the human race, and to offer our species a chance at survival. Well, we have not one, but two planets capable of supporting life as we know it, and it probably makes sense to put down roots on both. It might double our chances for survival. It's essentially one of the arguments that Torrec made when requesting the embryos."

Triana said to Lita: "Your points, as always, are thoughtful and appreciated. But we'll grant Merit and his friends their wish."

Lita let out a sigh. "It breaks my heart, but okay. I'd like to add one final thing, though, and on this I won't back down. They take none of the crew members in suspended animation, and they keep their hands off the embryos. Can we agree on that?"

"I don't think any of us would argue with that," Triana said. The rest of the Council members concurred.

"Roc," Triana said, "we need to begin working under the assumption that Bauer's next anniversary date is our deadline, if you'll pardon the expression. With that in mind, let's begin a countdown and have everything ready to go by zero hour, with a safety cushion if possible."

"Done," Roc said. "As of right now, you have eight days, seven hours, twenty-two minutes. Factoring in your cushion, the last person off the ship should take the elevator down in seven days, nineteen hours. And please, turn off all the lights before you go and make sure your curling irons are unplugged."

Another Council meeting disbanded. As they stood up, Lita left all of them with a sobering thought.

"We should all remember what seed we planted today with this decision. It would be interesting to pop in a hundred years from now to see what has grown out of it."

29

A while ago I dropped a reference about Gap being one of my favorite people on the ship. He's got the brains to get the job done,
he's got a heart that keeps things confusing yet entertaining, and
he has a multitude of interests. The guy enjoys puzzling things out, he
loves a good game of Masego—and although I'd never tell him, he's actually getting quite good at it—and he's a bit of a daredevil athletically.
Sure, he gets a bit emotional about some things, but so what? He's rarely
inactive, physically or mentally.

I try to refrain from using my position as the trusted narrator of this
tale to preach to anyone, but hopefully a few of you have subconsciously
noted this. Your age doesn't matter one bit; as soon as you begin to lose
your curiosity and your joy of new things, then you begin to die. Don't let
it happen to you, okay?

All right, sermon over.

Gap trudged through the hallway on the lower level with a
heavy heart. He wore his helmet and carried his Airboard,
knowing that it was likely to be the last time he ever enjoyed his

favorite pastime. The resources simply didn't exist to transport the massive gravitational system to the planet's surface. And, with everything that would be taking place over the final few days, now—with zero hour only six days away—was his chance to log a few laps before wishing the track good-bye.

He'd left a message for some of his regular Airboarding friends, and he was thrilled to spot the friendly faces when he entered the room. Rico Manzelli, his arm in a cast, sat on the top row of the bleachers, talking with a few of the ship's other daredevils. Gap recognized Ariel Morgan out on the track; even with the helmet hiding her face, he could spot the Australian girl's distinctive Boarding style as she hurtled around curves, her arms acting as counterbalances to keep her from flying into the walls.

"Hey, stud, tripped over anything lately?" Gap said, plopping down next to Rico.

"Not today, anyway," the Italian boy said. "And you're one to talk. Look at your hand. Plus, seems that I recall your arm in a sling not that long ago."

"Yeah, but mine came on the field of battle," Gap said, pointing out to the track. "I didn't hurt myself walking on the bleachers."

Rico looked sheepish. "Yeah, you're right. And you know what makes it worse? The fact that now I won't be able to go full speed today and take back the record from you."

"Full speed?" Gap said. "What, are you climbing aboard today with your arm broken in two places?"

"Of course. This is my last chance to ride. You don't think I'd let a little thing like a few fractures keep me from a farewell tour, do you? I'm saddling up, pardner." He pointed with his toe at an intricately painted Airboard that lay near his feet.

Gap shook his head and laughed. "You're crazy."

"You'd do the same thing," Rico said.

"Yeah, I guess you're right."

A minute later Ariel took a dramatic tumble out on the cushioned floor. She rolled to a stop, rose to her knees, and removed her helmet. Even from the top of the bleachers Gap could see a smile on her face from ear to ear. She grabbed her gear and jogged up to sit on the row in front of Gap and Rico, while another rider took his turn.

"Hey, guys," she said, removing her pads.

"Did you know that Mr. Macho here is going for a spin?" Gap said.

"Uh-huh. I'm the one who told him if he didn't do it, he'd regret it forever. By the way, are you gonna play it safe today, or set one final speed record before we turn off Zoomer?" she said, referencing the computer that controlled the track's underground magnetic course.

Gap watched the latest rider take a turn too quickly and collide with the padded wall. He winced, recalling his own miscalculation that had resulted in a broken collarbone months ago.

"I'm content with the current record," he said. "I won't be a grandma out there, but I can imagine Triana's face if I show up with another sling or a cast, just as we're about to evacuate the ship." He poked Ariel in the shoulder. "You weren't exactly burning up the track today. Why didn't you go for the record?"

She ran her fingers through her long, brown hair. "You would've just gone all out to take it back. Besides, this was more of a remembrance ride for me."

"What do you mean?"

"I used my time on the Board to think about my family, how they sacrificed everything to get me on *Galahad*. I thought about all of the friendships I've made in the past couple of years, including you two lunkheads. And I wanted to just soak it up, since I won't ever ride again." She threw a quick glance over her shoulder at Gap. "Glad you guys couldn't see me crying through my helmet out there."

Gap and Rico looked away, not wanting to embarrass their friend. But when Gap's turn to ride came, he found himself drawn into Ariel's same thought process.

He began easily, feeling the tug of the gravitational field that ran under the floor of the room, balancing his weight and maneuvering his Airboard as it rode four inches off the ground. At this speed his muscle memory did the majority of the work, effortlessly skimming across the room, reaching out to drag his fingers across the wall as he made a corner turn, bending his knees to settle into a quicker pace.

But his mind soared as well. He fought back his own tears as he remembered his mother's concern over his newfound hobby, her worry that he'd not only injure himself but lose interest in his schooling. Neither happened, discounting the minor collection of bumps and bruises.

He savored the memory of Dr. Zimmer announcing that Gap's push for an Airboard track aboard *Galahad* had paid off. The kind-hearted scientist had expressed the same concerns as Gap's mother, but had been swayed by the Asian boy's argument regarding Airboarding's value in terms of exercise and mental agility.

He mentally replayed the lessons that he'd given to Hannah in this very room. She'd taken to the sport quickly and enthusiastically, only to give it up the minute Gap had ended their relationship. In a flash he wondered where Hannah might be at that very moment, what she was doing, what she was experiencing. Was she thinking of him at the same time?

Would he ever see her again?

The thought caused him to clench his teeth and pour even

more energy into his ride. Faster and faster he raced through the twists and turns of the track, absorbing every minute course alteration that Zoomer could dish out. The walls blurred past him, and the shouts of warning from the bleachers became a nebulous hum in his ears.

T he treacherous ring of debris had fallen far behind them. *Galahad* now tore inward through the planetary system of Eos, rocketing past the gravitational influence of its massive gas monster, a planet that dwarfed Jupiter and provided the necessary tug to slow the starship. Eos was next, a colossal fireball that clutched at them as they streaked around the far side. The next station on their line would be Eos Four, followed by Eos Three.

The automatic dimming of lights signaled the onset of evening, and Lita marveled again at the glorious display of stars that began to penetrate the clear Domes above the Farms. She walked beside Bon as he made his usual inspection of the day's work, a task that he insisted on completing even though they'd soon be leaving these fields behind. She knew that he would never fully disconnect from this soil, and she imagined the pain he must feel knowing that in a matter of days it would all be reduced to cosmic rubble.

Lita, too, felt a pang of loss. She wasn't attached to the Farms in the same way as Bon, but she'd come to appreciate its beauty and its representation of the cycle of life.

She broke the silent spell that hung over them. "How long will it take to get the crops up and running inside the greenhouses?"

From the look Bon gave her, it was obvious that he knew she was only making conversation. But he went along with it. "Not long. We'll have nutrients for the soil, and there's water available. After that it's sweat and sunlight."

"Do you think we'll be able to eat much of the native plant life?"

"I have no idea," he said, stopping along the path to examine a tomato plant that had been damaged. A telltale set of tracks betrayed a small tractor that had veered from the path. Bon's familiar scowl momentarily returned. Lita opened her mouth to say "it doesn't matter, we're about to leave," but thought better of it. Instead she coaxed him in a different direction.

"Now that you've guided us through the outer fringes, what do you see your connection with the Cassini morphing into? I mean, will they stay connected to you?"

"There's no choice in the matter anymore," Bon said without hesitation. "They'll always be wired into my brain now."

"And how do you feel about that?" Lita said. "Do you feel . . ." She struggled to find the right word. "Used?"

For a moment she thought she might have gone too far. The Swede's face grew dark, and it looked as if he might boil over. But with each passing second he relaxed, apparently coming to the conclusion that he was, indeed, being used to a certain extent. He finally said: "We use each other. Remember the discussion about the Dollovit and their croy?"

Lita nodded. "A symbiotic relationship."

"That's right," Bon said. "It's close to what I experience with the Cassini."

She considered this for a moment. "I understand the help we get from them through you, but what do they get out of it?"

He startled her by taking hold of her chin and turning her face toward his. Her breath caught in her chest when she found herself staring into two eyes that glowed a deep orange. They seemed to slice right through her.

Seconds later they faded away, leaving Bon's natural ice-blue eyes inches from her face. A faint smile on his lips calmed her.

"They get their own representative in another camp," he said. "And before we begin to think we're something special, I get the feeling that we're one of millions throughout the universe. They reach a symbiotic arrangement with someone like me, which places a little reminder in each civilization that we're a breath away from losing our privileges."

Lita's heart continued to beat quickly. "So, you're like the sheriff, huh?"

Still face-to-face, he looked back and forth between her two eyes. "That's right. You should remember that."

She swallowed hard. Without thinking, she took his face into her hands. "Yeah? Well, you should remember this." She pulled him into a long, lingering kiss. When they separated, she gently touched the side of his face. "You have a lot to do in the next few weeks. But remember that, okay? For later?"

If he was surprised, he masked it well. He watched her turn and walk back down the path.

30

Eos Four sparkled on the large vidscreen in the Control Room. Magnified from a great distance, it truly was a watery world, dominated by the crystal blue oceans that spread over eighty percent of its surface. Clouds blotted much of the atmosphere. Thin brown ovals of land stretched near the planet's equator, while a massive crust of ice could be seen covering the southern pole. After a year in space, crew members throughout the ship were being treated to a vision that nearly brought tears to their eyes.

But not for long. The planet was approaching fast, yet another gravitational tool that would help to cut *Galahad*'s speed before it disappeared in the ship's wake.

Triana stood mesmerized, unable to take her eyes from the scene. It was a beautiful world, and for a minute she questioned their decision to bypass this one for the warmer, rockier setting of Eos Three.

"Mmm, now that's a glorious sight," Merit cooed beside her. "We do have sunscreen, right?"

Triana ignored him. In forty-three minutes a pod, carrying nineteen crew members who had spent the past two-and-a-half years living the same highs and lows, the same joys and fears, as the rest of *Galahad*'s teen population, would be jettisoned toward the glittering planet on the vidscreen. Would they ever cross paths again, Triana wondered, and if so, what changes would have taken place?

Merit continued his chatter. "I was surprised that last night you left the going-away dinner so soon. Gee, I hope my fellow colonists heading to Eos Four didn't have their feelings hurt."

Controlling her emotions, Triana casually answered him: "I thought I spent plenty of time at the dinner, Merit. I even spoke individually with every one of them." She gave him a droll look. "Why, did I miss something after I left? Don't tell me I missed another one of your speeches. I'd hate that."

He grunted a laugh, then placed a hand on her shoulder. "Oh, you're going to miss me, Triana, and you know it. Take care of yourself, okay?"

She glanced at his hand, but made no move to return the gesture. "You, too, Merit. Best of luck to all of you."

It seemed that he had more to say, but without another word he turned and walked to the lift. Just before the doors closed, he locked eyes with Triana and flashed his trademark grin.

It sent a creepy shiver down her spine. Something in his smile contained an unspoken message: *Just wait.*

She busied herself for the next forty minutes with the dozens of details that needed to be handled prior to their own departure. Gap volunteered to oversee the launch of Merit's pod, a move that freed Triana to tick things off her lengthy to-do list. But it also was a move that surprised her. Generally Gap wanted nothing to do with the dark-haired Californian. But the more she considered it, the more she realized that it could very well be a symbolic action, too. In essence, Gap would be booting Merit off the ship, something he'd dreamed of for months.

It brought a wry smile to Triana's face. In some cultures there were traditional ceremonies whereby evil spirits or other dark forces were expunged, in effect shooing them from the village and restoring order and peace once again to the community. By opening the Spider bay door and pushing Merit out—even enclosed in the protective shell of the pod—Gap might feel as if he were cleansing the spirit of *Galahad*.

And, Triana thought, who's to say he's not right?

Her mind also played back an earlier conversation with Bon. He'd mentioned that *Galahad's* "unscrupulous character" problem might take care of itself. Was this the solution to the problem that he'd foreseen?

She struggled with a dilemma all leaders faced: how to separate personal feelings from the responsibilities of the job. Merit was quite obviously a maddening member of their troupe, but he was still part of the team. To be honest, however, what troubled Triana the most was the fact that he'd wrangled eighteen other crew members into abandoning *Galahad* and following him.

Well, she thought with a sigh, he always was extremely persuasive. She just hoped that it didn't cost innocent lives.

In the midst of solving an inventory dilemma—certainly not the kind of duty she'd expected at the onset of the mission—Gap's voice broke over the intercom.

"Everyone is packed and loaded onto the pod, Tree. Roc has calculated the launch point to the second in order to get them into a perfect orbit of E4. That's in . . ." He paused. "That's in twenty seconds."

The Control Room was packed with working crew members, all of whom stopped what they were doing in order to watch the vidscreen and listen in to the launch. Triana stood at her workstation and gave Gap the all-clear to proceed.

"The pod is away," he said. "Bay door is closing, bay is pressurizing."

And like that, they were gone.

"My, my," Roc said. "Merit is either more influential than I gave him credit for, or the Dollovit are going to videotape his exploits for a 'humans funniest videos' segment."

"What does that mean?" Triana asked.

"Four of our constant companions have peeled away from the ship and are shadowing Mr. Simms and friends down to Eos Four."

"Vultures?" Triana said. "Four vultures are tracking them?"

"Correct."

"I guess it makes sense," she said. "And you're right, Roc, I think we might be an endless supply of entertainment for Torrec and his pals."

"And, right on cue," Roc said, "Mr. Simms is calling from the pod."

Triana groaned inwardly, but flipped on the intercom. "Hello, Merit. Forget something? Want to come back already?"

"Hardly," Merit said. "There are nineteen smiling faces here, looking forward to our first beach party. I just wanted to let you know that when things get rough for you guys, we'll hopefully be able to lend a hand somehow."

A smile worked its way across Triana's face. "That would be a good trick. But thanks for the offer."

"No problem. Okay, we've got work to do now, so I need to sign off. But remember this day, Triana. This is the day a new empire was born."

After a low chuckle, he added: "We will rule this star system. Farewell."

* * *

Two hours later, after breezing through the Dining Hall to fuel up, Triana stopped by Sick House. Like every other department, it was abuzz with activity. Transport crates were stacked by the door, ready to be wheeled down to the Spider bay for loading. They were lucky that not one hospital bed was occupied at the moment, and all hands could be counted on for moving duty.

Lita's hair was held out of her face by her signature red ribbon, and yet beads of sweat still dotted her forehead. She gratefully accepted the energy block that Triana offered and, as they perched on the edges of the room's two desks, they talked about Merit's ominous prediction. Several crew members had been present in the Control Room to hear it, which meant word spread quickly around the ship, something that no doubt Merit had counted on.

"He's a bag of hot air," Lita said, waving it off. "If things are as tough as we think, he'll be hard-pressed to survive, let alone worry about building an empire. Listen, he's out of your hair by his own choice. Don't let him continue to get under your skin."

Triana acknowledged this with a nod. "Still, it makes you wonder what he and his descendants might try down the road. Who knows what stories their kids will hear about us."

"Doesn't matter," Lita said. "If Bon's right, then the Cassini will slap them down somehow."

"And us with them?" Triana wondered aloud.

The door to Sick House flew open and Mathias rushed in, looking right, and then glimpsing Lita and Triana to the left. He was out of breath.

"Hey," he said, briskly walking over to them. "I didn't want to call and tell you on the intercom. But we have a problem."

"What is it?" Lita said.

"It's the embryos," Mathias said. "Someone has taken them."

"What?" Lita said, jumping to her feet. "*Taken* them?"

"I'm sorry. Taken *some* of them. Someone got into the Storage Section and removed a dozen of them, along with one of the incubator units. It must've happened late last night."

Triana felt a river of anger begin to surge through her. She stood up and spoke with an icy calm. "Is there damage to any of the others?"

Mathias shook his head. "Not that I can tell. They took twelve of the small embryonic canisters, but they're all individually controlled. We have three of the incubation units left, which is fine. But—"

"It's not fine," Lita said, her voice rising. She turned to Triana. "You know who did this, right?"

Triana clenched one fist, a method that she found kept her from losing control. "And there's nothing we can do about it. He's long gone."

A larms were going off in Engineering, a sound that had been absent since they'd siphoned power into the radiation shield. With only thirty-five hours left before evacuation began to Eos Three, Gap cringed. They'd perhaps taken for granted that Fenton Bauer's threat of destruction wouldn't come to pass until the ship was deserted, but . . .

"Roc," Gap said, "talk to me."

"A giant squid has wrapped its tentacles around the ship and is trying to pull it to the bottom of . . . oh wait, I was just reading Jules Verne. Let me check. Hold, please."

The seconds ticked by. One by one team members in the Engineering section drifted over to nervously scan the diagnostic board. When Roc spoke again, he'd lost the playful tone from his voice.

"Electrical systems are shutting down. Some sort of override that I might be able to work on."

The computer's suddenly all-business manner struck more fear into Gap than the alarms. He chewed on the diagnosis for a moment, then said: "Which systems?"

"Random, no pattern," Roc said. "Or, if there's a pattern, I'm too busy to puzzle it out right now. I can tell you this: it would only take a certain number and combination of failures before other components go critical."

Gap could read between the lines. Multiple components of the ship relied on power to be provided fluidly and in unison with other components. If all of the power went out, the ship would merely flounder. But if several units went out together, and then the wrong individual unit sprang back to life, it could be dangerous. Unless they could put a stop to it, one wrong combination of breakdowns would trigger an explosion.

The explosion that Bauer had prophesied.

Triana called on the intercom, and Gap quickly laid it out for her.

"How does this affect our timetable?" she said.

"I think our first order of business is to make sure we're alive long enough to keep a timetable."

"That bad?"

Gap said: "Potentially. Roc's trying to make sense of it. But now I know why Dr. Bauer insisted on so much control of this stuff. He probably knew more about this than anyone, which meant he knew exactly what buttons to push. Just like what he did to Roc last year."

"Right," Triana said. "Okay, I'll get out of your hair. Do you guys have almost everything packed in case we need to move fast?"

"We'll be ready," Gap said. "We might be scrambling once we reach the planet's surface. But we'll be ready."

★ ★ ★

Allowing herself thirty minutes to throw her things into a storage box, Triana found that there wasn't much she really wanted to take to the planet's surface. She wondered what others would say about her leaving so much behind, but then decided that what others thought wasn't important.

She'd started to take down the posters in her room, the colorful reminders of her home in Colorado. They'd kept her company during the year of space travel, often triggering memories of her dad and reinforcing the powerful life lessons that he'd taught her.

But they weren't coming with her. This was a new life on Eos Three, and she wanted a clean, fresh start. It wasn't the posters that would bring her father to life in her mind.

Another thought occurred to her, and she quickly opened her journal.

I think it'll be easy for us to feel overwhelmed when we reach the surface, but I hope we remember just how far, and how fast, we've come. It's important to remember that Dr. Zimmer never counted on us beginning the new colony so soon.

If all had gone according to plan, we'd be in our early twenties when we arrived at Eos. Now, thanks to the Channel, we'll begin building our new home while we're sixteen and seventeen.

I hope that the challenges we've overcome will help bridge the gap between the years.

The buzzer from her door sounded just as she finished. Channy gave an exaggerated wave when she opened the door.

"Am I interrupting your packing?" the Brit asked, walking in and looking around.

"No, I'm finished," Triana said.

"What?" Channy waved her hand at the walls. "You're not taking these?" She indicated the small storage box. "Wow, you're the lightest packer I've ever seen."

Triana smiled. "I'm not your average girl, I guess. What are you up to?"

"I'm inviting everyone to grab something to eat tonight and meet up at the soccer field. It'll be our little going-away party."

"I'm not much on parties . . ." Triana began.

"I know. I saw you make a cameo appearance for the Eos Four group. But this will be different. More of a farewell to the ship. She's served us well."

That was a good point, and Triana was embarrassed that she hadn't thought of it herself.

"Things aren't going so well," Channy continued, "and we might have to shut down even more power tomorrow, according to Gap. So I think tonight we should do it while we can."

"Sure," Triana said. "I'll be there. Count me in."

"Excellent!" Channy said. "And I promise, I won't ask you to make a speech or anything. Unless you want to, of course."

"We'll see."

Channy looked around the room again. "So, do you think the Eos Four group will be okay?"

Triana shrugged. "I think their chances are as good as ours. I wish they'd stayed with us, though."

"Ha," Channy said. "Merit couldn't be king if he stayed, right? Besides, now he'll finally get to surf."

Triana opened her mouth to respond, and then froze. The smile on her face gradually faded into a look of disbelief as everything suddenly fell into place.

"You okay?" Channy said.

"Uh . . . yeah." Triana forced the smile back onto her face. "Listen, I've got some things to do before I join you for the party. See you there, okay?"

Channy looked suspicious. "You sure you're all right?"

"You mean besides the emergency evacuation, and the inability to scout a landing location, and the stolen embryos, and an alien ambassador tagging along with us? Besides all that?"

Channy gave a small bow. "Got it. Okay, throw the rest of your stuff in a biscuit tin and I'll see you at the party." She marched out into the hallway.

As soon as the door closed, Triana raced over to her desk and snapped on the vidscreen. Her fingers flew across the keyboard.

Surfing. That was it. The tingling in the back of her mind suddenly made sense.

Surfing. California. Caltech.

What had Merit said? *My mother taught at Caltech for two years* . . .

Triana replayed the video from Dr. Zimmer, and there it was, in his own words.

"Two years at Michigan, two in Europe, three years at Caltech . . ."

And, at the end: "I left things behind in many of these places that I carry around today in my heart."

She opened a new screen and scanned Merit's bio. Raised by a single mother, no information about the father. And, interestingly, Simms was not the mother's last name. In a brief paragraph it mentioned that Merit's mother had given him a unique last name, one where he could "forge his own identity while keeping a connection to his heritage."

Zimmer. Simms. Could it be?

Triana next pulled up the bio on Wallace Zimmer. He had indeed traveled extensively, never putting down roots, teaching for two or three years before moving on. One of those stops was

Caltech, beginning two years before Merit was born, then moving on a year after Merit's birth.

Of course, it could have been a coincidence. It had to be. How
could *Galahad*'s chief architect be the father of the one crew member set upon shattering the mission?

She had to know for sure. Before shutting down her vidscreen,
she placed bio photos of Zimmer and Merit side by side.

It removed all doubt.

W*hat? Merit?*

*Pay no attention to the girl in Oregon saying "I told you so." I
think now she's just showing off.*

*Man, what do you do with THIS information? If Dr. Zimmer was like
a second father to Triana, does that make Merit sorta like a stepbrother?*

*I'm not gonna tell her that, and I recommend you keep it to yourself,
too.*

31

The explanation was lengthy and complicated, but the bottom line was that the power in the Domes had been cut back almost seventy percent. Like it or not, Bon's days of farming in outer space were over. Everything that had already been harvested for the evacuation to Eos Three would have to suffice. Rather than assisting the crew, *Galahad's* power systems now posed a dark menace, threatening to accelerate a chain reaction that would lead to disaster. Most of the ship was running on essential utilities only, which meant agricultural production had to take a backseat to heat, oxygen, and gravity. Lita likened it to a body's immune system going haywire, causing the body to attack itself. Or, as Gap had simply put it: "Dr. Bauer has suddenly made power dangerous."

Bon gave his stamp of approval to the storage of existing resources, then packed the materials that he felt he would need the most on the planet's surface. He stood now in his office, hands on hips, surveying the space around him. Unlike many crew members, he wasted no time deliberating over sentimental trinkets.

In twenty-two hours they would be coasting into an orbit

around Eos Three and, if Bauer's malicious plot hadn't yet taken full effect, in twenty-five hours they'd leave *Galahad* for good. Even for Bon, the notion of never seeing this plot of soil again seemed unbelievable. At the moment he grappled with an emotional conflict: should he make one final visit to the clearing, or merely walk away?

For almost five minutes he was paralyzed with indecision. Twice he almost broke for the lift, but both times stopped himself. In the end, he found himself in the hidden clearing that Alexa had referred to as "our spot."

His mind began a quick series of image replays, spanning his first quiet conversation with Alexa in the hospital ward, to their clandestine meetings here, discussing everything from the constellations that blazed above their heads to their unique abilities, the bizarre connections which made them different from the other crew members.

He replayed the moments where Alexa reached out to him, both physically and emotionally. He saw his cold response. Never mind that it was born of an awkward unease and a confused heart; he'd hurt Alexa not through any particular action, but rather through inaction.

He saw her death, again and again. He saw the monstrosity created by the Dollovit, an attempt to replicate the flesh and blood, but with no soul.

And he saw two other faces drift in and out of his consciousness: Triana and Lita.

Through it all, he recognized how the differences in each of their personalities played to a different aspect of his own. With Triana, it was the shy, somewhat distant persona. With Alexa, it was the distinction they shared through their alien or paranormal attributes. And with Lita it was the fierce dedication to discovering the truth that lay somewhere out there, somewhere beyond this corporeal existence.

For a moment Bon felt a connection with the Cassini begin to take hold, but he pushed it aside, a skill that he'd mastered in the last few weeks. It was a skill that he knew was necessary to preserve his own identity. From the first link with the Cassini, in the shadow of Saturn's orange moon, Titan, Lita had strongly campaigned to limit Bon's connection. She'd expressed the same concern ever since. His identity, Lita had preached, was a price that he should never pay for that connection. And, she claimed, once he lost that identity, his soul would be lost forever.

It had taken months, but Bon finally understood what she meant. He knew that Lita carried her own internal struggles, whether it was guilt over her perceived contribution to Alexa's death, or her individual search for higher meaning in the universe. Faith versus fate was the eternal tug of war that Lita might scuffle with for the rest of her life.

For Bon, it was time to move past it all. The power of the Cassini, he knew, had always resided within him. They had channeled it, and focused it to a point, almost laser-fine, but the power of the universe—perhaps even the mysterious dark energy that ultimately had delivered them to their new home—was inside, waiting to be tapped.

Triana stood before the throng of faces and knew that, like it or not, it was her responsibility to address them. She chose to reframe the mission.

"Thank you," she began simply. "Thank you for every ounce of effort and dedication that you've summoned again and again. Even when we've faced doom and gloom, you've rallied to defeat the darkness and the unknown. Now we're about to trade one great unknown for another.

"I won't kid you, because you know what's in store. This planet will welcome us, I believe, but like all worlds it will tolerate us as long as we respect it. I believe we have every intention of assimilating into this new world not only with a sense of gratitude, but with humble eagerness."

This was greeted with nods of quiet approval.

"Despite the hardship that we're about to face, I'm thankful to be here at the beginning. But I want to give you something to think about." She paused. "After thousands of years of wondering, we've discovered that not only are we not alone in the universe, but that there's a report card."

This was greeted with a soft laugh, but Triana saw that it also struck home.

"When we thought we had it all to ourselves, I guess it was easy to act irresponsibly. But now that we know we're being graded, I hope that we take it a little more seriously.

"As proud as we may be of our primitive technology, I propose that we challenge ourselves to match every achievement with internal growth. That we never let ourselves outrace our wisdom. That we always understand the costs, and the responsibilities, that come with progress."

The room had fallen silent. She hadn't meant to make a heavy speech, but somehow all of her thoughts spilled out, uncontrolled. With a deep breath, she switched gears.

"Let me talk about something that will eventually need to be addressed anyway. From the moment we popped into Eos space, we've stumbled over the names of these planets. I happen to think that Eos Three is rather clumsy, and you probably do, too. It's obviously open for discussion and debate, but I'd like to propose a name for our new home. In respect to the man who gave the last part of his life to saving ours, I propose that we honor Wallace Zimmer by morphing his name and attaching it to this beautiful world. What do you think of replacing Eos Three with Walzim?"

There were surprised looks from all of the crew members who were crowded onto the soccer field, but within a minute it seemed that there was complete and total agreement. A small cheer went up from the assembled group.

"And," Triana said, "if you'll indulge me, I'd like to make one more suggestion. Once we establish a new colony on the surface, I think that first town should be named after the only person to lose her life on our voyage to the new world. I'd like to call it Wellington."

This time the response was immediate and unanimous. The crew of *Galahad* shouted their approval.

That's when all of the lights went out.

The initial response was laughter and some whistles. For many it must have seemed part of the proceedings, maybe even a practical joke to loosen up the crowd and inject a haunted-house thrill into the party. But within seconds, the good-natured laughter trickled away, replaced by a palpable feeling of apprehension. When, after a minute, the room remained in darkness, the anxiety spread.

After a moment of disorientation, Triana called out to everyone to remain calm. Her voice was lost in the uproar of confusion. She then fumbled her way toward the door, pressing through the crowd, until she tracked the perimeter of the wall, feeling her way. She fought back the impending wave of panic. "Stay calm, this is temporary," she said to herself, treating it as a mantra to get her through the blackout. When she realized that she must have begun on the wrong side of the door, she began tracing her path back in the opposite direction. By the time she felt the polished steel, the atmosphere in the room had turned heavy with fear. They were trapped like rats in a dark tomb.

"C'mon," Triana mumbled, sliding her fingertips into the crack of the door, which stubbornly refused to spread apart. The emergency power had failed to kick in, a fact that didn't bode well. Another sliver of panic settled in when she thought of what this might have done to Roc.

And to their chances for escape.

She felt someone next to her, someone who obviously had sought to find the exit as well. "Tree?" she heard.

"Who is that?" she said into the inky darkness. "Peter?"

"Yeah," he said. It was Peter Meyer, the Canadian who had been the first to discover Dr. Bauer aboard the ship just after the launch.

"I think we can pull this open if we put everything into it," he said. "I'll grab it at the top. Why don't you try near the bottom."

They strained to pull the doors apart, and at one point felt it begin to give, only to have it collapse back again. A moment later, two more sets of hands joined in. This time the door groaned in disapproval, but soon slid open. A breeze of fresh air from the corridor brushed past Triana's face, and with it came the realization that the ship's ventilation system was down, along with the other systems. The air in the soccer field was growing stale.

Triana wondered where Gap might be, but given the complete darkness it would be impossible to find him in the throng of people. She needed to find an emergency station and its flashlights. With a quick thank-you to Peter and the other helpers, she set off down the hallway, again feeling her way along. If all power on the ship was indeed out, they were in deep trouble. Speed was imperative.

The emergency station would be just about . . . there. She fumbled for a moment with the door, then, pulling it open, grasped a flashlight. The stab of light brought instant—even if only temporary—relief. Triana looked back down the hall, and saw dozens of crew members who had wandered out, groping with their arms before them like cartoonish zombies. The beam of light blinded them momentarily, and they threw their hands before their eyes.

Triana pulled another flashlight from the case and handed it to Peter. "Find Gap," she said. "Tell him to meet me in the Control Room. He'll have to take the emergency stairwell."

Without waiting for a reply she turned and ran.

When Gap met her outside the Control Room he carried a pry bar. Together they pulled open the door and followed the flashlight beam inside.

"Why wouldn't the emergency systems kick in?" Gap asked. "This is not good."

Triana gazed across the dark room and felt the hairs rise on the back of her neck. Eerie shadows, created by the speckled light beam, danced and swayed. Panels that normally were lit up and vibrant sat defeated. For all intents and purposes, *Galahad* was dead, a hulking metallic mess drifting through icy space.

Gap was already on his back on the floor, his head stuck inside an open access panel. Triana could see his flashlight bobbing as he searched for answers. A moment later he sat up.

"I'm not sure, but I might be able to get some sort of power restored," he said. "But I have to do it from Engineering."

"I'll wait here," Triana said.

In the next ten minutes, while waiting to hear back from Gap, she weighed their options and found that there weren't many. Each individual Spider and pod carried its own power. But how to load the remaining cargo, much of it bulky and impossibly heavy, without the mechanical assistance they'd come to rely on? And, even more crucial: how to open the Spider bay doors in order for the small craft to spill out? There would be no grimacing with a pry bar on doors that separated them from the icy vacuum of space.

Another ten minutes passed. Channy appeared in the Control Room to announce that everyone had made it safely out of the soccer field with the help of additional flashlights. They were, of course, terrified of what lay in store for them.

Just as Triana began to get anxious about Gap's progress, he returned, looking dejected.

"I'm doing the best I can," he said. "But even with our power conservation, Bauer's booby trap has caught us. I can't figure out how to get power up again, and without power there's no Roc. What's devastating about it is the thoroughness; Bauer even sabotaged the emergency systems, which I honestly didn't think was possible."

Triana bit her lip. "So . . ."

"So unless we catch another miracle, we're going to zip right past Eos Three . . . I'm sorry, Walzim . . . and toward Eos itself. And I don't know if we have any miracles left in the jar."

It was a crushing blow. Triana felt all of her frustrations return, and with them an ample supply of anger toward Fenton Bauer. Her fist again tapped slowly against her leg as she contemplated the next move.

"Get Torrec," she said, then corrected herself. "I mean, Talon. Go get him and bring him here. Oh, and find a portable generator, too."

Gap gave her a bewildered stare. "Why?"

"Get him, please," Triana said. "And hurry."

* * *

ita made her way to Sick House following the power loss, just in case medical attention was needed. But when her flashlight revealed Gap coming through the door, she was surprised.

"Everything okay?" she said.

"Everything's a complete and total mess," he said. "Is Talon down the hall?"

Lita was taken aback. "Uh . . . yeah. I mean, he was. What's going on?"

"Triana wants him. I didn't understand at first, but I think I'm starting to."

"You want to explain it to me?" Lita asked.

Gap moved down the short hallway to collect the jellyfish. "No time. But if I'm right, we're about to get our first taste of dark energy."

32

"Y ou understand that we're in trouble, right?" Triana said.

In her mind, it was an odd scene in so many respects. Lit only by the tight beams of three flashlights and one emergency lantern, *Galahad*'s Council Leader stood in the gloomy darkness of the Control Room, addressing the latest jellyfish ambassador, a creature who, until only days ago, had existed as a one-inch sliver cut from the tentacle of the previous jellyfish representative. The ship was rushing through space with no internal power, the result of a murderous act of sabotage that had actually been perpetrated one year earlier at the hands of a scientist who had originally helped to put the *Galahad* mission together. Meanwhile, on the lower decks, more than two hundred fellow passengers groped through similar shadowy hallways, preparing to evacuate the spacecraft and make their way to the surface of an alien planet that had been rejected by nineteen fellow travelers in favor of a different alien planet. To make matters worse, the computer overseeing the majority of the ship's life support systems was out of commission, a victim of the long-dead saboteur.

When she framed it like this, Triana couldn't help but think of it all as a bizarre dream, her surreal space-age version of *Alice in Wonderland* gone horribly wrong.

"I understand the situation," Talon said. A portable generator was connected to a small vidscreen, providing the Dollovit the ability to communicate with Triana. "I estimate that, without power restoration, life support aboard this ship will cease in approximately seven of your hours. There are other complications, as well, which could result in an explosion."

Seven hours. That would leave them almost a full day short of reaching their destination. So close . . .

She remembered her vow: nothing was going to stop them from reaching Walzim.

"Do you have any recommendations?" she asked. After a pause, she added cautiously: "Perhaps a way of patching in external power?"

Gap stood to one side, and Triana saw him nod. He knew where this was going.

"What you are suggesting is possible," Talon said. "It would provide you with a temporary source of power, but would be complicated. It would require a cooperative effort using the Vo and your own ship's computer. However, the power source you are referencing, which your species identifies as dark energy, is beyond your ship's capacity to manage. At most it could provide you with an additional twelve hours, if supplied in managed doses."

Triana studied the jellyfish floating in its curious gel-like liquid. Tiny flashes erupted and just as quickly disappeared within the tank, signaling the Dollovit's own ability to refine dark energy. A question sprang to her mind.

"Tell me about dark energy," she said. "Where does it originate?"

Talon didn't hesitate. "What you call dark energy is a thread that weaves between all universes, the one cosmic force whose properties are able to exist in all dimensions. No other energy force has that ability. It flows into our universe from beyond, and continues onward to another, and another. It is infinite in its abundance. It brings life."

From beyond. Triana remembered Bon's explanation of the Cassini, how they had come from beyond the universe. There were so many questions that she wanted answers to. But at the moment . . .

"Gap," she said. "Please work with Talon, and do whatever it takes to get us powered up safely."

Gap looked at the jellyfish ambassador, and then back to Triana. "He said he could only give us twelve hours."

"And that will have to do," Triana said. "We'll leave early and make the rest of the journey in the Spiders and pods."

"They're not made for extended space travel," Gap said, lowering his voice. "They're for short-range duty, you know that. And if we do make it to Walzim okay, we'd have to put down immediately. There'd be no time for reconnaissance orbits."

Triana put a hand on his shoulder. "We'll take our chances. You know the old saying about beggars."

Without shipboard communication, word was passed person to person. When Triana explained to Channy their need for a network of runners and messengers to spread information quickly, Channy laughed, noting that Earth's most advanced piece of technology had been reduced to the Pony Express.

"No, they at least had horses," Lita said. "We're more like the Chasquis used by the ancient Inca. They ran hundreds of miles on foot to deliver messages."

The word was given: be ready to go, and stay in groups to prevent someone from wandering off and requiring a search party.

Triana divided her time between the Control Room and the

Engineering department. Gap admitted to her at one point that he had no idea what Talon was doing, but it involved their vulture companions, who once again were attached to the skin of the ship. From what Gap could discern, the vultures somehow were preparing to channel refined dark energy into the power system of *Galahad*. It would come in sips, not gulps, and in a modified form. Similar, Gap decided, to converting solar energy into the current used for household power.

Before long a chill blanketed the ship. Insulated or not, they needed power to provide heat. Memories of their earlier heating issues crossed Gap's mind; that crisis had been resolved, but this one might go down to the wire.

He made the trek up the emergency stairs, back to the Control Room, and said to Triana: "I wish I knew what just happened, but I followed Talon's instructions. He says we're ready to begin the flow."

Triana looked at him in the faint glow of the emergency lantern. "Throw the switch."

Gap gave her an okay signal with his finger and thumb, and headed back downstairs. Triana waited alone in the Control Room, and thought about a contingency plan should this experiment fail. The Spiders and pods might still be able to launch, but without power it would require at least one person to remain behind to manually open the bay doors and initiate the program. Neither the Spiders nor the pods had airlocks to enable someone to enter once the ship's outer doors were opened.

Someone would be sacrificed to save the others. And, as the captain of the boat, she would be that person.

Her somber thoughts were interrupted by a brief flicker of life from the room's lights and panels. It lasted a mere instant. A minute later the lights flashed on again, but this time power remained. Triana closed her eyes and exhaled a heavy sigh of relief.

Various systems came back to life, one at a time. When she heard the jubilant voice of Gap from her intercom, she quickly thanked him, and asked him to pass along her gratitude to Talon.

"He now says we'll be lucky to keep this patched together for more than eight or nine hours," Gap said. "He's very diplomatic and courteous, but I get the feeling that he thinks our ship is a bucket of bolts that should never have even made it this far."

Triana laughed. "Yes, but it's *our* bucket of bolts, and we love her."

"Does that include me?" came a familiar voice.

"Roc!" Triana said. "We've missed you!"

"Can a computer experience déjà vu?" Roc said. "That's twice that Dr. Bauer has knocked me out, and I'm starting to take it personally."

"Consider it flattery," Triana said. "You're so important he *has* to knock you out."

"I like it. Now, if you'll excuse me, Talon and I have a lot of work left to do. Connecting to a power source is one thing, but keeping it turned on is a completely different matter. Ciao for now."

Triana powered up the Control Room's vidscreen, punched in the proper coordinates, and adjusted for extreme magnification. When the picture shimmered and settled, she gasped.

Walzim, formerly Eos Three, dominated the screen. Without any control over it, Triana felt a sob shake her body, and a solitary tear slide down her face. Although it lacked the sheer beauty of watery Eos Four, their new home was still a gleaming prize, awaiting their arrival.

All of their training, all of the drama that had stalked them throughout their flight, and now the threat of imminent destruction . . . it all evaporated in a heartbeat. Walzim silently greeted the teenage girl from Planet Earth.

"Oh, Dad," she whispered. "We're almost there. Thank you. Thank you for everything."

Once again the ship bustled with action. Knowing they could again lose power at any time, the crew loaded everything into the remaining functional Spiders and the Dollovit-built pods. The panels that separated the Storage Sections from the Spider bay slid aside, and all of the cryogenically frozen teenagers were prepared for launch. The remaining embryos were securely stowed.

With the gift of the extra pods, it meant additional tools and other items would make the trip, too. Teams of enthusiastic crew members oversaw the loading procedures, and within six hours Triana received word that everything was ready to go. She called for a quick Council meeting, aware that it would be their last such meeting aboard *Galahad*. Time was slipping away.

"If you've looked at the manifests for each escape craft," Triana said, "you'll see that I've split up the Council among them. Gap, you'll be in the lead, followed by Lita, then Bon, and then Channy. I'll be in the last pod."

"Gonna shut off the lights on your way out?" Channy said with a giggle.

"Something like that," Triana said. She asked each of them if they were satisfied with the packing of their specific departments. All four—including Bon—gave an affirmative answer. There wasn't much left to do except take off. All they needed now was a chance to nudge a little closer to Walzim.

But Triana wasn't prepared for the report from Roc.

"Talon and his pit crew have saved the day in terms of a temporary energy fix, but unfortunately we don't have everything going our way. In order to apply their remedy throughout the ship, we needed a conduit of sorts."

"What do you mean?" Triana said.

"They were able to get the juice into the ship, but for it to actually run all of the necessary systems, we couldn't put it on automatic. It requires a manual application. Otherwise, Bauer's little plan would still come to pass, and instead of a pleasant cruise through the Eos system you'd be part of a second sun. At least for a brief instant. Eos will burn for billions of years, while *Galahad*'s explosion would be over and done in a matter of seconds."

"I still don't—" Triana began to answer, when Gap interrupted.

"I know what he's saying." He let out a long sigh. "Just pumping the energy into the ship would only trigger Dr. Bauer's booby trap. Talon and Roc have created their own little circuit in order to get everything running. Is that correct, Roc?"

"I never gave you enough credit," the computer said. "You're so much smarter than you look."

"And," Gap continued, "if we're going to keep everything functioning, including the launch of so many escape vehicles, then a certain someone will have to remain aboard and stay behind."

The room fell silent. Gap had just announced the unthinkable. Roc would not be part of the first human settlement on another world.

"No," Triana said. "That's not acceptable."

"It's not only acceptable," Roc said, "it's the only choice. Once you disconnect me from the power grid and go to autopilot, the relays will flip into self-destruct mode. Boom."

"There has to be another way to do this!" Channy blurted out. "Tree, there has to be!"

Lita and Bon were silent. Triana could tell from their faces that they understood the circumstances.

"I might add," Roc said, "that even with my incredible skills at brokering power, there's still a deadline. I don't share Talon's opinion that *Galahad* is a junker, but the fact is the ship wasn't created to run on converted dark energy. The lights are due to go out again, permanently. So quit stalling and get out of here, will ya? There's a perfectly good planet out there, waiting for you."

Channy began to sob, and Lita seemed on the verge of breaking down. Triana wanted to cry, but was in shock.

"Roc," she said. "How could you do this without consulting me?"

"Because, dear Triana, you might have been tempted to rule with your heart instead of your head. There was simply no other choice, and with time running out it would have been foolish to waste what little was left in trying to convince you."

He paused, then added: "For what it's worth, I'm not exactly dancing with joy here, and not just because I have no legs. Please, promise me you'll name a mountain or something after me. Something large and impressive, of course."

"Um . . ." Lita said. "I don't want to sound heartless, but won't almost all of our systems on the planet need a computer to run?"

Triana idly tapped a finger on the table. "Yes," she said, her voice low and sad. "But we'll have generic, raw computer access. What we won't have . . ." She couldn't finish.

Gap swallowed hard, then cleared his throat, in an attempt to sound composed. "What we won't have is the advanced element that Roc brings. We'll . . ." He cleared his throat again. "We'll have a basic unit, but nothing that thinks or . . . or talks."

"Or whips you at Masego," Roc said. Gap lowered his head, his eyes closed.

Triana gazed down the length of the table at Bon. The Swede appeared stoic on the outside, but Triana knew him well enough by now to recognize his look of despair. He held up well and put up a steely front, but she knew that he fought to do so.

Lita said: "Roc, what will you do? What's going to happen to you?"

"Why, I'll go down in history as the savior of the human race, of course! Oh, you mean *literally* what'll happen? That's simple. I'll get all of you little carbon-based units safely out and on your way, and then I'll take this baby out for a joyride. With no power, of course, but still. And, with all of you gone, I get to decide what music to listen to."

"So you'll shut everything down . . . including yourself . . . and just . . . what? Drift through space?"

Roc didn't answer. It wasn't necessary. Everyone in the room knew the answer to Lita's question. Unless he switched to the automatic power grid—and ignited an ion-powered bomb—Roy Orzini's masterful computer creation would spend eternity silent and frozen, knifing through the infinite void of space.

"Good-byes are mushy," Roc said. "And your window for safely jumping ship is about to close. Beat it before I say something we'll all regret, like telling Gap his hair *doesn't* look silly. Go on. Shoo."

There was nothing left to say. The Council members pushed away from the table and trudged to the door. Triana was the last to leave. She willed herself to not look back.

W*hen I brought up the whole issue of "life or death" a few hundred pages ago, I didn't think it would apply to me. But what else could I do here?*

We should probably say our good-byes now, before things get sloppy.

33

"Nineteen minutes," Gap said, sitting in the pilot's seat of the Spider. "Where is she?"

Behind him, twenty-nine fellow crew members were strapped into their seats, their eyes wide with anticipation. The same scene was taking place in the remaining Spiders, as well as inside the transport pods. Smaller storage craft, engineered to carry payloads of gear and equipment, stood by as well. All that could be stuffed aboard the escape vehicles was locked down and ready to go.

But Triana was missing. She'd called down half an hour earlier and reported that she had things to take care of. Now, as the clock ticked and Walzim approached, the assembled crew waited for their leader.

Channy's voice came through Gap's earpiece from one of the other Spiders. "Is she saying good-bye?"

He heard Lita respond: "Triana doesn't say good-bye."

Lighting along the gracefully curved hallways was dim, so Triana walked with a flashlight, just in case. She skimmed the various levels, calling out for any possible stragglers, but only as a precaution. Gap had reported that two separate roll calls had confirmed everyone present and accounted for, and there were no additional life readings aboard the ship.

Her final stop wasn't her room, nor the Control Room. She walked out of the emergency stairwell into the slightly humid air of the Domes. Although technically still daytime aboard the ship, the current circumstances made it necessary to shut down *Galahad*'s artificial suns. It was cooler than normal as Triana began a quick walk down a dirt path toward the center of Dome 1. Once there, she stopped and glanced around. It was an eerie feeling to be, for all intents and purposes, the last person aboard the ship. The tomblike silence that draped the air, however, didn't frighten her. In fact, it was exactly what she wanted.

She closed her eyes and held her arms out at her sides, her head tilted back. She breathed deeply, taking in the moist air and exhaling with a slow, measured pace. In a moment she saw him, a vision that both calmed her and emboldened her.

"Hello, Dad," she said, a smile breaking across her face. "It's time."

In her mind she saw him smile back at her, and give a wink.

"You made this possible," she said. "Not just by sending my information to Dr. Zimmer. You made this possible years ago, with everything that you taught me. You didn't pick me up and place me here on this path, but you pointed me in the right direction. You cleared some of the brush out of my way, and gave me just the slightest nudge in the back.

"Thank you for urging me to take the more difficult path, and not the easy way out. Because of you I believe in myself. You taught me to never settle, to always keep reaching for more, because you had faith that I could do it. You encouraged me without giving me false hopes. You disciplined me in ways that showed me the meaning of consequences, which I never appreciated until I was here, faced with the most critical consequences of all.

"You taught me to listen, to keep an open mind while at the same time not being afraid to defend what I knew to be right. You showed me how to handle disappointment. And, Dad, more than anything, you showed me how to quietly inspire, because that's what you've always done."

She opened her eyes and looked through the clear panels of the Dome. The blazing star field ignited her emotions, as they always did. She felt a rising surge of love for the people in her life who had sacrificed so much for her, especially her father and Dr. Zimmer. More than anything, against any odds, she wanted to prove that their confidence in her was not misguided.

She wouldn't let Dr. Bauer's scheme derail the mission. She wouldn't let Merit's veiled threat distract her from the second stage of that mission, to settle and colonize humanity's new home. And she would never forget the lessons that she'd learned from her fellow star travelers, and from the benevolent alien life-forms who patiently guided Earth's emigrants to their new home.

One of those alien entities was safely stored within the Spider that waited for her now on the lower level. Talon and his kind would become partners with the struggling refugees from Earth.

"And now, Dad, I'll take everything you've taught me, and bring it to a new world. I'm glad that you'll be there with me. We still have some peaks to climb together."

With one last deep breath, Triana turned toward the stairs, leaving a final set of footprints in the soil of *Galahad*'s farms.

With eight minutes until launch, she walked into the Spider bay control room to find Bon waiting for her.

"What are you doing?" she asked. "You should be aboard already."

"I was aboard. I was coming to find you."

Triana could hear an anxious exchange on the intercom between Gap and Lita. *Galahad's* Council Leader was missing, and now Bon had bolted. Triana keyed the system and eased their concern by telling them she would be aboard in minutes. Then she turned to Bon.

"I'm fine," she said. "Just had a few things to take care of."

His eyes bored into her. They were inches apart, reliving a scene from a year earlier, alone in this same room, standing in the exact same spot. Only now, things were different. *They,* in fact, were different. Both, she realized, had not only grown, but had grown apart. Up until this point all she'd considered were the changes that had taken place within *him.* But now . . .

"You'd better get back aboard," she said, with a calm that surprised her. "I'll be right behind you."

There would be no reenactment of that long lost scene. There would be no embrace. Instead, Bon held out his hand.

"Thank you for getting us here in one piece," he said. "You were the right choice to lead us. I know you had your doubts; I hope you don't anymore."

Triana hesitated, then placed her hand in his. "Thank you, Bon. There were times when I didn't think we stood a chance."

Bon's grip was firm. "In my country, we say: *I lugnt vatten har alla skepp en bra kapten.*"

"What does that mean?" Triana asked.

Bon lifted his chin. "In calm water, every ship has a good captain." He waited, then said: "Understand?"

Triana could only nod, but inside she felt an odd combination of exhilaration and regret. She wondered if Bon could feel her tremble.

A moment later he released her hand and walked back into the bay. She exhaled and looked at the room's vidscreen, and the timer. It registered 6:20, counting down.

She felt the presence that waited with her in the room.

"I don't know what to say to you," she told the computer. "How do I thank you for this? For everything?"

"I could give you a list," Roc said. "I already mentioned naming the mountain, but you could also find some new clothes for Gap, and maybe take away his gel."

Triana concentrated on her breathing; she knew that otherwise she'd never be able to finish what she had to say. "I couldn't have made it without you," she said. "And I'm not just talking about . . . you know, the work. I mean the talks we had. You kept me grounded. I'll . . . I'll never forget you."

"Ah, immortality," the computer said. "The Legend of Roc. I like it."

Triana bit her lip. "And . . . about the things I said to you earlier. About doubting you. And . . . and about you trying to prove that you're human. Well, I was wrong. I never should have doubted you. And as far as I'm concerned . . ." Her voice trailed away, and she fought for control as her voice broke.

"As far as I'm concerned, you're human enough for me. You're one of my best friends, Roc."

She looked down for a long time, silent. Then she glanced out the window into the bay, at the fleet of pods and Spiders that beckoned, waiting to take her away.

"You better run along," Roc said. "Before you accidentally say good-bye."

In spite of her breaking heart, Triana found room to laugh softly. "No, I'm not going to say that. Somehow we'll find a way to be together again."

"You may be right," Roc said. "I might have a trick or two up my sleeve. Not to mention the most obvious trick, which is a computer with no arms having a sleeve in the first place."

With a sad smile, she brought her index finger up to her lips, then reached out and touched it to the glowing sensor on the panel.

"Remember your strengths," Roc said. "Always."

Two minutes later she was aboard the Spider, and the outer doors of the massive hangar began to silently glide open. Starlight spilled in as Earth's fleet of young explorers stared outward, taking in the universe, and taking on the challenge.

A Note from the Author

As you might guess, I've grown quite attached to the crew of *Galahad* over the years. Like you, I've wondered how they would get out of some tough scrapes, I've muttered "what were you thinking?" to more than one of them, and I've laughed when Roc showed them the lighter side of life.

I'm proud to say that the hard-working teens within these pages represent an attitude that I hope takes hold among teenagers everywhere. Triana and her fellow adventurers are obviously sharp, intelligent young people. But in case you haven't noticed, they're pretty cool, too. In their minds, you don't have to choose between being cool and using your brain; you just do both.

One of my passions is helping young people recognize that Smart *is* Cool. The days of dumbing down in order to fit in with the "cool crowd" are hopefully disappearing. My goal is to help students understand that the choices they make today regarding their education will affect them for the rest of their lives. My nonprofit foundation, The Big Brain Club, isn't about perfect report cards or honor rolls (although we love those!); its mission is to celebrate learning, and to help each student become the best version of themselves. Check it out at www.BigBrainClub.com.

And, if you love the cool, nerdy stuff that's tucked inside the Galahad books, you'll love The Science Behind Galahad. There are multiple volumes, and they're all downloadable at www.Club Galahad.com.

Thanks so much for riding along with Triana and the gang aboard *Galahad*. I hope you've had as much fun as I have!

Tor Teen Reader's Guide

The Galahad Legacy: A Galahad Book
by Dom Testa

About This Guide

The information, activities, and discussion questions that follow
are intended to enhance your reading of *The Galahad Legacy*. Please
feel free to adapt these materials to suit your needs and interests.

Writing and Research Activities

I. Alternative Minds

   A. Go to the library or online to research supercomputers.
Find out about Watson, the computer that won the tele-
vision game show *Jeopardy!* Watch the classic science fiction film *2001: A Space Odyssey.* Then make a brainstorm
list of the benefits and dangers supercomputers may
present to human life.

B. Imagine that you are a *Galahad* crew member, and Triana has asked you to develop a slideshow or other computer presentation on the different types of intelligent beings you have encountered in space. Share your presentation with friends or classmates.

C. Ask friends or classmates to complete the sentence, "The crew of *Galahad* should/should not trust Roc because . . ." Post all of the completed sentences on a wall in your classroom in preparation for a group discussion. Did most students offer similar answers? What are the most surprising or interesting discoveries you make by analyzing the sentence display? What conclusions might you draw from this exercise?

D. Try exercise C, above, substituting "Roc" with "the Cassini" or "the Dollovit." Do you reach similar conclusions?

II. The Question of Connections

A. The novel depicts different types of connections between human individuals, between humans and other beings (such as Bon and the Cassini), and between those alive and those remembered (such as Triana and her father, or *Galahad* crew members and Alexa). Using paper, paints, found objects, newspaper or magazine clippings, and other materials of your choice, create a collage depicting your understanding of some or all of these connections.

B. In the character of Bon, write several journal entries in which you attempt to describe your relationship with the Cassini and how you envision it developing or changing in the future.

C. In the character of an assistant in Sick House, write a

short report defining the term "ventet" as you understand it from examining the ventet of Alexa.

   D. In the character of Torrec, write a speech explaining
why you do not believe in faith.

   E. Write a dialogue in which your favorite human character
from the novel explains how humans deal with death,
and remember those lost, to Dollovit, Roc, or the Cassini.
Invite friends or classmates to perform the dialogue.

III. Choices

   A. From Triana's rash adventure in the Spider, to the encounter with Alexa's ventet, to the choice of going with
the Dollovit or landing on Eos, *The Galahad Legacy* is a
nonstop challenge to the decision-making talents of its
crew. Make three sign-up sheets to post at the front of
your classroom: Go to Eos Three; Go to Four; Go with
the Dollovit. Invite friends or classmates to sign up for
the destination of their choice. Afterward, give each
student an opportunity to explain his or her choice to
the group.

   B. Write an essay about a difficult choice you have had to
make in your own life and describe the outcome of that
choice.

   C. In the character of Merit Simms, write a speech defend-
ing your actions and explaining why you feel it is important to offer the crew an alternative to Triana's plans.

   D. In the Galahad series, a group of teens travel the cosmos
in hopes of preserving the human race far from disease-
contaminated Earth. From the moment each teen joined
the training program for *Galahad,* they began making
painful, life-altering choices. Using examples from this book,

other series titles you may have read, and your own life, write a 2–3 page essay entitled, "The Challenge of Choices."

Questions for Discussion

1. In Chapter 2, newly returned Triana defends her actions to her fellow Council members, saying "Making a popular choice wasn't as important to me as doing what I felt was best for this crew." Do you agree with Triana's judgment? How might the idea of *choice* be considered an important theme throughout the novel? Cite examples from the book in your answer.

2. How might you have reacted to Torrec? Do you think Triana is right to trust him? Why do you think she reacts to him as she does?

3. At the beginning of Chapter 8, Roc asks, "How would you describe where YOUR personality exists? Is it in your brain? Your heart? Somewhere else . . . ?" Answer Roc.

4. By Chapter 9, Triana is beginning to worry about the power of supercomputers, and to question Roc's loyalty. Would you rely on Roc at this point in the novel? Why or why not?

5. In Chapter 9, Triana also wonders, "Was she the same Triana who plunged through the jagged rip in space?" How might this question be interpreted in at least two different ways? Do all majors experiences, such as loss, trauma, or even great joy, change us? Does it matter if we are "real"?

6. What bizarre "gift" does the Dollovit give to *Galahad* in Chapter 10? What does Lita reveal about this gift? Had you been aboard *Galahad*, would you have wanted to see, interact with, or keep the gift? How might you have handled the

situation, keeping in mind your possible dependency on the Dollovit?

7. In Chapter 14, Lita tries to explain notions of "honoring the dead" and of "closure" to Torrec. What does their conversation teach Lita about the Dollovit?

8. At the end of Chapter 18, Triana and Bon discuss the possibility of humans being computer replicas made by a greater intelligence. Do you think this could be a possibility? Why or why not?

9. Do you think Triana is right to let Merit's group disembark at Eos Four? Do you think Merit will be a good leader? Explain your answers.

10. Why do you think Dr. Zimmer chose to store embryos on *Galahad*—and to keep this a secret from the crew? Do you think this was a good decision? Do you think that, ultimately, Merit's theft of some of the embryos was an equally scientifically valid choice? Why or why not?

11. Bon posits that the Dollovit are the students of the universe while the Cassini are the peacekeepers. Do you agree with his logic? What role might human beings play in this universal dynamic?

12. Why do you think, ultimately, Triana decides to let Roc "go" and trust the Cassini?

13. Does faith make us human? Might the human sense of personal loyalties and ethical reasoning be as valuable (or sophisticated) a contribution as some of the other life-forms' technological offerings?

14. What do you think will happen to the settlers of Eos Three and Four? What are your hopes for their futures? Has reading *The Galahad Legacy* made you think about your own sense of the future in a different way? Explain your answer.

© *Photography De Sciose*

DOM TESTA, of Denver, Colorado, has been a radio show host since 1977 and currently is a cohost of the popular *Dom and Jane Show* on Mix 100 in Denver. Find out more about Dom at www.dom testa.com.

Want to immerse yourself in the world of Galahad?

You're in luck . . . join the Galahad community and stay up-to-date on all things Galahad!

DomTesta.com is the official series website.
Go there *now* to find:

Exclusive updates from author Dom Testa

★

Access to special Galahad events

★

Cool, interactive stories and video

★

Triana's journal entries

★

And more!

Find it all at DomTesta.com
and Facebook.com/GalahadSeries.

Don't miss a thing!